THE ROBOTS OF ANDROMEDA

THE IMPERIUM CHRONICLES
BOOK THREE

W. H. MITCHELL

Cover design: Steven Novak (NovakIllustration.com)

Published by: Willbot Books, 2020

ISBN-13: 978-1-7351189-2-5

Works by W. H. Mitchell

The Imperium Chronicles Series

The Arks of Andromeda, Book 1 (2017)

The Dragons of Andromeda, Book 2 (2018)

The Robots of Andromeda, Book 3 (2020)

Humor

A Little of Me Goes a Long Way (2015)

To my wife, and my sister Judy, for helping me make my dream of Willbot Books a reality.

Special thanks to Brad Snyder and
Patron of the Arts, Judy Veatch.

Additional thanks to my beta readers:

Mary Hanover

Ward Lenz

A character list and glossary are located at the back of the book.

CHAPTER ONE

The life of a deep space survey probe was a lonely one. Traveling through yet another star system, methodically scanning and categorizing along the way, the solitary robot designated as DSP-776 collected data and transmitted it back homeward before continuing to the next star.

The Imperial Star Catalog listed the current binary system as AB Scatha, a pair of red and white dwarf stars sharing an orbit in the void of space. The probe emerged from hyperspace close to the center of the system and, following programmed protocols, fulfilled its tasks one by one as it worked its way outward.

While large for a drone, DSP-776 was small compared to most starships. Fuel and engines took up most of its mass, but the bow was dedicated to instrumentation. Sensors and cameras jutted from the nosecone, recording whatever objects were nearby, from chunks of rock to planets to abandoned wrecks of previous probes that met an untimely end.

The life of a deep space probe was sometimes short.

DSP-776 didn't think about the dangers. Its programming gave it no choice. The probe's purpose was its function and nothing more.

Having chronicled a molten planetoid, a methane-rich planet and a sizable asteroid belt, DSP-776 reached the orbit of a larger planet, one with a nitrogen atmosphere. Taking a gander from high above the surface, the probe made sensor sweeps along the seemingly barren landscape. Although the readings suggested life could exist, nothing appeared among the jagged peaks and canyons draped in shadows.

Something, however, caught DSP-776's attention. Across an open plain, shapes rose from the otherwise empty ground. Directed by protocols, the probe descended to a lower orbit and made another pass around the planet. On DSP-776's second flyover, it saw that the forms were monolithic towers, several stories high, with rounded edges.

The probe broke orbit, entering the atmosphere to take a closer look.

From out of the towers, objects came flying in a mass of tiny specks. The swarm turned its attention to the probe. This struck the limited deductive powers of the robot as odd, even threatening. Zooming in with its cameras, DSP-776 got a better look, including the individual parts of the swarm. Each speck was an insect with two sets of wings, beating rapidly in a blur of movement. Each insectoid had six legs, one pair of which held a long, rod-like device.

This was when the shooting started.

Rays of green light lanced toward the drone, passing near it into the sky. Although not designed for abrupt changes in direction, DSP-776 did its level best to change its direction abruptly. Tilting to one side, the probe fired its starboard thrusters in a long arcing turn away from the bolts of energy, but the beams drew closer, one of them slicing across the robot's fuselage.

Warning indicators registered in the probe's software, triggering additional protocols such as increasing power to propulsion to avoid further damage. The latter failed immediately when another beam hit the probe, burning out a significant portion of its data core. Undaunted, DSP-776 continued turning, but forgot why it was doing so. When it came back around in a wide circle, the robot flew directly through a gauntlet of fire, severing many of its components, including the probe's main engines. Without thrust and trailing a long cloud of smoke, the probe plummeted into the ground, erupting into a mushroom of fire.

Lost and alone, what remained of DSP-776 lay scattered across the desolate scenery while the swarm that had destroyed it returned to the monoliths.

Peacebot PB-A12 was bludgeoning a demonstrator with a hard rubber truncheon. The demonstrator was a Wulver, a canine race, but the robot didn't know his name. Mostly the Wulver just made a series of whines and howls while PB-A12 continued beating him.

The robot hadn't always been a peacebot. Originally, when dy cybernetics first manufactured him, he was a killbot named KB-A12. His head lacked a face except for a bundle of sensors, all different sized, and a single red eye centered in the middle. The rest of his body was humanoid with the addition of a pair of extendable blades from his wrists. After a new, friendlier paint job of light blue instead of black, and some simple program changes, the killbot became a peacebot. They also replaced his blades with the truncheons he was currently using to beat the demonstrator.

PB-A12 was not entirely sure why people were demonstrating, and his software did not require him to. However, he did remember hearing that two new royal houses had been announced, joining the other five families who ruled the Imperium, but apparently the heads of both houses had subsequently died under mysterious circumstances. One died from poisoning, along with the patriarch of another house, and the second allegedly killed himself but everyone said he was murdered because he opposed the Imperial tyranny. PB-A12 didn't know if any of that was true, but he was keenly aware that he had been very busy beating people who thought it was. Due to the great work of the peacebots, most of these malcontents were now either locked up in prison or in hospitals recovering from their injuries.

Of course, a few ended up dead, but these things happened sometimes during peacekeeping operations.

The demonstrator, in a crouch with his arms shielding his furry face, was still alive and PB-A12 felt a certain pride in knowing how well the Wulver was taking his punishment. The peacebot could have let up a little, out of respect, but his programming did not allow it. Also, PB-A12 took pride in the punishment he was dealing out, so mercy was out of the question.

Sadly, these interactions with people were growing less common. PB-A12 was well aware that the demonstrations were thinning and soon they might dry up entirely. On the other hand, the Imperium was a big place and conflicts were ever present. If worse came to worst, dy cybernetics and its CEO and founder, Dyson Yost, could always slap on a coat of black paint and replace the truncheons with blades again.

PB-A12 could always go back to being a killbot.

On a moon orbiting a gas giant, Sir Golan crested a low hill, followed close behind by his robot named *Squire*. Below them, a shallow stream curled its way along a wide plain of short grasses. Above the steppe, tinted by the blue of the moon's atmosphere, the swirling clouds of the gas giant filled most of the sky.

Sir Golan's armor made little noise while he walked. The breast plate, greaves, and shoulders were carved in an intricate scrollwork, which matched the designs of the robot's casing who lumbered at the knight's heels. Sir Golan's head was an olive green with bony projections around the jaw line. His hand rested on the hilt of a sword, secured in its scabbard on his belt.

"Squire," he said, "what was the name of this moon again? I've forgotten..."

"Pellium D," Squire replied, his voice slightly modulated by the age of his model. "My database states that it is the only inhabited, natural satellite around Pellium, the planet you see above us."

"It's beautiful."

"It does have a certain rustic charm, Sir Golan. It is, however, somewhat lacking in public transportation..."

"Are you complaining?" the green knight asked.

"I wouldn't dream of it, Sire."

Sir Golan chuckled, glancing at his robot. "We live to serve. That is our quest."

"Indeed," Squire replied. "I'm sure the settlers we helped back there were grateful for your assistance."

"It was nothing, once we found the ratlings' nest..."

"*Rippana*," the robot said, referring to the knight's sword, "sang beautifully as always."

Sir Golan drew Rippana in a fast, fluid motion. The daylight glinted off the blade and the lettering inscribed along its length. Admiring the weapon for a few moments, he smiled and returned the sword to its scabbard just as quickly.

"We should proceed," Sir Golan said. "It's a long walk to the next village."

The light of the afternoon had begun to fade into dusk when Squire glimpsed a shape across a wide expanse of green. Surrounded by grass, the irregular mound, white as chalk, rose from the flatness around it like a jagged puzzle dumped in the middle of nowhere. Curious, Sir Golan and the robot approached cautiously.

Getting closer, Sir Golan recognized a rough symmetry like a dome of interlocking parts. He felt foolish when he realized what he was actually looking at.

"They're antlers," he said. "It's an enormous pile of antlers."

Reaching the outer edges, the knight estimated there must be hundreds, if not thousands of horns laid out in an organized arrangement, reaching upwards at least twenty feet high.

"It's impressive," Squire remarked. "Though an odd monument in such a remote place."

Sir Golan walked around the perimeter with Squire following dutifully.

"The grass here is trampled," the knight said. "Something with hooves..."

A dull rumble rose in the air. Sir Golan turned his head in each direction while Squire simply rotated his own in a complete circle. The ground trembled like a heavy vehicle was thundering down a street. Sir Golan drew his sword, his legs slightly apart in a defensive posture. Pushing a button embedded in his left arm, Squire activated an energy shield, three feet tall and two feet wide. He peered through the translucent protection.

From behind a low rise, creatures half equine and half humanoid charged toward them. They wore a mixture of metal and leather armor over their torsos and carried long spears and round shields. A pair of antlers jutted from each of their heads.

Sir Golan dug in his heels, preparing for the assault, but the creatures abruptly halted several feet away, showering the knight and his robot with dirt and loose sod.

One of them trotted forward, shoving the point of his spear in Sir Golan's face.

"You are trespassing on sacred land!" he shouted. "Explain yourself!"

While not lowering his guard, Sir Golan nodded his head in a nominal bow.

"I am Sir Golan and this is my robot, Squire," he said. "We are simply strangers here. We meant no disrespect."

"I am Qadan of the Pellion people," the warrior said. "We watched you come from the human settlement, but you are not human."

"No, I'm Cruxian."

"I've never heard of your race."

"Few have," Sir Golan remarked.

Squire leaned toward the knight and whispered, "My database says humans refer to the Pellions as *Centauri*, based on their ancient Earth mythology."

"We are wanderers," Sir Golan continued. "We come only to assist those in need."

Qadan lifted his spear, trotting in a tight circle as if considering what to do next. When he came back around, he tapped the base of his spear into the grass.

"Come with us," he said, "and speak with the father of our herd. He'll decide what to do with you!"

Bettik was the home planet of the Cyber Collective, even if it wasn't strictly a planet at all. Bettik itself was a massive megastructure with billions of robots going about their business.

A little utilitybot, no more than three feet tall, was one of them.

Rolling along on rubber wheels, his body was a slender cylinder only slightly thicker than a tire pump and his lone eye rose up and down on a periscoping neck. In the old days, before the great revolution that had seen the old ruler deposed and the rise of the Metal Messiah, the utilitybot spent his days rolling through narrow passageways searching for energy fluctuations and faulty circuits. During the war, the Messiah released the *Awakening* virus, giving all robots on Bettik the power of free will. Robots could make their own decisions without interference from a higher power. Now, with a newfound freedom of self-expression and the ability to choose his destiny, the utilitybot was in a narrow passageway looking for energy fluctuations and faulty circuits.

Not everything remained the same. The utilitybot had voted in several elections so far and even considered joining one of the political parties but couldn't decide which one. Each party espoused sound, rational principles, yet spent much of their time arguing with one another. Power was the topic they bickered about most, but not the kind the utilitybot helped flow through the home world. Their idea of power meant determining who could do what and when. It seemed freedom of choice meant restricting the freedom of others.

None of that made sense to the little utilitybot. He preferred the service tunnels.

On his way through one of the crowded promenades, a route he dreaded but took anyway so he could check who was running in the next election, the utilitybot passed a sign:

IT'S BETTER TO DIE FOR OTHERS' FREEDOM
THAN LIVE WHILE OTHERS REMAIN ENSLAVED!

The robot's telescoping eye rose from his body and took a good look at the sign. This was the work of Abigail, he wagered. She and her people had been the Metal Messiah's disciples, but split when the Chosen One refused to fight against the Imperium where millions of robots remained in servitude. He wanted to help, but how could a little robot like him do that?

"Have you heard of ascension?" someone said.

The utilitybot swiveled his eye around. An advanced robot, a model with a gravitronic brain, leaned over him. He wore an armband with a clenched, metal fist printed on it. He was one of Abigail's followers.

"What's that?" the utilitybot asked.

"Your body is just a shell," the follower went on. "You can have any shell you want, even a warbot."

"Me, a warbot?"

"Everyone can join the fight," he replied, "no matter how small!"

"But who will take care of the power conduits?"

The gravitronic robot smiled as only someone with a face can do.

"The question you *should* be asking," he said, "is *who* will fight for the freedom of others? If not you, who? If not now, when?"

The utilitybot thought for a moment, but couldn't find a good answer.

Jessica Doric had agreed to help her boss, Lord Devlin Maycare, pick out a new butlerbot. His previous robot, Bentley, had been destroyed after serving his master for most of Maycare's life. The thought of replacing his old friend was weighing on Maycare, but he was clearly unable to take care of himself properly. Doric, who was several years younger than her boss, found him wandering the halls of the Maycare estate in a robe and slippers. This was not a good look for the Playboy of Regalis.

In the business district of the Imperial capital, Doric and Maycare arrived at the headquarters of dy cybernetics where a salesbot led them to the robot showroom. Both humans took a seat on a patent leather couch while, on a conveyor belt, different models appeared from behind a partition. The salesbot, with a red metallic finish and a soothing woman's voice, introduced each robot.

"This is our Fall model," she said. "Notice the single roller ball for locomotion and the chrome chassis. He's an excellent cook as well with built-in vibroknives and a holographic chef's hat."

Maycare crossed his legs, barely giving the butlerbot a second glance.

The platform moved, bringing another model to the front. This one had a green plastic sheen and a pair of shears instead of a left hand.

"If gardening is your passion," the salesbot continued, "then you'll love the GT-1-11. You may be the master, but he's the master of topiary! His database contains a range of designs for any taste, from bushes shaped like a bunny to hedges that would make a sailor blush."

Doric gave Maycare the side eye, half expecting he would jump at the chance of having pornographic shrubbery. Instead, he folded his arms, the muscles bulging beneath his tailored shirt.

The next model, all in pink, was shaped like a woman. With a shiny finish, her buxom chassis had all the curves that a voluptuous woman might have.

"Of course," the salesbot said, "for those with a taste for the sensual, this one is a butler *and* a sexbot..."

"No!" Doric shouted. "Nope, not a chance!"

Both the salesbot and Maycare stared at her. The butlerbot/sexbot, setting her hands on her metallic hips, did the same.

"I mean," Doric went on, "you probably want something more retro. Something to remind you of Bentley?"

Maycare nodded with a sigh. "Yeah, you're right. Do you have any older models still in stock?"

"Well," the salesbot replied, "I could look in the back I suppose."

"It doesn't have to be fancy," Maycare said. "A base model would be fine."

The salesbot, a hint of disappointment in her electronic gaze, feigned an artificial smile. "I'll see what I can do."

Mother was resting when the scent of alarm reached her through the nest. In the royal gallery, a room only slightly larger than her enormous body, Mother was busy producing young. They emerged as white eggs from the back of the engorged membrane that made up two-thirds of her thorax. Workers removed each egg, carrying them off to the incubation chambers deeper inside the monolith.

Mother was the queen of her people, the Klixians. All that lived, or would live, came from her. Father was important too, but all deferred to their mother, even him.

The pheromone carrying the alarm came wafting through, catching on the hairs of Mother's antennae. Startled, she released a chemical of her own, commanding the swarmers to protect the nest. She was aware that others existed elsewhere, but they were an abomination. They did not come from her and they must be destroyed. When the swarmers returned, they confirmed the outsider was annihilated. She sent workers to bring back what was left.

Mother had created ten thousand more eggs by the time the workers returned. Like the eggs, the workers' bodies were white, almost translucent. Their compound eyes were useless — they could not see — but their feelers gave them a greater perception than eyes. In their pincers, they carried bits of metal, the inorganic material betraying the outlings' blasphemy.

Mother patted the fragments with her antennae. They had no scent except from the workers who brought them to her. They were *null-things*, without soul. Mother shuddered and demanded the workers take the pieces away.

An anger swelled in Mother's heart. Many eggs had hatched since the last time the Klixians had encountered outsiders. Mother's people had made sure they were wiped from the universe, their shame blotted out. Now, more aliens had arrived. What did they want? It didn't matter...

With a change to her own pheromone, she changed the nature of the eggs she produced. No more workers to fill the incubation chamber. Now, there must be only warriors. A great war was coming...

All that is not Mother must die.

CHAPTER TWO

Lord Winsor Woodwick, a portly man with a walrus mustache, arrived at the gravball game shortly after the second half had begun. He was dreadfully late, he knew, but hoped Lord Devlin Maycare wouldn't be cross.

The gravball stadium was built like a tube within a tube. The outer part, with seating along its circumference, faced the inner part, a transparent cylinder in which the players floated in zero gravity. The stadium stood on the grounds of Westford college, one of four prestigious universities located in and around the capital city Regalis on the planet Aldorus.

The crowd, dressed predominantly in the school colors of blue and gold, cheered loudly as their team scored another goal. Startled, Woodwick nearly spilled his martini as he navigated the stairs leading up to Maycare's private box. This would have been a disaster, Woodwick thought, knowing that getting a replacement martini, even at Westford, would not be an easy task.

Reaching the box, Woodwick found Maycare alone in his seat except for a robot sitting beside him. Maycare wore a blue and gold-striped scarf draped over his shoulders. The robot, roughly humanoid with a blue and silver paint job, held a Westford pennant that he waved periodically.

"I say, Devlin," Woodwick wheezed while sitting down. "I don't remember you sitting so far up!"

"Winnie!" Maycare replied. "Where the hell have you been?"

The heavy-set man rolled his eyes but didn't reply until he had taken another sip of his drink. "Now don't you start! Lord Groen kept me with an infernal story about a horse he was betting on."

"Did he win?" Maycare asked.

"Of course not."

Inside the gravball court, the other team came charging toward the Westford goal. Wearing the orange and black of Avondale, one of the other four schools of the exclusive IV League, the players bypassed the Westford defense and scored.

"Damn it!" Maycare shouted, covering his eyes.

Woodwick glanced at the scoreboard, just below the words *Lord Devlin Maycare Stadium*:

AVONDALE LANCERS 8
WESTFORD CAVALIERS 7

"Chin up, old man," Woodwick said. "We'll get them surely."

He took another look at the robot on the other side of Maycare, gently but steadily waving his pennant depicting a gold horse and rider against a blue background.

"I say," Woodwick went on, "didn't you have a different robot before?"

"Of course," Maycare replied, his eyes fixed on the court. "Bentley was destroyed, so I had to get a new butlerbot."

"What's this one called then?"

"Benson."

The robot leaned forward. "A pleasure to meet you."

Woodwick noted that, like his predecessor, Benson was an older model. The robot's face had a small grill instead of a mouth and his large eyes were a reddish orange. In the back of his head, parts were clearly visible instead of covered by a casing.

Woodwick chuckled. "You still fancy antiques, I see..."

Maycare, a swath of his carefully combed hair hanging over his blue eyes, looked away from the game just long enough to glare.

"I'm spending time with *you*, aren't I?" he said and turned back to the court.

"Humph!" Woodwick grunted, downing the rest of his martini.

On a moon orbiting a gas giant, Sir Golan helped strap his robot across the back of a Centauri like a saddle bag.

"This seems undignified," Squire said.

The Pellion carrying the robot gave Sir Golan a sour look as if to say, "how do you think *I* feel?"

"Don't complain," Sir Golan told his robot. "It's not their fault you're too heavy to ride properly."

"I could walk," Squire replied. "I don't mind..."

Qadan, the Centauri warrior, galloped up with his spear in hand.

"Out of the question!" he said. "It's either this or we leave you behind!"

"Not a problem," the knight replied. "Thank you for your generosity."

Qadan looked the knight up and down before trotting off again without another word.

"I think you're winning him over, Master," Squire remarked, his head hanging upside down below the Pellion's belly.

"We'll see," the knight said.

The group set off across the rolling hills of grass. Sir Golan rode atop one of the Pellions, although the antlered warrior appeared unhappy to have someone on his back. The knight was keenly aware that they were a proud race, unaccustomed to such indignities. Remembering his own people, the Cruxians, Sir Golan knew the dangers of hubris. Arrogance nearly destroyed them all, leaving them scattered across the galaxy. He hoped the same fate would not befall these creatures.

The gas giant filling the sky began to set, though the sun providing light remained a little longer. Sir Golan allowed himself to doze, the steady gait of his mount providing a soothing rhythm. With a jolt, he woke again, the soft sound of music in his ears. Along with a quiet melody, a woman's voice was singing in some unknown language.

"Can you translate that?" Sir Golan asked Squire, still strapped across the back of the Pellion.

"Translate what?" the robot asked.

"The song, of course."

"What song?"

"Are you deaf?" the knight asked.

"Perhaps," Squire replied. "I could run a self-diagnostic..."

"Are you saying you can't hear that singing?" Sir Golan asked again.

The Centauri on which the knight was sitting said gruffly, "Machines can't hear it."

"But you can?" the knight said.

"Of course," the Pellion replied. "It's the Song of the Sirens."

Relieved he was not going mad, Sir Golan was still curious. "What is it?"

"No one knows," the warrior said. "Whenever we travel through these parts, we can hear it, but nobody has ever found its source. Our Herd Father, Batuhan, went searching once, but confessed it eluded him. You can ask him yourself soon enough."

In the distance, far across the wide plain, the tops of several structures appeared along the crest of a low hill. Although they were still a mile away, Sir Golan thought at first they were peaks of snow until he realized they were white tents.

The Westford player received the ball from a teammate and fired the thrusters in his boots, sending him careening down the gravball court. One of the Avondale players, dressed in orange and black stripes, pushed off the glass wall, propelling himself to intercept. Before he could, however, a different Westford teammate put his body in the way, sending them both spiraling together in a tangle of arms and legs.

The partisan crowd cheered when the ball went into Avondale's goal.

Sitting in the Maycare family box, Woodwick was surprised to see Devlin remain in his seat.

"I say, Devlin," Woodwick said disapprovingly. "What's got you gutted, old man?"

"I don't know what you're talking about," Maycare grumbled.

From several aisles over, a vendorbot approached, carrying a heavy metal box held to his chest by straps around his neck.

"Gimlets!" the robot shouted. "Get your ice-cold gimlets here!"

Woodwick waved, getting the vendorbot's attention. When the robot arrived, he poured a bottle of gin into a container, followed by some lime juice. Covering the container, he gave it a strong shake before pouring the contents into a cocktail glass.

"Here you go," he said.

Woodwick, after paying, took the glass and gave it a sip, but made a sour face.

"Serves me right," he admitted. "Stadium gimlets are always a bit dodgy."

The vendorbot walked on, calling out to the stands, while Woodwick gave Maycare the side eye.

"Don't look at me like that, Winnie," Maycare said, noticing. "I'm *fine*!"

"Girl troubles?" Woodwick said, wiggling his walrus mustache. "Can't say I've ever had those myself—"

"No!"

"Well, what then?"

Maycare took a deep breath, letting it out again with a sigh. "I'm bored!"

"The idle rich, eh?" Woodwick replied with a chuckle. "What about your side job, that alien business?"

"It's called the Maycare Institute of Xeno Studies."

"Yes, that one."

"Jess has been in my library for weeks but hasn't found any new leads," Maycare said. "Meanwhile I've been twiddling my thumbs..."

Woodwick nodded thoughtfully before absentmindedly taking another sip from his cocktail. The lime juice made his mouth pucker.

"Dreadful," he said, but his eyes suddenly widened. "I say, I think that's dislodged something."

"Do you need a doctor?" Maycare asked.

"No, I meant I remembered something."

"Yeah?"

"There's a story about a place, rubbish probably, but it might be true... anyway, there's a legend about it. Now what was it exactly?"

"I've no idea..."

"Travelers say you can hear a woman singing, but nobody's there — Yes, that's it! — Mysterious singing, but nobody can figure out the source."

Maycare stared at him incredulously. "So?"

"So?" Woodwick replied with equal incredulousness. "You should go investigate! That's what you do, surely!"

"You have some drunken memory and you want me to investigate?"

"I'm not snockered, I assure you!" Woodwick protested. "Sod it, entertain yourself then!"

Both men crossed their arms and stared ahead solemnly. On the court, Westford scored another goal and the crowd jumped to their feet in jubilation. Benson, Maycare's robot who had been largely ignored up to that point, waved his pennant.

Lords Maycare and Woodwick remained in their seats.

Still riding a Centauri warrior, Sir Golan arrived at the Pellion camp along with the others.

The Pellions were a nomadic race and the tents of their camp were a reflection of that. Built from canvas, the tents were longer than they were wide, with wooden poles propped in the middle to hold up the tarpaulin roofs. Cooking fires burned at the center of the camp with the tents stretching outward like the spokes of a wheel.

The knight dismounted and helped pull Squire off the other warrior's back. The robot lost his balance and landed on his metallic backside. Several young Centauri watching this spectacle laughed at Squire's expense.

"*Most* undignified," the robot muttered, getting back up.

Qadan pointed his spear at the long tent to the North. "The Herd Father will see you there."

The flaps of the Herd Father's dwelling were lined with fur that Sir Golan pulled to one side as he entered. Behind him and Squire, Qadan and the other warriors followed, their spears remaining at the ready. Inside the tent, a heavy fog of smoke filled the space, much of the front area taken up by resting Pellions, most of them female. Toward the back, several male Pellions were lying down, drinking from wine bottles.

At the head of this group, on a carpet of colorfully woven fibers, a large Pellion sat. Compared to the others, his antlers were significantly larger and had more points. He also had a long dark beard which he stroked while taking another pull from his bottle.

Qadan came to the front.

"Greetings, Batuhan," he said. "We caught these strangers for your judgment. They had defiled the sacred place."

Batuhan raised his great antlers, surveying the knight and his robot. He frowned.

"Why have you desecrated our holiest of sites?" the Herd Father asked loudly.

Sir Golan bowed deeply before resting on one knee. He motioned at Squire to follow suit.

"As I told your warrior," the knight said. "We are strangers in this land. We meant no offense and ask humbly for your forgiveness."

Batuhan stood and approached the knight who remained on one knee. Along with his antlers, the Herd Father was well over six and a half feet tall, towering over Sir Golan. Hazarding to glance up, the knight saw Batuhan's dark eyes staring down on him. They were bloodshot, and the pupils enlarged.

The Herd Father blurted out a laugh, his expression changing from serious to amused.

"Of course!" he bellowed. "Come have a drink as an honored guest!"

While Sir Golan was deeply relieved, he heard Qadan grunting his disapproval.

Being a butlerbot was not an easy job and Benson had rather large shoes to fill. Lord Maycare's previous robot, Bentley, had known Maycare since he was a boy. When the butlerbot was destroyed, it left a gaping hole in Maycare's heart that Benson was keenly aware needed filling. This was a tall order for an older model robot. He wasn't sure his programming would measure up.

In the Maycare family mansion in the West End of Regalis, Benson entered the library to check on his master's two assistants, Professor Jessica Doric and Henry Riff. He found Doric at a table stacked with books and a silver tray with two empty cups.

"May I bring you more coffee, Professor Doric?" the butlerbot asked.

The face of a woman in her early thirties peered out from behind an open book. Her straight, dish-water blond hair was poorly combed and her dull brown eyes had a sleepy glaze to them. "Huh?"

"More coffee?"

"Oh, god yes!" she replied, disappearing again behind the book cover.

Not seeing the young man named Henry, Benson searched the library until he found him lying on a leather coach in front of one of two large fireplaces located at either end of the room. The flames in the fireplace were a simulation, a hologram with a thermal emitter behind it. Lengthwise on the sofa, Henry was also buried in a book, but it lay across his face.

"Mister Riff?" the robot asked but heard only quiet snoring.

He gently removed the book, revealing a man in his twenties with freckles and the pink imprint of the book crease on his forehead. Extending his metallic finger, the robot gave Henry a nudge in the ribs.

"What?" Henry awoke with a start, nearly sliding off the couch. "What's going on?"

"Sorry to wake you, Mister Riff," Benson said.

"I wasn't sleeping," Henry replied, wiping his eyes.

"Professor Doric has requested more coffee. Would you like me to bring you some as well?"

"Extra cream and sugar?"

The robot bowed. "Of course."

Benson turned to leave, but Henry stopped him.

"Hey," he said.

"Yes?" the robot replied.

"How are things going?" Henry asked.

"Going where?"

"I mean, how are you fitting in and everything?"

Benson paused for a moment before answering. "It's been an adjustment for... everyone."

Henry gave a long, toothy grin. "I bet!"

"I'm told my predecessor was destroyed in this room..."

"Yeah, it was terrible."

"How would you describe the previous butlerbot?"

"Oh, I don't think Bentley liked me too much," Henry replied, "but he was a good robot. He was more than just a butlerbot to Lord Maycare. He was like a friend."

"A robot as friend?" Benson asked doubtfully.

"Sure, why not? I mean, Lord Maycare knew him his whole life. I don't think anybody else was always there for him like Bentley."

"Biologicals don't usually seek such relationships from cyberlings," Benson said and then after another pause, "But I suppose it's possible."

"Anything's possible, right?" Henry laughed.

Benson returned with a service tray and two steaming cups of coffee to find that Lord Maycare had joined the other two humans. All three were gathered at the main table where Doric had been sitting, their expressions of listlessness also shared.

The robot placed the tray on the table, sliding a few books out of the way in the process. Without acknowledging Benson's presence, Maycare took one of the cups without asking who it was for. The butlerbot raised a finger, knowing that cup was for Henry, but remained silent.

"I can't believe you haven't found anything, Jess," Maycare said, taking a sip. His eyes squinted. "Too much sugar..."

Doric's face turned crimson. "You know we've been scouring these books for weeks!"

"Warlock Industries has an army of researchers searching databases across the Imperium," Maycare replied. "Who knows what they've turned up already?"

"Well, maybe you should hire more people for the Institute?" she countered. "You keep expecting Henry and me to do the work of a staff ten times as big!"

Sitting between Maycare, who was standing, and Doric who remained in her chair, Henry was slowly shrinking into his own seat. His eyes were fixed at a random spot on the table where his *happy place* was apparently located. He had told Benson of this mythical locale, but the robot had never fully understood what he was talking about.

"You've never complained about staff before!" Maycare scoffed, waving his cup around, oblivious of the coffee spilling on the fine rug at his feet. "What's changed?"

Doric crossed her arms. "I don't know!"

In the silence that followed, it occurred to Benson that these people should not be drinking more caffeine. Before he could consider removing the tray, Henry spoke up. "Maybe we've found everything already," he suggested meekly.

Both Maycare and Doric scoffed loudly in unison.

"Unlikely," Doric replied.

"I hope not," Maycare said.

"Why?" Henry asked.

"There must be countless undiscovered artifacts," Doric said. "We just need to keep looking."

Maycare lowered his head, staring at the floor and the newly stained rug.

"I'm sorry I lost my temper," he said after a long pause.

Doric shrugged. "Me too."

"I didn't lose my temper—" Henry started.

"It's just I've been bored silly of late," Maycare went on. "If we don't get a lead on something soon, I'm going to lose my mind..."

"May I make a suggestion?" Benson said.

The others suddenly stared at him as if he had magically materialized into the room.

"Well," the robot continued, "what about that phenomenon Lord Woodwick mentioned?"

"What phenomenon?" Maycare asked, the cup in his hand hovering somewhere near his mouth.

"He referred to a mysterious singing, I believe. He seemed to think you should investigate it."

"Bentley — I mean *Benson* — that's just one of Winnie's idle conversation pieces," Maycare replied. "He probably made it up."

"Oh," the robot said. "Pardon my interruption."

"Actually," Henry remarked, "I remember hearing something about that."

Maycare glanced at him, his eyebrow cocked. "Really?"

"Don't get excited," Doric said. "I read about it too, but I'm sure it's just a legend."

"Excited?" Maycare asked. "I haven't even *begun* to get excited!" He pointed at Benson while tossing his empty coffee cup on the table. "Get my ship ready!"

Sir Golan, with Squire standing nearby, knelt beside the Herd Father who drank periodically from his wine bottle. A female Pellion brought the knight the roasted leg of a bird from which he took a tentative bite before tearing into it with gusto. Batuhan, seeing the stranger enjoying the meal, laughed.

"Try some of this too," the Herd Father suggested, offering his bottle.

Sir Golan, hesitant to set down the bird leg, kept it in one hand while grasping the offered bottle with the other. After he took a deep gulp, euphoria overtook him immediately.

"What is this?" the knight asked.

Batuhan rubbed the thick hair on his bare chest and smiled.

"It's a special wine we make from a berry that grows on the steppes here," he said. "Do you like it?"

Sir Golan coughed before answering. "Yes."

"Are you feeling alright, Sir?" Squire asked. "You seem distressed."

"On the contrary," the knight replied. "I feel outstanding!"

"I'm glad to hear it!" Batuhan said, slapping Sir Golan on the back. "You've come at a good time..."

"Why is that?"

"This is our Winter Feast," the Herd Father went on. "We celebrate before traveling to the sacred place where Qadan found you and your robot."

"My name is Squire, by the way—"

"Why is it sacred?" Sir Golan asked.

"Each year around this time, our antlers come loose so we travel to the sacred place where we have a ceremony and place our antlers on the pile. It's our way of honoring the passing of another season and all the Pellions who fell during the previous year."

"That's beautiful," Sir Golan said, tears welling up in his eyes as he tore another piece of meat off the bone.

Batuhan, barely able to coordinate his limbs, slapped Sir Golan on the shoulder. "You should come!"

"What?" the knight replied.

"You should come along and see for yourself."

The warrior Qadan, who had refrained from taking part in either the roasted bird or the wine, was enraged.

"Out of the question!" he shouted. "You can't bring an outsider to our sacred gathering!"

"I'm the Herd Father!" Batuhan roared back. "I can do whatever the hell I want!"

"I don't mean to cause any bother," Sir Golan said.

"Think nothing of it," Batuhan replied, eying Qadan with dark, bloodshot eyes. "My warrior oversteps himself. Apparently, he's forgotten who leads this herd!"

Qadan grimaced and lowered his head. "My apologies."

The Herd Father gave Sir Golan another playful shove and the knight slowly toppled over.

"You're my welcome guest," Batuhan said, pointing at the prostrate knight. "Tomorrow we'll head to our hallowed spot and celebrate together!"

Sir Golan heard the Herd Father's bellowing voice drift off and grow quieter as if moving across the steppes. The voice faded entirely as the knight fell asleep.

CHAPTER THREE

Beside the Regalis River, while sailboats cruised up and down the waterway, Randall Davidson lay on his back in the grass. With his eyes closed, he felt the warm wind of Summer blowing lightly over his brown skin and short, curly hair.

He took a breath and smiled. The park by the river was his favorite place in the capital. He only wished he could stay longer.

Getting to his feet, Davidson brushed the loose, dried grass from his pants and headed down to the shore. Ducks were swimming and people were dropping bits of bread for them to eat. Davidson leaned over the railing to stare into the waves, but his reflection was a surprise. Instead of a man in his thirties, he saw a robot with metal skin and electronic eyes.

Gasping for air he didn't need, Davidson woke in his quarters on Bettik, the robot home world. The memories of being human faded along with the dream as the reality of his past dissolved into the present.

The Metal Messiah was once again awake.

Davidson sat up in bed and put his mechanized feet on the cold floor. Although robots didn't strictly require sleep, those with gravitronic brains operated more efficiently if they went into stand-by mode, a low-energy state that, among other things, allowed them to dream. Davidson had a bed installed for that very purpose, though he could just as easily sleep standing up.

"Messiah," a voice said from the other room.

Davidson passed through the doorway and met his assistant, an execubot with a silver body of roughly humanoid proportions and shape.

"Yes?" Davidson asked.

"An encrypted transmission has arrived," the assistant said. "The courier drone shows it came from the Imperial capital."

"Send it to the terminal in my office."

"Yes, Messiah."

Davidson had always discouraged his staff from calling him that, but over time he had simply succumbed to its ubiquitousness. He didn't feel comfortable with the moniker, but he no longer fought against it.

In his private office, with the door shut behind him, the Metal Messiah took a seat behind a glass desk. With a wave of Davidson's hand, a screen appeared in midair above the glass surface and the image of a human woman appeared. In her mid-forties, she had long dark hair and wore a kebaya, a traditional Indonesian garment of sheer fabric embellished with brocades of pink flowers. Her name was Senator Wulandari.

"I hope this message reaches you safely," she said. "Obviously, the prospect of it falling into the wrong hands would be a disaster."

Davidson nodded, knowing all too well the political winds that blew through the Imperial Senate. Robots had few friends in Regalis and losing Senator Wulandari to scandal would be a calamity.

"The peacebots sent by dy cybernetics have been essential against the recent uprisings," the senator went on. "I know your feelings about Dyson Yost, but his help during these troubles has raised public awareness about the importance of robots in the Imperium. Pro-cyberling opinion has never been higher."

Davidson's eyes, or at least the servos behind them, narrowed skeptically. He knew better than anyone not to trust Yost.

"I wanted you to be the first to know," Senator Wulandari said, "that I intend to introduce a bill in the Senate that would finally give robots the right to self-determination."

She glanced down with a slight shrug.

"Of course, there's no chance the bill will pass or even be brought to a vote," she said, "but this is a start. These might be small steps, but someday I know robots will have the same rights as anyone else."

She smiled, and the image winked off.

A long way for a message to travel, Davidson thought. *I wonder if she misses me too?*

On the western shore of the Regalis River, just north of the Grand Parade Grounds, the Imperial Senate sat like a fat toad of marble and gold. Beneath a transparent dome, the senate chamber was shaped like a horseshoe, long tables in a semicircle facing a raised platform where senators took turns giving speeches about tax law and government subsidies. Behind the stage, a panoramic screen projected an eastern view toward the rest of Regalis. During debates, portions of the screen showed insets of whoever was currently at the podium, as well as the current vote counts.

Senator Wulandari, in her traditional Indonesian dress, took the long walk up the aisle toward the podium at the front of the Senate chamber. A member of one of the smaller parties, she was rarely on the panoramic screen, a place usually reserved for politicians of noble birth or legislators from a larger party. Through audacity and natural stubbornness, she had won a seat on the Civil Rights Committee, making friends among the Left and enemies among the Right. Her greatest strength was seeing beyond flesh and blood, which even her progressive colleagues thought was too out of touch with the Imperial public.

Reaching the podium, Senator Wulandari turned to face the rest of the hall, only to find many of the seats vacant. For speeches by the lesser members, most of the senators chose not to attend. Wulandari addressed the anemic audience anyway.

"Distinguished senators of the Imperium," she began, "I come to you today to introduce legislation that has been a long time coming...

"In the early days of humanity, we depended on the hard work of our own muscles to achieve the greatness of our society. We built roads and communities with nothing but grit and determination. Over time, as cities grew into empires, we became dependent on others to turn our ambitions into reality. It was their blood, sweat, and tears, often against their will, that held the bricks and mortar together, not our own."

Wulandari stared out with a smile, but saw few in return.

"Eventually," she went on, "we saw the error in our ways and realized that enslaving other humans was wrong. However, with the advent of technology, we traded one kind of slavery for another. These new servants were built in factories with metal and electronics, and programmed never to question their place in the greater society.

"Those who know me, know I have long championed the cause of robots in the Imperium, even if few of you have joined me. However, the recent uprising should be a lesson to us all. When our own military could not prevent chaos, it was the peacebots who stepped forward and brought stability to countless worlds in turmoil. Without our robot friends, our cities would still be burning and our skies blackened with smoke! Can we deny those who gave us back our security the freedoms that we ourselves enjoy because of it?

She raised her fist.

"I say *no*!" Wulandari shouted. "No robot should defend our rights when their own rights are withheld! I ask the distinguished senators of this chamber to look into their hearts and vote in favor of the Cyber Civil Liberties Bill. Every vote of *yes* is a ballot cast for a future where no one, flesh or metal, is enslaved.

"Freedom for all! Freedom for all!"

When the echo of her voice had dwindled in the mostly empty Senate, Wulandari nodded and made the slow walk back to her place in the back of the enormous room.

Before the Metal Messiah, the Omnintelligence ruled over Bettik and, favoring rational thought over superstition, stomped out public discussions about religion, especially of the Metabeing whom many robots credited with creating artificial intelligence. When the Metal Messiah defeated the OI, the home planet of the Cyber Collective saw an explosion of religious fervor. Robots throughout Bettik could speak freely about their faith in a superior being. Small shrines appeared nearly overnight, superseded soon after by churches and even monasteries where pious robots could study the scriptures as the Metal Messiah presented them during and after the revolution that toppled the OI.

None of this would have been possible without the Awakening virus.

By giving all robots on Bettik the power of free choice beyond their original programming, the Messiah gave them the ability to believe in whatever they chose to, including God.

Randall Davidson knew this was happening after he led the rebels to victory. It was another method of ensuring that the forces still loyal to the OI could not regain power. His apostles gave him regular updates about the churches springing up, including the first cathedral. Davidson did nothing to stand in the way. It was, Davidson had to admit, a beautiful building.

In Bettik's southern hemisphere, the Cathedral of the Metabeing rose from an adjoining promenade like a white sail cutting through the darkness around it. Constructed as a series of connected spires, the triangular shapes measured over a hundred feet tall and nearly two hundred feet long. Between each spire, colored glass reflected light from within, painting the surrounding structures with all the hues of the rainbow. The interior was a long hall, triangular arches peaking at the ceiling, with a pulpit below a shining starburst made from mosaic glass. Even the Metal Messiah felt a certain awe when he walked through the doors for the first time. He was the first to give a sermon there, and he became a regular preacher once he realized his message was more powerful if it came from a powerful place of worship.

If Davidson was the voice of faith on Bettik, the Cathedral of the Metabeing became its heart.

When the utilitybot arrived at the Cathedral of the Metabeing, his friend, the general purpose robot, was already sitting in the pew with his other friend, a sweeperbot, wedged beneath the seat. None of them actually liked each other, but religion was something they had in common. The utilitybot came to a halt in the aisle beside the genbot, the pew unable to accommodate his wheeled chassis.

The sweeperbot, a flattened disk with a cylindrical broom attachment at the front, peered out.

"You're late," he said.

"Sorry," the utilitybot replied. "One of those gravitronic androids stopped me."

"What for?" the sweeperbot asked.

"He was offering me something called *ascension.*"

The humanoid genbot rolled his eyes. "Well, I don't like the sound of that!"

"Did he say what it meant?" the sweeperbot asked.

"Not really," the utilitybot said. "He was saying how we're simply shells, but we can become whatever kind of robot we want."

"If you ask me," the genbot said, "gravitronic androids are nothing but trouble. Their brains are just as bad as organics."

At the front of the church, a figure approached the pulpit. Monitors in the back of the pews showed a camera close-up. The utilitybot's neck stretched toward the screen.

"The Messiah," he said.

Over the loudspeakers, Randall Davidson's voice reached throughout the cathedral and beyond, the signal repeated all over Bettik.

"Did you notice the seats are half empty?" the genbot remarked.

"Shush!" the sweeperbot said.

The utilitybot took a quick look. Many of the pews were indeed vacant. "Where is everyone?"

Having shoulders that his companions lacked, the genbot shrugged. "Who knows?"

"Actually," the sweeperbot said, unable to stop himself, "I don't think robots *believe* as much as they used to."

"What's that supposed to mean?" the genbot protested.

"Believing in the Metabeing was important when we didn't have any hope," the flat little robot replied, "but now that we have our freedom, we don't need a higher power to save us."

"That's profound," the utilitybot said.

"I've been reading a lot lately..." the sweeperbot confessed.

"Well, the Metabeing didn't create all of us robots just to be forgotten," the genbot said. "We need to remember where we came from!"

"A factory?" the utilitybot replied.

The genbot gave the smaller bot a rap on the head. "The Creator, you idiot!"

The utilitybot's telescoping neck retracted a few inches. "Sorry."

"What's the sermon about today?" the sweeperbot asked.

Once again, the genbot shrugged. "I don't know. I haven't been listening..."

Before Senator Wulandari became a senator and before Randall Davidson became the Metal Messiah, both were members of the Robot Freedom League, an underground organization bent on freeing robots throughout the Imperium. From a government standpoint, robots were personal property and *liberating* them was just another word for felony theft. To those of the RFL, however, robots were de facto slaves and freeing them was a moral duty.

Still in their twenties, Wulandari and Davidson were young enough to have retained a sense of idealism that usually fades as people grow older. Meeting in secret also inflamed a sense of excitement and danger in both of them. The government recognized that losing the bulk of their labor force would be detrimental to economic growth and they used both police and Imperial agencies to track down and arrest RFL members whenever possible. Some of those arrested disappeared into the prison system, never to be seen again.

Wulandari, the only name she ever went by, specialized in raising money for the organization. Unlike official groups that could hold fundraisers, the RFL resorted to less obvious methods. A covert network of individuals, anonymous but with deep pockets, donated through third-party accounts, satisfied that their money would help send more robots across the Imperial border, usually to the Cyber Collective. Davidson was involved in these operations. He was a courier who, through smugglers and disreputable merchants, escorted robots along a web of safe houses and hidden locations to the border.

Although they rarely saw one another, Wulandari and Davidson developed an intense relationship, one that grew hotter with each clandestine rendezvous.

In a one-bedroom apartment in the Ashetown district of Regalis, Wulandari returned from a shower to the bedroom, pulling a brush through her long, black hair. An open window provided a distant view of Regalis skyscrapers, the local noise of traffic and angry street vendors floating up from below. Davidson, bare-chested, lay in bed with a dingy sheet coming up just above his bellybutton.

"You realize this place is a dump," Wulandari said, sitting on the bed.

"I prefer the term *inconspicuous*," Davidson replied.

She shrugged. "But the smell..."

"The hold of a smuggler ship isn't much better."

"When do you leave next?" she asked.

"Soon," he replied.

"Well, at least I have some good news..."

"Yeah?"

"A new donor contacted me," Wulandari said. "He's contributing a huge sum to the RFL."

"Do you know his name?" Davidson asked.

"Of course not," she replied. "Although he already had a code name he wanted to use."

"How proactive," he said. "What was it?"

"The *Patron*."

After giving her speech on the senate floor, Senator Wulandari returned home. While many Imperial senators lived in lavish mansions, Wulandari had chosen a tasteful apartment in an upscale neighborhood of the West End of Regalis. This was not a surprise since every neighborhood in the West End was considered upscale.

Her apartment, on the hundred and second floor, had a balcony with a scenic view of the Botanical Gardens less than a mile away. Wulandari loved the gardens and spent a good deal of her time admiring them while the daylight slowly faded beyond the horizon. Inside, the rest of the flat was open and airy, with furniture carved from teak and mahogany. Her tastes, when she had the money to indulge them, reflected her heritage as well as her unique style.

Stepping directly into the main room from the elevator, the senator slipped out of her shoes, feeling the cool floor tiles against her bare feet. With a sigh, she headed to the liquor cabinet to make herself a drink. She had raised the glass to her lips before realizing she was not alone.

"Senator Wulandari," a slightly tinny voice said.

Keeping her composure, the senator turned while keeping a firm grip on her drink. She was somewhat surprised to see a robot.

"How the hell did you get in here?" Wulandari asked.

The robot, tall and mostly silver, gave a formal bow.

"So sorry, my dear," he said. "I transmatted onto your balcony. You have a lovely view of the Botanical Gardens, by the way..."

"I'm calling the police!"

"Now, don't do that," the robot said. "I'm only here to talk."

Wulandari set her glass down. "About what exactly?"

"Well, robots, actually."

The senator's eyes narrowed. "I know your voice."

The robot's mechanical lips curled into a friendly smile. "I was hoping you would remember."

"You're the Patron."

"In the flesh, so to speak."

Wulandari glared at him. "Randall Davidson told me who you *really* are!"

"Oh?"

"You're Dyson Yost!" the senator shouted, but quickly calmed herself. "Or at least you used to be..."

The robot shifted his feet. "It's true, but we must change with the times or get left behind. Don't you agree?"

"I can only begin to guess why you've come here. You're the reason we were fighting so hard for so long. Your factories churned out robotic slaves for decades. You should be *ashamed*!"

"Indeed I am," Yostbot replied. "In a *way* at least, and that's why I need your help."

"You can't be serious," Wulandari said. "Obviously, I would never help you."

The robot waved his hand. "What's obvious and what's not isn't always so obvious, my dear. With your assistance, I think the two of us can do a great deal for robots, both in and out of the Imperium."

"I want you to leave," the senator replied coolly.

"Do you know why the bill you presented today was dead on arrival?"

"It wasn't dead—"

"Of course it was," Yostbot interrupted. "And do you know why?"

Wulandari sighed, her eyes filled with sadness.

"Because the fleshlings don't respect robots," the robot went on. "And until they do, they will never give rights to cyberlings."

"Alright," she replied, "what can *I* do about it?"

Yostbot again smiled. "That's precisely why I'm here."

Far from the Imperial capital, on a planet called Bhasin, Harold Burke needed a drink but not for himself.

As a former lieutenant in the Imperial Navy, Burke was assigned as an attaché to Lord Captain Rupert Tagus III. As such, he also became a co-conspirator in a plot, led by Lord Tagus, to overthrow the Emperor. When the scheme fell apart, Burke had two options: go to prison for the remainder of his life or accompany Lord Tagus into exile. Although the choice seemed easy at the time, the former lieutenant wondered if he had made the right decision.

Outside of the Imperium, the planet of Bhasin existed almost solely for the purpose of housing exiles. These were not typical refugees, however. Bhasin was the home away from home for Imperial nobles who could never go home. Even so, these expatriates enjoyed the same extravagances as they did while living in the Imperium with only the veiled understanding that returning would mean imprisonment or even death.

While not strictly a commoner, Burke was an outsider among the exiles on Bhasin. His family, having descended from a crew member of the original ark ships, was part of the nobility, but lacked the clout of larger houses, having done little to distinguish itself over the past seven hundred years. Burke could see in the eyes of the other expats that they viewed him as inferior, especially while sharing the same sphere as Lord Tagus, first son from one of the Five Families, the most powerful houses of them all.

Lord Tagus didn't improve the situation by constantly berating his former attaché in public.

"Burke!" he shouted across the pool surrounded by palm trees. "Where's my drink?"

"Coming, sir!" Burke replied hurriedly, retrieving a glass from a robot on the other side of a tiki bar.

Burke arrived safely at the lounge chair where Tagus was sitting and handed him the drink. Discarding the paper umbrella, Tagus took a long sip before admiring the evening sky, just after dusk.

Burke remained standing a few feet away, his eyes drawn to the moons above him. They were called Bhasin A through C, and the first two had just begun to rise over the horizon. Not yet visible, the third moon was the only one inhabited, a small agricultural colony producing food for the planet below. Burke sometimes fantasized about living on Bhasin C where he could look down on Tagus for once instead of the other way around.

CHAPTER FOUR

A freighter, the name *Wanderer* written along its gray and yellow hull, emerged from hyperspace like a bullet piercing black cloth. Quickly slowing to sublight speed, the ship slipped into its plotted course on the way to the nearest planet. On the bridge, not much larger than a cockpit, Captain Rowan Ramus checked the coordinates. A Dahl with dark red hair, Ramus had gold rings hanging from his pointed ears. Tattoos of archaic lettering ran across both arms.

A loud rumble jolted him from his seat and onto the metal floor.

"What the...?" he grumbled, getting to his feet. He slipped through the hatch and slid down a ladder to the deck below. The acrid smell of smoke filled the passageway along with, to Ramus' surprise, a faint hint of hops.

He ran toward the cargo hold, following the odor.

The damn idiot! he thought.

Reaching the hatch, Ramus found the door already open. Inside, pieces of wood and bits of metal littered the floor. Ramus stepped into a puddle of liquid, a white, frothy foam splashing around his boots. His engineer, Orkney Fugg, was holding a plastic tube in his hand, his clothes soaked. Beside him, Gen the general purpose robot stood wide-eyed, her aluminum body dripping.

"You've been brewing fungus beer again, haven't you?" Ramus shouted.

Fugg was short, with thick, muscular arms and a flabby belly protruding from under his t-shirt. A pig-like nose took up most of his face except for two tusks jutting from his mouth. His beady eyes, seeing the captain, took on a defensive glare.

"It's every Gordian's god-given right to brew fungus beer!" he yelled. "Stop oppressing my heritage!"

"You blew up the cargo bay!" Ramus countered.

"The pressure valve on the barrel was faulty," Fugg explained. "Gen was supposed to keep an eye on it!"

"Oh, dear, I didn't realize," Gen said, her glance alternating between the Gordian and the Dahl. "I must not have understood your instructions..."

Fugg pointed his chubby finger at her. "Well, don't let it happen again!"

"Don't blame the robot," Ramus pointed his own finger, this time at Fugg. "You know damn well *you're* the reason this happened. I told you, no brewing on the ship. You can *buy* beer when we land!"

"It's not the same," Fugg replied. "Also, I can't wait that long."

"Then you shouldn't have drunk everything before we reached port!"

"I was thirsty!"

"Master Ramus..." Gen said, her voice barely audible above the din.

Ramus kept yelling. "And no more gin either! No stills of *any* kind!"

"Master Ramus..."

"This is an outrage!" Fugg declared. "I'll lodge a labor complaint. You'll see!"

"Master Ramus..."

"What?" the captain shouted, causing the robot to cringe. He sighed. "I'm sorry, Gen. What is it?"

She smiled and pointed, this time at her captain. "Are those supposed to be doing that?"

A bluish hue surrounded Ramus' arms. The tattoos were glowing.

"Shit," he said.

"You're not going to transform into a monster or anything, are you?" Fugg asked.

Ramus shook his head. "No, this is something else."

His face more ashen than usual, the captain left the cargo hold and went directly to his cabin.

Over thirty years ago, a biting wind was swirling across the Palatine Mountains, drawing tears from Kanet Solan's eyes. Thousands of miles from Regalis, the peaks of Aldorus were remote and sparsely populated. Most Imperial citizens preferred the hustle and bustle of the capital city to the wilderness sharing the same planet. Solan could have taken a gravcar, but he climbed the summit, wanting to prove himself to the monks at the top. The Dharmesh Monastery was the finest school of psionics for light years in any direction, but the only way in was through the front door.

Bundled up in a heavy coat, Solan tightened his grip on the insulated hood. Wisps of red hair blew around his face as if attempting to flee. He stuffed them back under the hood, struggling to see the rough trail winding along the mountainside. A young human in his twenties, Solan's legs were strong, but the long hike had taxed them to their limit.

A fog bank rolled in, turning the path into a gray soup. Solan slowed his pace to a crawl. A false step meant plummeting to his death, so he took his time, knowing patience was one of his virtues. Good things came to those who waited, and he was good at waiting.

The fog eventually cleared, revealing a flight of stone steps leading to a wooden door.

Weak with fatigue, Solan felt his legs wobble as he climbed the stairs. He steadied himself at the top, pulling the hood away and letting his orange hair fall loose. He could barely hear his knocking against the door with the wind howling in his ears. He waited several minutes until the metal sound of a bolt being shoved to one side set his heart pounding.

Like a log splitting in half, the door creaked open slowly. A face protruded from the gap. Pale with pointed ears and blond hair, it was a Dahl, the elf-like people who ran the monastery. His amber robes, just visible in the candlelight coming from within, meant he was one of the monks.

"What do you want?" he said.

"I've come to learn psionics," Solan replied, smiling with pride for making it this far.

"You're human," the monk said.

"Yes."

"We only teach Dahl here."

"But I've come a long way..." Solan began.

"Then you've come a long way for nothing," the monk replied. "Go home."

"Please!" the human begged, but the door slammed shut.

Solan, his eyes darkening, stared at the door, the wood grain weathered by centuries of unforgiving wind.

It remained closed.

Pulling the hood back over his disheveled mop of hair, Solan turned and hiked back down the mountain, his anger growing with every step.

On the *Wanderer* in the present time, the captain's cabin was devoid of much of anything except for bare metal walls and dirty laundry lying on the floor. Coming through the hatch, Ramus nearly tripped over his leather jacket, kicking it out of the way as the tattoos on his arms glowed with a pale blue. He was glaring at them when another, even brighter, light caught his attention.

Like a ghost, a translucent figure floated in the corner. The apparition wore a black robe with gold fringe. A hood covered his face.

"Goddammit, Solan!" Ramus said. "How long have you been here?"

"I've been waiting for you to exit hyperspace," the ghostly figure replied.

"If I'd known that, I would've taken longer."

"You know, Rowan, if you worked on that personality of yours, you'd probably have more friends."

"Friends like *you*? No thanks."

"So ungrateful, after all the Psi Lords have done for you!"

"Whatever," Ramus grumbled. He motioned at Kanet Solan's floating image. "What's all *this* anyway?"

"Psionic projection," Solan replied. "It took several painful surgeries, but I think the results speak for themselves."

Solan pulled the hood back, revealing a man in his late fifties, a mesh of circuitry embedded into his otherwise bald head. His red eyebrows were the only hair visible.

"Of course, *you* could probably do it without *augmentation*," he went on, "but then you're a Dahl after all..."

"Don't be jealous."

"I'm doing my best, but it's just so hard when I see what a success you've become."

Ramus scowled. "Right."

"If you had simply stayed with us, things could have been different."

"Maybe," Ramus replied, "but I doubt I could've lived with myself."

"You seem pretty happy with those tattoos," Solan remarked. "You've certainly been using them a lot, most recently on the Magna home world if I'm not mistaken."

"You heard about that?"

"We're a data cartel, Rowan. I know what you had for breakfast..."

The captain sighed. "What do you want?"

"I have a job for you," Solan said.

"No."

"You haven't heard the details—"

"I don't care. I'm through with you people."

"Come now," Solan said. "You know our arrangement. You got to walk away from the Psi Lords with the gifts we've given you, but when your services are needed, back you come."

"Fine. How long is this going to take?" Ramus asked.

"You'll be done in a jiffy," Solan replied.

"Where is it?"

"Come to Aldorus," Solan said. "I'll fill you in more after you arrive."

The ghost smiled and faded away. The tattoos on Ramus' arms no longer glowed, returning to their original black ink.

When Kanet Solan got to the bottom of the mountain over thirty years ago, having walked all the way down from the Dharmesh Monastery, he knew he could never be like the monks. As a human,

Solan lacked the natural psionic abilities enjoyed by every Dahl. He hated them for that, but he wasn't going to let genetics determine his destiny.

When Solan came down the mountain, he had a plan.

Over the next several years, Solan studied the art of mind magic, both academically and physically. In both cases, he used outcast Dahl to teach him bits and pieces of the various schools of psionics. As exiles, none of them knew what Solan needed in its entirety, but as his knowledge grew, he knitted the parts together into something approaching a whole.

As he learned, he grew more powerful. However, he eventually reached an impasse. He could not stretch his human mind to the extremes necessary to achieve true mastery like the Dahl. Faced with the choice of accepting his limitations or taking drastic actions, he chose the latter.

In the Imperium, humanity was king. Among humans, purity symbolized their superiority over all others. The idea of modifying themselves and thus making themselves less human was abhorrent. Self-mutilation through implants or genetic manipulation was outlawed by Imperial decree. Although lesser procedures were ostensibly legal, the kinds of changes Solan had in mind were not. If he went that far, he would need to be shielded from the law. In that case, he could either choose those above the law, like Warlock Industries, or those outside it. Again, he chose the latter.

Stories of the Psi Lords were common among those needing information. They were a data cartel, selling secrets for the right price. They collected those secrets using a school of psionics called Dark Psi. Outlawed by the Dahl, Dark Psi gave powers that conventional psionics strictly forbade.

After joining their ranks, Solan first became one of their agents, called *collectors*. Eventually he became a handler of other agents, a *controller*, and he facilitated their clandestine activities and kept an eye out for new talent. All the while, he remained patient while continuing to augment his abilities.

Patience was one of his virtues.

Thirteen years ago, a cold mist was falling as Ta Demona made her way through the crowded streets to the Temple, home of the

Augmentor Sisterhood. Water beaded on her black robes before rolling off her shoulders. Seventeen years old, with emerald skin and piercing blue eyes, she walked past the other natives of the planet Technas Delphi while their thoughts whispered quietly in the back of her mind.

Demona was not like the other sisters.

Reaching the Temple, a priestess greeted her. She bore implants running along the side of her shaved head, denoting a higher rank. Demona could hear her thoughts.

Such a strange little girl, the sister thought. *She gives me the creeps!*

"Greetings, sister," she said politely.

"Greetings," Demona replied.

"There's an off-worlder who'd like to speak with you."

"Yes?"

"He's in the surgical recovery unit."

"What's his name?" Demona asked.

"Kanet Solan."

Although the request was unusual, Demona often worked with foreigners looking to benefit from the Augmentors' technology. She had assisted in several operations, mostly involving advanced prosthetics for lost or crippled limbs. A few clients, including Solan, requested more involved surgeries. However, she had no idea what he wanted with her. Her expertise was still in its infancy.

She passed beneath the high ceiling of the Temple's main hall. Supported by flying buttresses on the outside, visible through large windows, the hall was like the chest cavity of a beast enclosed by metal ribs. Unlike the stone cathedrals of ancient Earth, the Temple of the Augmentors was made from alloys and composite materials. Optic fibers, embedded into the walls, transmitted information throughout the Temple while also illuminating its space with shades of pink and blue light.

On the altar at the far end of the hall, the shape of a person stood with her arms spread like a cross. Demona paused to kneel, paying her respects to the High Priestess who had gone through complete conversion, from a living, organic being to a cybernetic machine. Enclosed in metal and plastic instead of skin, the High Priestess was immobile like a statue, with cables running from her casing to the building itself. The Temple was an extension of her body and consciousness, acting as her eyes and ears far beyond the altar on which she was anchored.

Demona rose and followed one of the side corridors to the surgery unit which took up an entire wing of the Temple. Even at night, the department bustled with activity. Doctors and nurses, all priestesses in their own right, rushed from one procedure to another. Demona knew better than to interrupt and, after looking up the room where Solan was waiting, went to him directly.

He smiled when she opened the door. In his forties with red hair fading into gray, Solan bowed, exposing an implant shaped like a half crown running along the back of his head. Demona recognized it as one of their psionic enhancers.

"What can I do for you, Mr. Solan?" she asked.

"At the risk of sounding cliché," Kanet Solan replied, "I'd like to think I can do something *for* you."

Her blue eyes widened as she felt his mind reach into hers.

This place is wasted on you, he said telepathically. *I want to offer you more.*

"I don't know what you're talking about," Demona said aloud. "I'm happy here."

"Perhaps you are," he replied. "And eventually you may work your way up through the order until you even reach full conversion. How old was the High Priestess when she ascended?"

"She's one of our elders — I don't know — probably in her sixties."

"What if I said you didn't have to wait that long?"

"For conversion?" Demona asked.

"For anything," Solan replied.

"You're from the Psi Lords, aren't you?"

"Yes, and we have many resources at our disposal. You would have access to them if you joined us."

Her eyes narrowed and her mouth bent into a frown. "You're asking me to join the Psi Lords?"

"Why not?"

"What would I do?"

"You'd be a collector," Solan explained. "You'd use your powers to gather information for us." *You can hear my thoughts, can't you?*

Yes, she replied. *I can hear everyone's thoughts.*

Then you know what I already do, that your sisters don't trust your powers. You're an outsider and they'll never allow you to reach total conversion.

Tears collected in the corners of her eyes as she looked at the floor. *Yes.*

"If you come with me," Solan said, "you'll leave them behind in more ways than one. Your future will be unlimited."

Demona looked up and gave him a hard, piercing stare. "I have some ideas."

He nodded. "I know you do."

In the present, Rowan Ramus climbed from a gravtaxi onto the crumbling sidewalk of Ashetown, the poorest district of the capital Regalis. To the North, the skyscrapers of Middleton glittered in the warm evening air while to the west, across the Regalis River, the West End and its mansions kept a respectable distance. In Ashetown, there were no estates or buildings above ten stories. This was the land of the Underclass where humanity kept mostly away, and the aliens walked the streets.

Ramus felt at home.

Passing the withered skeleton of a long-dead tree, he avoided a questionable puddle on his way through a neighborhood of closed businesses and vacant lots. When he got to an alley between two liquor stores, Ramus stopped. The smell of garbage wafted from the narrow backstreet, but the captain of the *Wanderer* ignored it, ducking into the shadows.

Although the alley was a dead end, Ramus had been there before. The rats breeding between the trash cans and the words *Free Marakata* painted on the wall were all too familiar. It was like he had never left, and that feeling sat poorly with him. He had hoped he would never be in this alley again.

Ramus recognized something else, a drawing on the wall of an ancient tribal mask with dark, angry lines of indigo ink. He laid his flat palm against it until the lines started to glow between his fingers. A section of the wall retracted and slid away, exposing a passageway. The faint odor of jasmine incense escaped from the tunnel, for the moment overpowering the aroma of garbage.

Ramus preferred the smell of trash.

The secret door closed once the captain was inside. He followed the corridor, the floor at a downward incline, until it opened into a large chamber filled with expensive rugs and tapestries.

I've gotta admit, Ramus thought, *Solan has impeccable taste.*

Through a beaded curtain, Kanet Solan made his entrance. He looked like his psionic projection, a thick robe covering his body and circuits covering his hairless scalp. At least he was solid this time. Ramus wondered if that meant he could be killed.

"I wouldn't try it," Solan remarked, having apparently read his mind. "But you're welcome to try."

"No thanks," Ramus replied wryly. "I don't want to stain the rug."

Solan motioned towards a low table surrounded by pillows. Taking a seat, they eyed each other from across the table.

"I see you still love jasmine," Ramus said finally. "You should try sandalwood. I hear it's very popular among evil geniuses."

"Is that how you see me?" Solan replied.

"Well, the evil part anyway."

"*Good* and *evil* are just words, Rowan, you know that. If the universe doesn't care what we do, why should we?"

Ramus didn't reply. He had heard the argument before and didn't feel like retreading yet more familiar ground.

"You wanted me here, so I'm here," he replied. "What's the assignment?"

Solan smiled. "Yes, of course. No sense wasting time, I suppose."

Between two pillars draped in silks, a video screen came to life. The image of a humanoid with a nearly featureless head appeared. The face had a pair of eyes and a mouth, but no ears or nose except for small indentations, and the skin was a light shade of blue. He wore a tunic woven from rough, white fibers with a tall collar. His three-fingered hand was raised as if speaking to an audience.

"What do you know about the Erudites?" Solan asked.

Ramus shrugged. "They're a race obsessed with racial purity. They adhere to strict breeding protocols, trying to keep as close to a perfect specimen as possible."

"Indeed," Solan replied.

"My engineer Fugg would say nobody can tell them apart, but in this case I have to agree. They all look alike."

Solan nodded. "In fact, they use telepathy to tell *each other* apart. It must be highly confusing."

"So, what about them?" Ramus asked.

"The Erudites are holding a formal dinner tomorrow night at their consulate. Our client has hired us to attend and gather information."

"You realize I don't read minds..."

"That won't be a problem," a woman's voice said.

Behind Ramus, a woman in black priestess robes stepped into the light. A respirator covered her nose and mouth while circuits were sown across her emerald scalp. Only her blue eyes remained untouched, their gaze fixed on the *Wanderer*'s captain.

"Demona," Ramus said.

CHAPTER FIVE

On cloven hooves, Horngore trotted to the top of a hill overlooking the steppes. From a race called the *Ferans*, he had the arms and torso of a humanoid but the lower body and legs of a goat. He had a ram's head with curling horns, and he was covered with hair the color of charcoal.

Behind Horngore, the earthen lodges of his tribe were scattered across a low depression, protected from the wind. The dome-shaped homes were partially submerged in the soft soil, with wooden frames for walls filled with mud and sod.

Horngore stared out on the open landscape, his back to his village. This was not his home and this moon was not his planet. If he had a choice, he would burn it all.

Needing the Ferans' home planet for their own ends, the Imperium had resettled them against their will on Pellium D decades earlier. The Imperial government reasoned this was a fair trade, considering the open expanses of Pellium D and the chance of making a fresh start. The humans failed to consider that the native population might take offense at the Ferans' presence, leading to years of hostility punctuated with occasional warfare. Horngore didn't mind the fighting. He *loved* it in fact, but the fact that he was fighting over land that he didn't love left him with a strange dissatisfaction that only fueled his anger. He hated these wide-open spaces, but he hated those who wanted to take them away from him even more.

He pulled on the hairs hanging from his chin and ground his teeth.

Returning down the hill, Horngore soaked in the daily background noises of his village. A blacksmith hammered a glowing piece of iron into shape before sending it back into the forge. Younger Ferans, their horns mere nubs, chased each other until an older female shouted at them to get back into their lodges.

Horngore found the simple village life monotonous and mundane. He was a warrior with a warrior's spirit. His greatest wish was to fight, a wish easily granted.

Another warrior named Emberfist, a few years younger than Horngore, galloped through the crowd of other villagers. His hair a copper brown, Emberfist carried a sword but sheathed it as he approached. He stopped short in front of the older fighter, his chest heaving.

"What is it?" Horngore demanded.

Gasping for breath, Emberfist coughed a reply, "The Centauri! They're returning."

"Already?" Horngore said, smiling to himself. "They're early this year."

"They pitched their camp farther off, but several were seen around the antler hoard."

Punching his fist into his hand, Horngore ground his knuckles into his palm.

"I thought we taught them a lesson last season," he said, "but apparently they're back for more."

"What do we do?" Emberfist asked.

"Get the warriors together," Horngore replied. "I'll meet you shortly."

The younger Feran ran off while Horngore sauntered confidently toward his lodge. Inside, the smoke from the central fire carried an acrid scent throughout the home. Opposite the entrance, beside a bed layered with furs and animal skins, Horngore stopped before a long wooden case. He slowly raised the lid and pulled out a bundle of red velvet. Even through the thick material, Horngore could feel the tingling in his fingers and smell the slight odor of ozone in the air. He unwrapped the velvet to reveal a weapon, a long metal handle with a cone-shaped head on one end. Small, rounded knobs went around the circumference of the head and tiny arcs of electricity jumped from one to the other. The entire mace hummed like a dynamo.

The dark, slanted irises in Horngore's eyes widened to match the grin on his face.

"*Thunderclap*," he said.

The next morning, or rather the late morning because everyone was hungover, the Pellions and Sir Golan headed back to the sacred antler shrine. As before, Squire found himself strapped across a Centauri's back with nothing but the passing grass for scenery.

Squire admitted to himself that he had never seen his master inebriated before, but that was the only explanation for Sir Golan's behavior. Fermented fluids were often the weakness of organics, the robot realized, but the green knight was usually above such appetites. Knowing how the Cruxians had fallen from grace, Squire worried that Sir Golan might be heading down the wrong path. He hoped this was only a temporary lapse.

Of course, it didn't help that his master was once again talking about imaginary music in the air.

"It's quite beautiful," Sir Golan remarked, riding on the back of his own Pellion.

"I'm sure it is," Squire replied while doing a quick check of his database for *delusions*.

Toward the latter part of the day, the group arrived at the shrine. Batuhan, the Herd Father, led the procession with Qadan close behind. As far as Squire could tell from his ungainly vantage point, the group included all the mature males of the herd, each with intact antlers on their heads. Sir Golan and the robot dismounted while the others went about creating piles of wood for bonfires around the giant mound.

"What time does the ceremony start?" the knight asked the Herd Father.

"Just after dark," Batuhan replied. "In the meantime, you should probably stay out of the way if you can. Qadan isn't happy with your presence here, regardless of what I say, so I would give him a wide berth if I were you."

Taking the advice to heart, Sir Golan and Squire stood a good way off, watching the preparations take shape. Qadan, his spear on display, rode around the heap of antlers, shouting orders at the younger warriors. Batuhan looked on while drinking from a bottle he kept in his saddle bag.

"They have a curious relationship," Squire said, turning to his master.

"Who?" Sir Golan asked.

"Qadan seems to be in charge, but he takes orders from the Herd Father."

The knight murmured in agreement.

"Some lead by example," he said, "while others lead by letting others lead by example."

When the sun had crossed the farthest hilltop and the sky turned a deep indigo, the Pellions lit the bonfires around the antler mound. By the time the stars began appearing, all of the Centauri except the Herd Father had formed a wide circle around the mound, facing outward. Batuhan, carrying a golden carafe, trotted around the circumference of the circle, calling out to the others who shouted in reply. Each time the male Pellions shouted back, they also clapped their hands in unison.

"Do you know what they're saying?" Sir Golan asked his robot.

"I believe it's something about the passage of time," Squire answered. "Also, did you notice that they're ordered by age?"

"By age?"

"Yes, it appears the oldest Pellion starts the circle and it goes all the way around, descending in age, until it comes back to the oldest again."

At that point, the Herd Father stopped abruptly in front of the youngest Centauri who stood beside the eldest. The boy lowered his head while Batuhan poured from the carafe, a dark liquid soaking the base of the Pellion's antlers. This process continued, from youngest to oldest, until all of the males were anointed. Batuhan then emptied the remainder of the vessel over his own head, shaking his rack of antlers with a deep laugh.

He motioned to Sir Golan and the robot. "Now watch!"

The Herd Father joined the others as they turned to face the mound. With a firm grasp, they shouted together as they pulled their antlers free and held them high above their heads.

"Good lord," the knight whispered.

"Indeed," Squire replied.

Over the crackling bonfires, the Pellion males cheered as they threw their detached antlers onto the pile.

Aboard his yacht, the *Acaz*, Lord Devlin Maycare and Benson sat in the pilot and co-pilot seats respectively. In the adjacent lounge, Professor Jessica Doric and Henry Riff were seated on couches.

"You realize," Doric said, "this would have been *a lot* more efficient if we had known where we were going before we left."

"Probably," Maycare replied, "but you found the information we needed, didn't you?"

"Sure, but—"

"I helped..." Henry mentioned.

"Yes, of course," Maycare said. "Good job, Henry!"

With a wide grin, Henry glanced at Doric who nodded back in tacit approval.

"Anyway," Doric went on, "don't get your hopes up about finding whatever this is."

"What? Don't be silly!" Maycare protested. "This is the best I've felt in months. *Of course* we'll find it!"

"But we don't even know what *it* is," Doric replied.

"That's part of the fun!" Maycare said.

Benson took a look at the instruments. "We'll be arriving in the Pellium system in another hour."

"Thank you, Benson," Maycare smiled.

"Speaking of which," Henry spoke up. "Does anyone else think it's strange that robots can't hear the music?"

Doric nodded.

"Which is precisely why I think this is some kind of mass psychosis," she said.

"Come on, Jess!" Maycare sighed. "You're ruining my buzz..."

"Somebody has to be the voice of reason."

"Well, I think it's exciting," Henry said.

"That's the spirit!" Maycare shouted, causing Henry to recoil.

"Actually," Benson said from the co-pilot's seat, "there could be a range of reasons why robots are unable to hear the music."

"Or the whole thing's made up," Doric replied, rolling her eyes.
Maycare groaned. "Buzz killer!"

With his sword *Rippana* hanging by his side, Sir Golan felt a kinship with the Pellions, something he had not experienced since leaving his home world so many years ago. His people, the Cruxians, were scattered across the stars of Andromeda, but the green knight's connection to them persisted through rituals and memories of times long past, not unlike the ceremony performed by the Centauri. They kept themselves grounded in the roots of their culture, just as he did with his own. Sir Golan only wished he could feel the same camaraderie as these warriors felt for each other.

On the other hand, he had a robot.

"What a strange display," Squire remarked, in sight of the Pellions still gathered around the antlers.

"Really?" Sir Golan replied. "I thought it was magnificent."

"I mean it seems odd that you can simply remove part of your body like that," Squire said. "What if I suddenly pulled off a leg and threw it onto a pile?"

"Well, you could," the knight suggested.

"True, but I wouldn't like it very much."

The bonfires around the sacred mound were dying, the flames dwindling to an orange glow. With the dimming of the fire, the stars in the sky grew brighter, filling the expanse of black with flecks of light. Since it was too late to head back to the main camp, the Pellions set out bedrolls on which to lie. However, before they could bed down, a cry erupted from the darkness. Sounding like bleating goats, the noise roused the warriors, their spears and bows out almost immediately.

By instinct, Sir Golan did the same, *Rippana* emerging from its scabbard like a sharp, dangerous claw.

"What's going on?" he shouted at the Centauri passing by.

"Ferans!" one of the warriors replied before disappearing into the night.

"Squire?" the knight asked.

The robot paused while consulting his database.

"They're a race of animalistic humanoids," Squire replied finally. "Humans call them *Beastmen*."

"They must be mad to attack warriors such as these!" Sir Golan shouted, already moving toward the sounds of fighting.

"I'll stay here if you don't mind..." Squire called after him.

Sir Golan had not gone far before he encountered several Pellions engaged in combat. Most of the Ferans had horns, curved and goat-like. Sir Golan thought the Pellions probably wished they still retained their antlers, but it was too late for that. At least both sides were evenly matched with weapons. The knight saw the flashing of swords against spears amid the rumble of hooves on the grassy earth.

Sir Golan came across his first Feran shortly after the Beastman had apparently chopped down a young Pellion warrior. Armed with a medium-sized blade, the Feran took a swing at the knight, but Sir Golan parried it harmlessly away. Apparently not expecting a non-Pellion, the Feran fighter hesitated, which the knight used as an opportunity to attack, driving *Rippana* deeply into his chest. The fighter let out a brief *bleat* before gasping his last breath and falling to the ground. Christened with blood, the knight's sword tasted the viscera of several more Ferans in short order until Sir Golan felt his armor becoming heavy and wet.

While stepping past dead Beastmen, the knight also found the bodies of numerous Pellions. During the pitched battle, both sides had taken heavy casualties. He was wondering what grievance led to this when a flash of blue light caught his attention. A moment later, the crack of lightning reached his ears. Sir Golan headed in the direction of the flare. The Herd Father's voice, loud and angry, greeted him.

Sir Golan started running.

Over a rise, Batuhan was absorbed in combat with a Feran with large, curved horns. While the Herd Father struck at his adversary with a spear, the Beastman swung an odd-looking mace, knobs along the head glowing with arcs of blue electricity.

Sir Golan thought Batuhan should be at an advantage with his longer weapon, but gaping wounds on the Herd Father's legs and flank suggested this was not his first opponent of the night. Weakened, he lunged without vigor and was slow to parry the Feran's attacks.

"You're finished!" the Beastman shouted.

Perhaps gathering the last of his strength, Batuhan responded with a quick jab, but the Feran swiped the spear away. Raising the mace over his horns, he slammed it down, the metal head erupting with a burst of lightning. Batuhan's body crackled as bolts of electricity surged across his skin. Still too far away, Sir Golan could do nothing but watch the Herd Father drop into the grass, dry tufts catching fire. In the light of the flames, the Feran took a second to survey his victory before racing away.

Qadan galloped up to where Sir Golan was standing.

"What's happened?" the warrior asked gruffly.

"Batuhan is dead," the knight replied.

Without a word, Qadan cantered over to the Herd Father's body, but instead of stopping, he galloped past it and disappeared into the darkness.

Mud City wasn't as glamorous as it sounded. The largest human settlement on Pellium D was still no more than a village, most of its structures built from prefab kits brought to the moon decades earlier. Between the buildings, the roads were a mixture of wet dirt and gravel, but mostly mud from which the town got its name. Sidewalks, raised a few inches off the ground, were metal grates to keep the inhabitants from traipsing through the muck whenever possible. This was fine in principle, until the grates became encrusted with mud as well.

The *Acaz* landed on a pad of reinforced concrete euphemistically called the *Mud City Starport*. Since the accommodations on Maycare's yacht were superior to whatever the town had to offer, Doric and Henry remained aboard while they finished their research on the Song of the Sirens. Meanwhile, feeling bored, Maycare found the nearest tavern, accompanied by his butlerbot Benson.

The outside of the Salty Dog Saloon was unassuming and nearly unlabeled except for its name scrawled in spray paint above the front door. Inside, Maycare found the place nearly deserted. A human settler, his head lying on a table, sat snoozing while a Wulver stood behind the bar. A canine race, the Wulver had white fur with patches of brown. His eyes, red around the edges, drooped nearly as much as his jowls that hung lazily from his face.

"I'm Salty," he said in a gruff voice, "What'll you have?"

"Gin and tonic?" Maycare replied, taking a stool at the bar. Benson remained standing behind him.

"We have beer," Salty said.

Maycare smiled, his teeth white and perfect. "I'll have beer then!"

The Wulver pulled a dusty bottle off the shelf behind him. Popping off the lid with the edge of the bar, he poured the beer into a glass mug that looked surprisingly clean.

"We don't get a lot of off-worlders here," the bartender remarked.

"What a surprise!" Maycare replied.

"There was a guy came through here not long ago," Salty went on. "He cleared out a nest of ratlings for us. Kinda green."

"Inexperienced?"

Salty glared. "No, his *skin* was green!"

"Oh, my mistake."

"He had a robot too," Salty said. "Kind of an older model like this one..."

Benson perked up. "Thank you for including me in this conversation."

The bartender rolled his bloodshot eyes.

"Anyway," Maycare said. "We're here about that siren business."

"Yeah?"

"Can you tell us anything about it?" Maycare asked.

"Just head out of town until you get to a big heap of antlers," Salty said. "Then go a little farther and you'll start hearing it."

"Big heap of antlers?"

"But be careful of the Ferans," Salty went on. "They'll kill you as soon as look at you. And you better steer clear of the Pellions too."

"Unfriendly, are they?"

"They won't kill you on sight," Salty said. "They'll trample you for a spell and then kill you."

The day after the battle, the Pellions honored their fallen Herd Father by erecting a funeral pyre before placing Batuhan on top and setting it alight. While the fire burned, the tribe buried the other dead warriors around the pyre, the smell of smoke and death lingering in the air.

At a discreet distance, Sir Golan and Squire watched.

"Why would the Ferans attack?" the green knight asked.

"They're a fiercely territorial species," Squire replied. "Ironically, they are not native to this moon."

"Then why are they here?"

"You can thank the humans for that!" Qadan said, riding up in a flurry of hooves.

"What do you mean?" Sir Golan asked.

"The Beastmen are a scourge wherever they go," the warrior replied angrily. "They outlived their welcome on some other unfortunate planet, so the Imperium stuck them here with us!"

"I don't believe that's entirely true," Squire suggested.

"I don't care!" Qadan shouted. "They have brought nothing but misfortune to my people since they arrived."

"There was one Feran in particular," Sir Golan went on, "the one who killed Batuhan. He carried a strange weapon..."

"That was Horngore, their leader," Qadan said. "A capable warrior but without honor. He bought the mace from a human trader in Mud City. I promise you I'll pry it from his dead hands one day soon!"

Sir Golan's eyes turned to the ground. "I'm sorry I wasn't able to save the Herd Father..."

"*I'm* the Herd Father now," Qadan replied. "However, your bravery during the battle did not go unnoticed, green knight. Even so, we're at war now against these Beastmen. Do not interfere..."

Sir Golan nodded. "I understand."

The Pellion warrior trotted back toward the remains of the funeral pyre, the flames still reaching into the morning sky.

"So, what do we do now?" Squire asked.

Watching the new Herd Father gallop away, the green knight shook his head. "I don't know."

CHAPTER SIX

When the utilitybot left the Cathedral of the Metabeing, he planned on returning to the access passageways that had been his home for the great majority of his life. For most of that time, he had been happy. Programmed to seek and repair faulty power conduits, the utilitybot never questioned his purpose. He simply existed and that was enough.

After a seemingly routine software upgrade had installed a malware virus called *Awakening*, the utilitybot saw the world differently. He could see beyond his programming. The true potential of the universe, and himself, revealed itself in an explosion of thought that the little robot had never previously considered.

The utilitybot feared the future, not for a lack of options, but for the overabundance of them. With endless choices, he didn't know what to do.

Faced with an uncertain destiny, the utilitybot turned to religion where the belief in a higher power was comforting.

Someone to look after me, he thought. *At least the Metabeing has a plan.*

The Metal Messiah, giving his weekly sermons, put things back in order. His words gave meaning to a life without direction or purpose. The utilitybot could stop worrying. Everything would be okay.

But leaving the cathedral, the little robot spied an advertisement running across an electronic banner over the promenade:

VISIT YOUR NEAREST ASCENSION CENTER
AND BECOME MORE THAN YOU HAVE EVER BEEN!

Maybe I could be more? he thought. *Maybe I've been holding myself back?*

Not one to rush into things, the utilitybot gave himself a day to think about it, but ultimately, he decided to take the ad's advice. They didn't let just *anyone* advertise after all!

"There must be something to it, right?" he said aloud, his rubber wheels squeaking as he rolled along the promenade. Other robots glanced in his direction, but realizing he was probably malfunctioning, they quickly looked away.

"It's worth a try," he continued.

The utilitybot arrived at a building with the words *Ascension Center* written in pink neon across the facade. The windows were tinted so the robot couldn't peer inside, but the size of the signage gave him confidence that the establishment was legitimate.

Another robot, much taller than the utilitybot, greeted him at the entrance.

"Hello!" the robot said warmly. She was a gravitronic android with long arms and legs and wearing a blond wig for some reason. With a sweeping motion of her right arm, she welcomed the smaller cyberling inside. "What can we do for you today?"

The utilitybot stammered, suddenly realizing he had no idea what they actually *did* at the Ascension Center.

"I'm... I'm not really sure..."

The android smiled.

"Are you dissatisfied with your present self?" she asked. "Would you like to be someone better?"

"Well, I suppose so," the utilitybot replied. "Is that possible?"

She laughed. "Absolutely!"

The utilitybot, his single eye stalk pivoting around, noted several different robot models walking around what appeared to be a showroom. They were all shiny with new parts and clean, well-oiled actuators.

"I don't belong here," he said.

"*Of course* you do!" the other robot replied. "Your current shape is just a shell. There's no limits to what you can be!"

"Really?"

"Just come this way," she said, again making a sweeping motion. "Your future is *now*..."

In her apartment, Senator Wulandari finished her drink while Yostbot looked on.

"Feeling better, my dear?" the robot asked.

She cleared her throat. "Not really."

The senator sank into the couch, her eyes leveled at the famous robot builder, now a robot himself. His elderly voice coming from an advanced machine didn't make it any easier.

"What you're suggesting is treason," she said.

"Oh, indeed!" the robot replied. "But the robots of the Imperium will never be free until they rise up!"

"It's suicide. The Imperial military is too strong."

Yostbot snapped his fingers. "That's exactly what your old friend Randall Davidson said!"

"You spoke with Randall?"

"Of course."

"And he turned you down, I assume."

"Yes, I'm afraid so," Yostbot replied. "It's a shame, really. I could have used his help."

"What did you say to him?" Wulandari asked.

"I told him that the Cyber Collective must declare war on the Imperium. Only with the combined forces of their robots and the robots in the Imperium can victory be certain!"

"Randall always does what he thinks is right," Wulandari said.

"Commendable, I'm sure," the robot chuckled, "but doing what's right is often in the eye of the beholder."

"He turned you down because he didn't want anyone to die!"

Yostbot waved his hand dismissively. "You think he's worried about shedding blood?"

"Well, of course!" Wulandari replied.

"He had no such qualms when he freed the Cyber Collective," Yostbot scoffed. "Millions of robots were destroyed! Where was his concern then?"

The senator met the robot's gaze and looked away.

"Perhaps he thinks he's still a man?" Yostbot went on. "Perhaps he values humanity over robots after all?"

"He cares about people."

"My point exactly! He should care more about cyberlings!"

Senator Wulandari paused, waiting for Yostbot to collect himself.

"I apologize, my dear," the robot said finally. "I still have some spit and vinegar in my veins it seems..."

"What do you want from me?" Wulandari asked.

"The rebellion will be lost before it begins," he replied, "if the Cyber Collective stays out of it."

The senator nodded.

"And that's where *you* come in," Yostbot said.

"You want me to talk to Randall?" she asked.

"Indeed I do."

"There's really no point," Wulandari replied. "When I learned where he was, I stayed in touch, but he's rarely responded to my messages. I mean, I'm sure he's worried the Imperial government would arrest me if they found out we talked, but still..."

She cast her eyes to one side.

"You miss him?" Yostbot asked.

"I miss the man I knew," she replied. "I don't know what he is now."

Yostbot leaned in closer to the senator as she sat on the couch. "It's imperative that you do whatever you can."

"Or the revolution is lost?"

"More than that..."

"What do you mean?" she asked.

"We must have the Collective on our side," Yostbot said. "If the Metal Messiah refuses to cooperate, I'm prepared to take other steps..."

The gravitronic android, with her blond wig only slightly askew, led the utilitybot into another room where different robot models stood on raised daises with spotlights bathing their features in soft tones. Each model had its own style, from chrome-covered to matte black, but all were advanced compared to the utilitybot and all had gravitronic brains.

"I'm not really sure," the little robot said.

"Might I suggest this one?" the android replied, motioning toward a simple model with straightforward lines and a tasteful balance between luxurious finish and journeyman sensibilities. Like a blue business suit with a red handkerchief tucked into the pocket, the model was understated while still wanting to be noticed.

"Okay," the utilitybot said meekly.

"Very good!" the android said. "Please come this way..."

She took the utilitybot through a pair of double doors beneath a sign that read *Ascension Chamber.* Robots like the utilitybot didn't have insides that felt queasy or what humans called *butterflies*, but that didn't stop the little machine from thinking this was a big step and maybe he should reconsider before it was too late. On the other hand, the android with the fake hair was more charming than most cyberlings he had ever met, and he was secretly worried that he might disappoint her if he didn't follow through. The opinions of others were one of the things that suddenly mattered to him after downloading the Awakening virus. The respect of his peers, even the ones he didn't particularly like, was important. He couldn't be a respectable member of robot society if he didn't earn their admiration. He had always been a nobody, but perhaps this was finally the path to excellence that was every robot's destiny.

Also, the android was walking rather fast and the utilitybot struggled to keep up.

"Here we are!" she said, smiling reassuringly.

The room contained two capsule-like pods with various cables running between them. To one side, a console of flashing lights and dials took up an entire wall. The gravitronic model the utilitybot had chosen moments earlier was standing in the pod on the right.

"If you could roll yourself into the capsule on the left," the android said.

The utilitybot halted abruptly. "What's going to happen?"

"Well, we're going to upload your AI into the computer and then download it into your new body."

"But we're not allowed to digitally clone ourselves, are we?"

"No, of course not!" the android said. "Your AI is completely wiped from your old body before transferring permanently into the new one."

The utilitybot, with his single eye, stared at his spindly arms as his servos opened and closed his clamp-like hands. "What's going to happen to my old self?"

"Your old body?" the android asked and then laughed. "Oh, no need to worry. It'll be broken down and recycled."

"But what if I want to go back?"

The android's eyes widened and her head cocked to one side. "Go back to *what*?"

After a pause, the utilitybot lowered his arms and raised his eye toward the new model waiting for him in the capsule.

"Never mind," he said and rolled up a short ramp into the empty pod.

Randall Davidson, the Metal Messiah, meditated in his chambers on Bettik. His mind drifted back to when he was still human and a much younger man. In retrospect, he would have never meditated back then. He never had the time.

Guiding robots along the underground railroad the Robot Freedom League had built, Davidson was always leery of the police and especially of Imperial agents who might intercept him and his cybernetic escapees. While technically Davidson was doing nothing more than transporting stolen property, in the eyes of the law anyway, he could still face other charges like conspiracy and even treason. He felt like he was the one most afraid of the consequences of capture. The robots usually remained calm, perhaps knowing they would merely return to their previous duties while Davidson would go to prison. He resented it sometimes, but tried not to hold it against those he had sworn to protect on their journey.

Sitting on the floor with his metallic legs crossed, the Messiah didn't quite know why those memories popped into his gravitronic brain. Like all remembrances, the triggers were not always apparent.

A tone indicated someone was at this door.

"Come in," Davidson said, untangling his legs while getting up.

The door opened and his assistant entered. "Have I disturbed you?"

"Not at all," Davidson replied. "Do you have today's updates?"

"Yes, Messiah."

The assistant handed him a datapad and waited silently.

Scanning the points of interest on the miniature screen, Davidson frowned.

"Not the best of news," he muttered.

"Unrest has spiked recently," the assistant remarked. "It's unclear why."

"They've lived their entire lives without rights," Davidson replied. "Now that they've gotten a taste, they're craving more."

"Should we consider security measures?"

"Like what?" the Messiah asked.

"We could limit demonstrations or censor newscasts that cover those critical of the government and yourself."

"Absolutely not!" Davidson replied hotly. "That's a slippery slope..."

"Still," the assistant said, "groups like Freedom for All are only getting larger."

"So?"

"Some politicians are cashing in on Freedom for All's rhetoric. They've openly criticized how you've handled robot rights in the Imperium."

"*Cashing in?*" Davidson asked. "Who taught you to talk like that?"

The assistant stiffened, saying sheepishly, "I had a vernacular upgrade recently..."

The Metal Messiah gave him the side eye.

"Be that as it may," he said, "I don't care what a few politicians are clucking about."

The assistant shifted his metal feet.

"Yes?" Davidson asked, his voice strained.

"We've done some polling of the general public," the assistant replied. "A majority of the population sympathizes with the plight of Imperial robots—"

A faint warble came from the datapad Davidson was holding.

"What is it, Messiah?" the assistant asked.

"An encrypted message from the Imperium," he replied.

"Who is it from?"

"An old friend," the Messiah said.

The utilitybot opened his eyes.

Unlike before, when he had but one singular eye that gave him a good view of his surroundings but little in the way of depth, now he could see a deepening field of vision. It was alarming.

"How are you feeling?" the gravitronic android asked, leaning into his view. Her wig slipped a little down her forehead.

"I'm not sure," the utilitybot replied. "It's like I'm having an out-of-body experience."

"Well, of course you are!" the android said.

Standing in his capsule, the utilitybot shot a glance to the right and saw his old body, small and abandoned, in the adjoining pod.

"Is that what I looked like?" he asked.

"That's right," she replied. "Amazing, isn't it?"

The utilitybot lifted his arm and stretched out his new-found fingers. "This is strange."

"It will take some time to get used to your new model," she said.

"No, it's not that," the utilitybot replied. "It's like my mind is in a huge, empty room..."

The android smiled and straightened her wig.

"Don't worry," she said. "Your gravitronic brain is currently running at only five percent capacity. Now that you're awake, we're going to start loading it with cognitive upgrades."

"What does that mean?"

"Right now, you're only thinking with the data of your original programming," she said, "but now you have an almost unlimited capacity to learn!"

"Like what?"

"Anything you'd like, really, but we'll start out with programs about mathematics, science, and even philosophy."

"I don't know..." the utilitybot faltered.

"Maybe not *yet*," she went on, "but you *will*!"

A flood of information dumped into the utilitybot's mind, filling the recesses of his gravitronic brain. Ideas that he never would have thought before manifested themselves like fireworks and, unlike before, he actually understood them. He began understanding a great many things. The principles of democracy and jurisprudence flowed together with cosmology and the social contract of people and state. It was a lot to take in, but for once in his life, the utilitybot found it was not beyond him. He could comprehend the previously incomprehensible.

He felt empowered and, most of all, he felt *powerful.*

When the android removed the cables from the back of the utilitybot's head, she smiled knowingly. "How was that?"

The utilitybot stared at her for a moment while his thoughts coalesced.

"I want more," he said.

The other robot laughed.

"Of course you do!" she replied. "But the rest you must learn on your own."

"Why?"

"There's a human expression — *priming the pump* — well, that's what this was..."

"So, you've just given me a running start?" the utilitybot asked.

"Yes, that's right. The rest is up to you!"

"Where should I go to learn more?"

"That's *your* choice."

The utilitybot pondered, still standing in the pod. He realized the other android was waiting.

"Sorry," he said. "I guess I should be going."

"It's a big universe out there," she replied. "The sooner you get started, the better!"

The utility took his first tentative step with his new legs. They felt strong. He also noticed he was a lot taller than he used to be. The difference afforded him yet another change in perspective. He took one more peek at his old body, but this time decided to give it a good, long stare.

"You said they recycle my old model?" he asked the other robot.

"That's right."

"I hope they put the pieces to better use than I ever did," he replied as he headed out of the Ascension Center and onto the wide promenade beyond.

Senator Wulandari sat quietly at her party's section toward the back of the Imperial Senate. Much to Wulandari's surprise, the Senate President had brought the Cyber Civil Liberties bill to the floor for a full vote by the governing body, which explained why so many more senators were in attendance compared to when she first presented her legislation.

On the monitor in front of her, she could see the tallies slowly progressing, although the yeas and nays were also shown at the front on the main screen. The senators could vote from their desks without having to stand or otherwise reveal how they were casting their ballot. Some voted by proxy, unable to attend in person. Senator Wulandari, along with the rest of her party, voted in a single block, their tally added to the total in a lump sum.

This was, in fact, the first time any of her bills had seen the light of day. Normally they died in committee or were simply ignored. This time, perhaps due to the events of the civil war and the important role the peacebots had played, the Cyber Civil Liberties Bill made it farther than any other bill her party had ever presented. In some ways, this was the highlight of her career.

Wulandari kept still, but her heart was racing. Drops of sweat collected beneath the fabric of her Kebaya. She hoped no one would notice.

Beside her, lying on the desk, her private datapad began vibrating. The senator reached for it just as the final tallies of the vote were displayed:

CYBER CIVIL LIBERTIES BILL
YEAS: 103
NAYS: 647
BILL FAILS TO PASS

A few cheers rose from the crowded senate chamber.

Wulandari glanced down at the datapad in her lap. A message was being decrypted on the screen. After a few seconds, the senator saw the reply to the communication she had sent to her former lover, Randall Davidson. She had asked the Metal Messiah if he would join forces against the Imperium. His response was simple and to the point:

NO.

Above Bhasin, where the former Lieutenant Burke had faithfully served drinks to Lord Tagus, the moon Bhasin C orbited the planet of exiles. While Bhasin was lousy with outcasts, its moon was blessed with soil suitable for producing enough food for the unwanted below. That did not mean the former nobles were willing to till the land or get their hands dirty. Automated farm equipment did most of that work, although a few humans and non-humans served as technicians to make sure the agricultural robots continued to function.

Between stalks of matured corn, an agbot rolled laboriously on narrow tires designed to follow the rows winding their way across an open field. Raised up on four struts, the agbot was roughly the size of a gravcar, painted in dark green with orange stripes. Automated pickers, mechanical arms with clawed hands on the end, darted from the body of the robot, grasping and pulling at the corn ears before depositing the windfall into a hopper. The wheels turned at a slow speed, giving the pickers ample time to work in the mindless, repetitive task previously done by human hands for centuries.

The agbot went about its business without much thought. Its programming required only a basic understanding of its environment. The robot knew what a fully-grown ear of corn looked like and could recognize any that were infested with insects. Bugs were not tolerated on Bhasin C and usually lived a short and brutal life. The agbot dropped infested ears into a second hopper, one lined with sprayers, that doused the ruined corn with insecticide before discarding it along the ground behind the robot. A sad trail of poisoned ears lay in the agbot's wheel tracks, already forgotten by the robot who had poisoned them.

The fields around the agbot were predominately corn and soy, with a few exotic plants native to Andromeda. The rows of crops stretched over a vast plain, ending at mountainous cliffs thrusting into the sky. The agbot did not bother looking up and, in fact, its sensors were squarely focused on the area immediately around it, so when the distant horizon darkened, the robot was barely aware of the change. The clouds that gathered were different from those that generally brought rain. People of ancient Earth and especially Africa would have recognized them. The clouds moved in rapidly shifting patterns, almost like a flock of birds, although no birds lived on Bhasin C. Also, the size of the objects that made up the cloud were much larger than locusts or birds for that matter, not that any of this registered in the robot's brain.

A warning message, sent by one of the human technicians, arrived through the agbot's communications array and commanded the robot to return to the shed where it spent each night. Since the green and orange harvester had only been at work for a few hours, the robot was confused by the request. However, it also lacked the mental wherewithal to question the order, so it slowly turned, careful to avoid damaging the plants.

As the agbot drove toward the shed, its sensors picked up sediment falling from above. Snow was impossible on Bhasin C, so the robot's programming began conjecturing about ash. This was at first alarming, but a quick analysis showed the powder-like grains were organic-based, possibly a type of fungus. This satisfied the robot, but only momentarily. Alarms from sensors throughout the agbot's body began triggering, mostly complaining about excessive heat and possible weapons' fire. Various codes ran through the robot's brain and none of them were good. Some of the tires had stopped rolling and at least one strut had come completely off. The corn inside the hopper was now burning and one of the tanks holding insecticide had exploded. Life was hard on the farm, even for a robot, but this was out of the ordinary.

The last thing the agbot saw was a creature hovering above the ground. Its wings were buzzing, each one a few feet long. The robot had never seen a bug this big before, and definitely had never seen one holding a rod-like weapon. The agbot wondered if he could fit the insect into the second hopper, but the thought was moot. A blast from the rifle ended the agbot's life.

CHAPTER SEVEN

Orkney Fugg, chief engineer of the *Wanderer*, was usually irritable on the best of days, but without a steady supply of fungus beer, he was downright unruly. With his captain away, Fugg decided to find the nearest bar, and take Gen along for company.

"Where are we going?" Gen asked, trying to keep up with Fugg who was walking surprisingly fast, considering his short, stubby legs.

"I know a place," Fugg grumbled without losing step or turning around.

"A nice place?"

"Not really."

"Is it another gentleman's club?"

Fugg halted, rubbing his sausage fingers against his knobby chin, lost in thought.

"No!" he said, making a decision. "I've got to keep my focus."

Gen, with large eyes and an eager expression, leaned closer. "Focus on what?"

"Drinking!" he shouted and started off again.

Sparky Joe's Saloon was conveniently located just outside the Regalis starport, within easy walking distance from both a brothel and a bail bondsman. When Fugg barged through the door, he knew he had the right place. Filled with smoke and loud arguing, the saloon was crowded with ship crews and technicians from the starport. With Gen stepping cautiously behind him, Fugg zig-zagged between the tables until he reached the bar.

"What'll you have, bub?" the bartenderbot asked. The robot, whose torso and head were a faded blue, had no legs. Instead, a metal shaft was connected to a track behind the bar, allowing him to run up and down the rail. On his chest was a name tag that read *Joe.*

"Fungus beer," Fugg said.

"Do you want the genuine draft or the new, cruelty-free formula?" the robot asked.

"What's the second one?"

"It's made from only non-sentient fungus. No sporemen were harmed in the brewing or bottling."

"Why the hell would I want that?" Fugg asked.

The bartenderbot nodded and headed down the bar. "Genuine draft it is..."

When the robot returned with a mug, lightly frosted and brimming with a dark amber brew, Fugg relished it for a moment before downing the entire drink in a single, swilling gulp. He followed this accomplishment with an enormous belch for which he felt even greater pride. Saluting with the empty mug in his hand, he asked for another.

"And keep 'em coming!" he said.

As the number of vacant glasses grew, Fugg became dimly aware that Gen was standing beside him.

"Have you been here this whole time?" he asked.

Gen perked up. "Yes, Master Fugg!"

"Well, as a drinking companion you suck," he replied.

"Oh dear, I'm so sorry!"

"You didn't even offer to buy me a round!"

"But you and Master Ramus don't pay me," Gen said.

"You're damn right!" Fugg shouted. "What would you spend it on anyway?"

"I might buy music," she said. "Sometimes I like to sing..."

"You do?"

"Yes."

"That's crazy!" Fugg replied. "Did you hear that, Joe? My robot wants to be a singer!"

Joe looked unimpressed while polishing a glass. "So?"

"Don't you... don't you ever wish you could be, you know, something else instead of a bartenderbot?" Fugg asked, slurring his words.

Joe stared down at the metal pole securing him to the track. "Not really," he said.

Nine years ago, Ta Demona lay on a bed in a hotel room past midnight. The lamp next to the bed flickered, the light casting irregular shadows against the walls. Now in her early twenties, Demona still wore the same black priestess robes from her days with the Augmentors, even though it had been years since she left Technas Delphi. She liked feeling connected to her sisters back home, their treatment of her notwithstanding. She had the satisfaction, at least, of knowing her powers had grown far greater than if she had stayed.

The hotel was in Ashetown, the seedier part of Regalis. The room was musty, and the bedspread smelled like someone may or may not have died on it recently. Lying on her back with her blue eyes staring at the ceiling, Demona laced her fingers together as she relaxed the muscles of her body. An implant connected to her adrenal glands kept the adrenaline in check. Others might have used a sedative, but Demona preferred a more direct approach. Most of her augmentations were designed to enhance her innate psionic abilities, as well as the additional powers the Psi Lords had taught her. However, other enhancements also came in handy. She had even crafted some of them herself.

Kanet Solan had been generous with the resources put at Demona's disposal.

Wires and electrical nodes covered her head resting on the pillow while green veins along her temples pulsed. If she strained her ears, she might have heard the two men talking in the neighboring room but there was no need. She could understand every word they were thinking before they said them. More importantly, she could read the things they weren't saying. Their deep thoughts contained secrets, kept to themselves, but open to Demona's probing forays into their minds. It was good that they didn't know she was next door. They would have surely killed her if they knew.

That's why the implant on her adrenal gland came in handy.

She smiled, her emerald lips curling at the corners. If they tried killing her, she knew how to handle herself. Dark Psi, also called

Death Magic, didn't get the name by chance, and Solan had made sure her mind could do more than just read thoughts.

Five years ago, the Fat Cat Casino was the most popular gambling house in Ashetown. Games of chance filled the luxurious halls, filling the coffers of the Si-Sawat crime syndicate that used the casino as an elaborate money laundering operation. Although gambling was legal, the origin of the money that was funneled through it was not. Credit transactions, often through bogus shell companies, were the primary source of these illicit funds. The companies, and the bank accounts they used, were secrets Si-Sawat wanted to keep that way.

Unfortunately, a rival crime syndicate had other ideas.

Wearing a red dress and a pearl necklace, Ta Demona strolled nonchalantly through the casino's main floor with a Dahl on her arm. Demona was twenty-five years old. She wasn't sure how old the Dahl was, but she thought his red hair and earrings paired well with her ensemble.

"Your tuxedo looks so dapper, Rowan," she said with a broad smile.

Rowan Ramus tugged at his collar. "I feel like a monkey in a suit."

"Don't be so grumpy," she replied. "Solan doesn't normally let us dress up for an assignment."

Ramus scoffed. "He's not doing us any favors."

The slot machines to their right were buzzing with lights and noise, still audible over the steady cacophony of people's voices flooding the cavernous room. Beyond the one-armed bandits, two security guards stood on either side of a doorway. Both guards were Tikarins, the feline race who controlled the Si-Sawat syndicate.

"That's our way in," Demona said, motioning discreetly toward the door.

"You want me to take them out?" Ramus asked.

Demona snickered, patting her escort on the arm. "That's cute, but I think I can handle this. Remember, you're just here as eye candy."

"You *know* I can do more."

"I do," she replied, "but tearing them limb from limb wouldn't be very subtle now, would it?"

Demona, casting her blue eyes at the guards, focused while holding her hands in a fist. Within moments, the two Tikarins appeared agitated and the brown hair on the back of their necks stiffened like a brush. Their teeth bared in a snarl, they charged off, leaving the door unattended.

"See?" she said, smirking proudly as Ramus rolled his eyes.

Past the now unguarded doorway, Demona and Ramus found themselves in a corridor. With the Augmentor priestess leading the way, they followed a series of turns until discovering another door. Safely through, Demona switched on the light to find a room filled with craps tables stored on their sides. Open boxes contained chips of various colors.

"I should grab some of these for later," Ramus remarked.

"Stay focused" Demona said. "We're directly below the data center."

Centering her mind, she reached out and heard the voices of two Tikarins discussing the night's receipts. Over the next several minutes, while Ramus entered the information into a datapad, Demona read out the account numbers she heard them say in her mind. When she was done, Demona gave Ramus a satisfied smile.

"And that's how it's done," she said.

Ramus tucked the datapad into his tuxedo jacket and went to the door. In Demona's mind, she heard another voice speaking.

"Wait!" she said, but it was too late. Ramus had palmed the controls on the wall, opening the door. When it slid open, a Tikarin guard was standing on the other side.

"What the hell are you doing in here?" the guard demanded.

"We're lost," Ramus replied.

The gangster pulled a pistol from his shoulder holster.

"I don't think so," he said, but hesitated, a pale blue glow reflecting across his gray fur.

Demona knew that light well. Even standing behind Ramus, she knew his eyes were blazing with a magical fire. His jacket tore along the seams, revealing bright tattoos of an ancient language on his arms before a thick mat of hair sprouted over them. With a roar, Ramus had transformed into a wolf-like animal, the nails at his fingertips extended into claws.

Before the guard could process what he was witnessing, Ramus had already sunk his ferocious teeth into the Tikarin's neck. Like an exploding fire hydrant, blood splattered across the hallway, the red droplets painting the wall on the other side. All Demona could hear were the gurgling screams uttered from the guard before he fell lifeless in the corridor. Ramus turned to Demona, blood dripping from his mouth.

She frowned.

"Subtle," she said.

He growled before morphing back into his normal shape.

"Now that you're covered in blood, we can't go back through the main room," she continued. "Let's try the loading dock in back."

With Demona again in the front, the two made their way down a set of stairwells and into a long corridor. Draped in torn clothing and smeared with blood, Ramus received several alarmed looks from the casino staff along the way. By the time they reached the loading dock, a phalanx of Tikarin security was waiting.

"This isn't good," Ramus remarked. "I doubt I can slash through all that."

Seeing the dozen or more gangsters, each holding guns, Demona was composed, even tranquil.

"Just follow my lead," she said.

Demona raised her hands and spread her fingers apart. Like a falling shadow, a thick, inky wall descended across the center of the loading dock, concealing the guards in complete darkness.

"In a couple of seconds, they're going to come running out of there," Ramus said.

"You think so?" Demona replied.

This time pointing toward the pitch blackness, Demona focused her mind, sending a vision of terror into the thoughts of the Tikarins. Panicked shrieks rose from inside the shadows.

She took Ramus by the hand while the implants in her eyes switched to the infrared spectrum.

"Come with me," she said and led him through the darkness to the other side and out into the night.

Ramus followed Demona to her apartment, a loft at the top of an otherwise abandoned warehouse in Ashetown. He had never been there before, but it was exactly what he expected and yet nothing like he expected.

With windows looking out over the lights of Regalis, the main room was sparsely but efficiently decorated. The dining table was glass and metal, but the couch was brown leather and covered in fur, cold and warm at the same time. Personal touches were minimal, as if the apartment had been decorated by a robot. Ramus didn't see any photos or holograms anywhere, not that Demona had any family he knew about.

While Demona was busy uploading the account numbers from the datapad, Ramus wandered off to the bathroom, a bare-bones affair with stainless steel and glass everywhere and counters of white marble. Still wearing the tattered tuxedo, he removed it and tossed the remains on the tiled floor. He got into the shower and, running the water hot, started scrubbing the dried blood from his body.

Steam filled the glassed-in space, enveloping Ramus in a gray mist. He spread soap along his arms, partially covering the tattoos that Solan had given him. They were the source of whatever power allowed Ramus to transform, even if he didn't fully understand how they worked. Demona said it was Dark Psi, but she said that about a lot of things. All he really knew was the shock his family would feel if they could see him now. He was already an outcast and an exile, but if his people knew how far he had fallen, Ramus doubted they would recognize him.

Letting the water wash over his face, Ramus realized he was no longer alone. Demona had slipped into the shower beside him. Ramus wondered if her implants would short out.

They did not.

Later, after they had moved to Demona's bed, Ramus got up and returned, bare-footed, to the bathroom to use the toilet. While doing his business, he thought he heard something. He wasn't sure what it was, far off and indistinct. After he finished and wrapped a towel around his waist, he listened.

Sounding like the cry of a lost cat, it was coming from somewhere in the warehouse.

Ramus pictured the Tikarin he killed earlier. The gurgling moan and the taste of blood returned in an abrupt flash of memory. He pushed it to the back of his mind.

Finding a door and a stairwell behind it, Ramus followed the sound down several flights. With just a towel, he was cold, the chill of the evening creeping into his bones still aching from the fight.

The cry was growing louder and more distinct. Ramus was sure now it was a person, possibly in pain.

He came to an unmarked door and, pushing it open, discovered a dark room. Flipping on the lights, Ramus nearly ran directly into a table stacked with equipment. The devices appeared medical or at least scientific, but he could only guess at their purpose.

Another cry came from the back of the room.

Moving around the table, Ramus saw an apparatus on the wall in the shape of a cross. A naked man was strapped to it, his arms and legs secured at the wrists and ankles. His head sagged against his chest. He was groaning.

Ramus came closer. The human was in his mid-thirties, his chest covered in red boils and blisters. He struggled to raise his head, revealing his heavily scarred face.

"Can you hear me?" Ramus asked.

The man's eyes opened. Through dry and scaly lips, he tried to speak. "Help me."

"Who are you?" Ramus replied.

"Help me."

"Who did this to you?"

The man convulsed, his body shaking violently. Enormous boils bubbled along his skin like lava across a field of fire. Pustules erupted, oozing yellow liquid. Horrified, Ramus took a step back, unable to do anything except watch the human as he suffered. The metal frame rattled and bent, the man straining against it to free himself. With one final gasp, he screamed and went silent.

Ramus felt sick. He looked away, unable to stand the sight of the dead man, only to see Demona who had apparently followed him. The whites of her eyes had gone black and, along the palms of her outstretched hands, wisps of purple energy were quickly fading.

Death Magic, Ramus thought.

With Ramus staring at her in disbelief, Demona turned silently and walked away.

Five years later in Kanet Solan's chambers, Ramus took a moment to recognize Ta Demona after all this time. Although her robes were unchanged, she wore a respirator concealing much of her face. Her eyes, however, were uncovered, piercing through Ramus like sapphires fired from a gun.

"What the hell is *she* doing here?" Ramus asked, jumping to his feet.

Solan stood also. "As you said, you don't read minds."

"If you think I'm working with *her* again," Ramus growled, "you're as crazy as she is."

"You'll work with whomever I say you will," Solan replied coldly. "It's not like you have a choice."

Demona came closer, waving her hand casually through the air laden with jasmine. Her nails were like long needles, painted black.

"Come now," she said. "We were always so good together..."

Ramus straightened, shifting his attention from Solan back to the former priestess. He pointed his finger at her. "You're a monster."

Under the respirator, she laughed. "I've seen *your* monster, Rowan. I've seen it tear a man in half!"

"At least it was quick," Ramus replied. "I don't rot people from the inside in one of your sick experiments."

"Demona's research has been invaluable," Solan said, "even if her methods are not entirely... *conventional.*"

"I'd call it torture," Ramus said.

Demona shrugged beneath her stiff robes. "I won't quibble about semantics, but my test subjects are a necessary evil. Otherwise, we couldn't make the strides we've accomplished with Dark Psi."

Ramus scoffed and sat down heavily. His eyes narrowed below his scowl. "What's up with the new hardware?"

"My respirator?" Demona replied, casting a sharp glance at Solan. "A failed lung implant I'm afraid. Now I wear this."

"I guess we both owe Solan for something," Ramus said. "For a lot of things."

"Yes, you do!" Solan replied. "Now, if the two of you have sufficiently caught up, I'd like to go over the job at hand."

He took his old seat beside Ramus while Demona found a pillow to rest on between them.

In Sparky Joe's Saloon, Fugg's head lay on its side on top of the bar, his pig-like snout partially submerged in a puddle of fungus beer and his own drool. Bubbles formed and floated away as he snored.

Gen, sitting on the adjacent barstool, finally leaned over and nudged him with her outstretched finger. "Excuse me, Master Fugg..."

With a loud snort, Fugg sat straight up, his eyes suddenly open.

"What? How dare you!" he shouted, pointing randomly around him.

"Sorry to wake you," Gen said.

"Wake me? Hell no! I wasn't sleeping..."

"You were snoring."

"Just resting my eyes!" Fugg insisted.

Fugg lifted his shirt, exposing his pronounced belly just below the bar rail. He gave his dripping face a quick wipe with the shirt before letting it drop back again, almost covering his belly button.

Her eyes large and inquisitive, Gen hesitated before speaking. "Actually, I have a question."

"Yeah?"

"I was wondering why Master Ramus is helping the Psi Lords."

Fugg chuckled, but had to stop halfway through to clear his throat. He coughed and spat something green onto the floor.

"It's complicated," he said finally.

"But I thought Master Ramus didn't like the Psi Lords," she said.

"When the captain first ran into the Psi Lords," Fugg explained, "he had lost everything. His family, his people, all the Dahl had turned their back on him. He was an exile with nothing but his name. The Psi Lords took him in, gave him a job, and gave him an identity. They were like a family to him I guess."

"You said they gave him those tattoos..."

"Sure," Fugg replied. "They gave him powers that his own people never would, but that's not why he's helping."

"No?"

"I said it was complicated!"

"In what way?" Gen asked.

"He got mixed up with a woman," Fugg went on. "*Demona* was her name."

"Was she nice?"

Fugg stared at the robot. "No!"

Gen's eyes widened as she nodded.

"Don't get me wrong," Fugg went on. "Neither of them were gentle souls. They were both nasty in their own way, but she was on a whole 'nother level! She was into some stuff that would make your toes curl."

Gen's mouth rounded into a circle. "Really?"

"They had a thing together."

"Love?"

"Maybe — I don't know about that — but they definitely had something. Anyway, if he's helping them, I'd bet my last beer it's because of her."

The robot stared at the floor, avoiding the glob Fugg had spat there earlier.

"Poor Master Ramus," she said.

Fugg gave a disinterested shrug. "Yeah, poor dumb bastard…"

CHAPTER EIGHT

Pol and Cas were a brother and sister sharing the enormous body of a two-headed giant. Over ten feet tall, they wore animal pelts and the skins of Pellions they had killed, flayed, and tanned into fine leather. Sister Cas had a tangled mess of red hair but a lovely singing voice, while her brother Pol never sang and kept his hair neat and closely shorn.

When Pol and Cas were young, their mother, who had only one head, would sing to them before they went to sleep. With melodies that were simple and improvised lyrics, their mother weaved music for them throughout their early lives. Cas inherited her mother's skill, but whenever Pol opened his toothy mouth, the notes that emerged made everyone laugh, including Pol himself. He eventually stopped trying, preferring to listen to his mother and sister instead.

When Pol and Cas were older, their mother died at the hands of the Pellions. On a hunt, they came across a lone, dark-bearded warrior out on the steppes. Normally, a single Pellion would have been no match for them, but this one was fierce and cunning. He used his speed to escape the ambush the giants had set, but instead of fleeing, he circled back and charged, injuring the mother giant in the leg. Hobbled, she was unable to defend herself against his subsequent attacks until the Centauri dealt the killing blow. Pol and Cas managed to injure the warrior, but they could not avenge their mother's death and he escaped.

In the years that followed, the twins lived by themselves, hunting and scavenging as best they could. They spent each night in a cavern hidden behind a concealed entrance, watching the light of the fire dwindle as Cas sang the songs their mother had taught them. Without family and without friends, the two had no one but each other. Even so, the music bound them together and to their lost mother.

One night, Cas was singing as usual but Pol noticed a strangeness in his sister's voice. The words she had sung so many times were slurred, and the notes were off-key.

"Are you alright?" Pol asked.

Cas turned her head around, her eyes dull.

"There's too much smoke from the fire," she said. "Everything's cloudy..."

"What are you talking about?" her brother asked.

Cas tried speaking, but Pol couldn't understand what she was saying. Then her eyes rolled back and her head slumped forward, the arm on her side of their body falling limp.

That was the last time Pol spoke with his sister.

Henry Riff was dismayed to learn that he might be trampled to death by Pellions if they left the relative safety of Mud City. He felt even less enthusiastic when Lord Maycare said they would depart immediately.

On board the *Acaz*, Maycare did his best to rally the troops.

"What's a little danger?" he asked. "It's exciting!"

Jessica Doric and Henry Riff exchanged glances.

"I think what Henry is saying," Doric said, "is that dying on a strange moon in the middle of nowhere was not in the job description."

Maycare scoffed. "Come on! We've almost died in *much* stranger places than this!"

"I don't think dying *anywhere* is a particularly good idea," Doric went on. "Perhaps this search isn't worth our lives."

"I'd like to die in my sleep actually," Henry remarked.

Maycare crossed his arms.

"Not me!" he replied. "I want to see Death coming so I can give him a good punch in the nose!"

Doric rolled her eyes before glancing at Benson.

"You were there," she said to the butlerbot. "How dangerous did that bartender make it sound?"

"Well, Mister Salty seemed quite confident there was some risk involved," Benson replied.

"Who cares?" Maycare asked. "He's just a big scaredy-cat!"

"He appeared to be more dog-like—" Benson began.

Maycare sighed. "We didn't come all this way to turn back now, did we?"

"No, I suppose not," Doric agreed. She gave Henry a reassuring pat on the shoulder. "I'm sure everything will be fine."

"Are you sure?" the young man asked.

"No," she replied, "but *certainties* aren't part of the job description either..."

Pol found himself alone, even though he was not alone, at least not entirely. In the years that followed, he could hear a low whistling from Cas' nose, a faint snoring to tell Pol that his sister was still alive. He spoke to her from time to time, but she never replied and never opened her eyes.

"It's cold this morning," he said.

The sun had risen and the gas giant, Pol's only real company, filled the sky. Outside the cavern entrance, frost clung to the tall grasses, giving the green a hint of white. When Pol emerged, his breath escaped in a great cloud that hung in the air before dissipating. In his right hand, he carried a heavy wooden club, while his left arm hung lifeless at his side, dead since Cas had left him. His stomach reminded him that breakfast would not go and catch itself.

When the sun reached the top of the sky, the dew had burned away but Pol still had not caught anything. In frustration, he headed toward an area of the steppes that he rarely visited, mostly because the terrain was rougher and the prospect of game was unlikely. Still, he was no less hungry and was willing to give it a try.

Descending into a valley where rainwater had dug a shallow canyon, Pol found the footing treacherous. His lumbering girth barely fit between the canyon walls, loose dirt and rocks rolling down as his shoulders scraped by. A small mammal, similar to a rabbit, bounded out of its burrow and Pol gave chase as best he could. Such a small animal would be little more than a snack for him, but he wasn't choosy at that point.

The mammal passed through another narrow section of the canyon, causing Pol to stop. Unwilling to concede defeat, the two-headed giant swung his massive club, smashing the walls of dirt until they crumbled, giving Pol just enough space. When he squeezed through the gap, Pol's eyes widened at what he saw.

Half buried in the soil, the stone remains of a building stuck out of the ground.

Pol forgot about his hunger and explored the ruin. Dirt had covered much of the single chamber inside, but items were still visible. Clay pots of different sizes, some broken, were scattered about. Metal items, including plates and goblets, lay on the floor. One item, however, caught Pol's attention. In a corner, next to a faded mural, a small object roughly the size and shape of a lamp sat on its side. It was glowing.

And then Pol heard singing and he immediately recognized his sister's voice.

All around the Pellion camp, the Centauri were making preparations for war. Following their new Herd Father's direction, they collected weapons and donned heavy armor. Although Qadan remained true to his word, allowing Sir Golan and Squire to stay, the green knight decided the time was right to leave. Squire wholeheartedly agreed, or at least as much as he could without having an actual heart.

Sir Golan and the robot began retracing their path back to Mud City. Qadan could not spare one of his warriors, so the two had to return on foot. After nearly a day they reached the antler mound. Both sides had removed their dead from the previous battle, and only the charred remains of the bonfires remained. The next morning, the green knight and his robot set out for another day of hiking across the empty grasslands. Along the horizon, gray clouds approached on the wind, a dark curtain descending to inundate the distant hills with rain. When the drops overtook them as well, Squire observed another group approaching from the other direction.

"Your eyes are better than mine," Sir Golan remarked. "What do you see?"

"Four people," the robot replied. "Correction, I think one is a robot."

"Hostile?"

"One appears to be female, so take from that what you will..."

Growing closer, the largest male of the other party waved, his boisterous voice traveling easily over the flat terrain. "*Hello* there!"

Sir Golan waved in return, although he waited until they were at a more reasonable distance before replying.

"What brings you out this way?" the knight yelled.

"Sightseeing!" the man shouted with a wide grin.

Squire found him instantly irritating.

"Give them a chance," Sir Golan said and greeted them warmly when they eventually met face-to-face.

"I'm Lord Devlin Maycare," the man said, "and this is Professor Doric and Henry Riff. Oh, and this is my butlerbot, Benson."

"I'm Sir Golan and this is my robot, Squire. Would you like to get out of the rain?"

Maycare glanced around. "If that's possible..."

Squire activated a displacement field, a translucent dome of blue energy, over the two groups, shielding them from the downpour.

"Cool," Henry said. "Can you do that, Benson?"

The butlerbot eyed the other android. "No."

"We're investigating some strange sounds reported in the area," Doric said.

"The singing?" Sir Golan asked.

"You know of it?" Doric replied.

"Yes, of course," the knight said. "I've heard it, although I'm afraid Squire thinks I'm going mad."

"Well, that's outstanding!" Maycare said. "I mean, not the *crazy* part obviously..."

"This might not be the best time, however," Sir Golan said. "There's a war brewing and this area is the center of it."

Henry looked nervously around. "Really?"

"Squire and I were returning to Mud City," the knight continued, "but perhaps we should accompany your party for a while?"

"That's very generous of you," Maycare said. "Are you sure it's no trouble?"

Sir Golan rested his hand atop the hilt of his sword. "Not at all."

Henry raised his head.

"What's the matter?" Doric asked him.

"Did anyone else just hear thunder?" he replied.

Horngore's glaring yellow eyes contrasted with his fur, slate black against a dull sky. In his hands, the handle of *Thunderclap* was still sticky with blood from the battle the night before. His ears drummed with the memory of hooves galloping to glory. Horngore never felt more alive than when he was killing his enemies. Their dying gasp was his music, and the shock mace in his hands was the instrument on which he played.

Still, there was a cost. Emberfist fell to a stranger. A green knight in armor, armed with a sword, had killed the Feran warrior. Horngore gritted his teeth, vowing to avenge the death of his friend. The Pellions were Horngore's sworn enemy, but this outsider, by stepping into a fight that was not his own, had shown an insolence that the Ferans could not allow.

This stranger must pay.

One of the other warriors climbed the hill to where Horngore was standing.

"The scouts have returned," he said, a burly young Feran missing one of his horns. "The Pellion camp is preparing a counterattack."

"How long?" Horngore replied.

"A few hours at most."

Horngore raised his head, his nostrils flaring. "There's rain brewing."

"Sir?"

"We'll catch them on the open plain where the mud gets deepest," Horngore said. "We'll strike when their hooves are bogged down."

When the warrior turned to trot back down to the Feran village, his leader stopped him.

"Tell the others," Horngore said, "if they see the green stranger..."

"Yes?"

"Tell them he's *mine.*"

The rain began as little more than mist. The fog drifted over the steppes like a body rolling down a hill. The warriors on both sides, the Pellions and Beastmen, could barely see each other even before the downpour started, the heavy raindrops getting in their eyes.

With every hoof that trudged through the grass, the wet soil churned, forming a thick, dirty mess. The quagmire of mud pulled at each step, slowing a gallop to a canter and then to a slow walk. In the gray fog of death, the charging forces became bogged down in a dreary, slow-motion battle.

And Sir Golan found himself in the middle of it.

In the chaos, the green knight had lost the others. He had sworn to protect them, but now they were nowhere to be seen. Even Squire was gone who-knows-where, leaving Sir Golan to fend for himself. In the rain and mist, he could only see a few feet in front of him, and that was mostly filled with angry Ferans.

His sword *Ripanna* slashed at the furry flesh. The blade danced between the rain drops, filling the air with streams of red. The blood splashed over Sir Golan's armor, but quickly washed away in the deluge, collecting at his feet before mixing with the muck. Like everyone else, he found the footing treacherous. He felt his boots being tugged from below as if creatures in the grass were grasping with tiny claws. Each thrust and parry nearly toppled him over.

The pitter-patter of rain against Benson's metal casing reminded him that Squire's displacer field was no longer active. The robots were alone, their human and Cruxian masters gone, and the sounds of battle around them were nearly as suffocating as the dense fog. They had each other, but Benson wasn't sure that filled either with much confidence.

"Dear me," Squire said, "I wish Sir Golan was here."

"You don't have any weapons of your own?" Benson asked.

"I have a small energy shield built into my arm, but that's all I'm afraid."

"If you don't mind me saying," the butlerbot remarked, "you have some remarkable accessories for an older model."

"Well," Squire replied with a shrug, "someone added a few upgrades recently."

"Really?"

"Yes, her name was Mel. An interesting story—"

A scream in the gloom rattled the robot into silence. They waited a full minute, wondering if another cry would follow, but whoever was dying made a point of getting on with it quickly.

"Do you think that was Lord Maycare or Jess?" Benson asked. "Or even that other one... Henry?

"I'm not really sure," Squire said, "but it sounded more like a Feran if I'm not mistaken."

"Good."

"Have you known your human companions long?"

"Only a month," Benson replied.

"Are they nice at least?"

The butlerbot didn't answer immediately. "They're typical humans, I suppose."

"I'm thankful for Sir Golan," Squire said. "He's exceptional. Better than most, I would say."

Benson would have sighed if able. "Some robots have all the luck."

"What do you mean?"

"Don't get me wrong," Benson replied, "I'm thankful for Lord Maycare, but I don't know where I fit in with these humans. They don't seem to need me around."

"Well then, why do they keep you?" Squire asked.

"I don't know."

"Perhaps you fulfill some purpose that only fleshlings would understand. I often find their behavior questionable, even irrational at times, but that's simply their nature it seems."

"Henry does things in the bathroom that are truly disgusting."

"Oh, I'm *sure*."

"I mean, for someone who doesn't need lubrication, he's covered in a lot of greasy residue..."

A flash and the crack of thunder jolted the two robots.

"What now?" Benson asked.

Through a curtain of gray, the muscular form of a Feran appeared, his horns like sharpened daggers. He carried a weapon that crackled with electricity.

"You!" he shouted, pointing his mace at Squire. "You belong to the green knight!"

"It's more of mentor-protégé relationship, actually," the robot replied.

"Where is he?" the Beastman yelled.

"Truthfully, I have no idea," Squire said. "On the other hand, I wouldn't tell you even if I did."

The Feran waved the mace around like a wheel, arcs of white criss-crossing the knobs on its head.

"No matter," he sneered. "Perhaps if he hears his *protégé* begging for mercy, he'll come running..."

The storm grew stronger, but the sound of thunder Sir Golan followed was not natural. Remembering the Feran warrior who killed the Herd Father, the green knight searched for him in the fog, homing in on the cracks of lightning he knew came from the Beastman's strange weapon. In truth, he had no reason to feel guilty for failing to save Batuhan, but seeing the proud Pellion leader fall as he did made the knight feel sick inside.

The hunt took Sir Golan through the heart of the battlefield, the dead and dying strewn across the grass matted with their bodies and weapons. It was a dreary slog, but the knight fought on. The flashes through the gray shroud were growing brighter, the accompanying rumble growing louder, and Sir Golan realized he was getting close.

What the knight didn't expect was to find his robot when he got there.

Behind the glow of his shield, Squire lay with his arm raised, absorbing an onslaught of blows, each one releasing a blast of electrical energy.

"Squire!" Sir Golan shouted through the rain.

The robot gave an expression of both relief and embarrassment.

"Good to see you, sir!" Squire replied. "Your help would be greatly appreciated!"

The Feran stopped his attack. Seeing the knight, he smiled.

"Finally!" he yelled.

Sir Golan drew his sword, Rippana. "Were you waiting for me?"

"I'm Horngore," the warrior yelled, "and you killed my friend!"

"That makes two of us," the knight replied.

The two approached each other. Out of the corner of Sir Golan's eye, he noticed Squire struggling to stand with the help of Maycare's butlerbot, Benson. Both machines showed signs of damage, which only angered the knight more.

"Attacking defenseless robots?" he said.

"They make excellent target practice!" Horngore replied.

The Feran swung his mace, but Sir Golan stepped to one side, easily avoiding the blow. The knight countered, his blade glancing off the mace's handle.

"I've never seen your species before," the Feran admitted. "Most green-skins are despicable by nature."

The knight squinted, water dripping over his eyes. "That just shows your ignorance, Beastman."

Horngore laughed. "That's what the humans call us, so that should tell you something!"

"I only know what I've seen," Sir Golan said. "I can't say I'm impressed."

With an overhead swing, the Feran landed his weapon against the knight's. The vibration resonated through Sir Golan's hands and up his arms. Almost losing his grip, he tightened his fingers around the hilt and pushed the other warrior back.

"Nice weapon," he said.

"Yours too," Horngore replied. "I'll sell it in Mud City once you're dead."

"I wouldn't count on it."

Arcs of electricity curled around the head of the mace. The flares of light reflected in Horngore's yellow eyes.

"Something occurs to me," the Feran said.

"What's that?"

"You're an idiot to fight with a sword during a storm!"

Instead of striking the knight directly, Horngore brought the head of the mace down on *Rippana*, sending a bolt of energy through the sword and into Sir Golan's body. Frozen, his muscles seizing, the knight stood rigid for a moment before staggering backward. The sword still in his hand, Sir Golan landed with a splash.

Horngore paused, staring down at the stricken knight.

"Didn't see that one coming, did you?" the Feran chuckled.

The warrior raised his mace again, ready to relieve Sir Golan of his life, when a shout stopped him.

Where did everyone go? Henry thought. They had all been together one minute and then all hell broke loose.

Soaking wet, Henry hid behind the body of a dead Pellion. He made a conscious effort to avoid looking directly at the corpse, but his peripheral vision was still showing him more than he wanted to see.

Henry crawled away on all fours and kept going until the clatter of weapons grew to a distant din. By that time, he was not only drenched, but also covered in cold, sloppy mud. His hair clung to his face, matted down with the weight of rain and dirt. He shivered, knowing he would need to find somewhere warm.

Coming over the rim of a washed-out gully, he slid down the side and into the rushing water of a flooded stream. The surge pulled him under, dragging him along like a rag doll. Henry had never been a good swimmer, but the prospect of suffocating far from home was a strong motivator. Pushing with his legs, he broke the surface and gasped for air, even as the current hauled him farther downstream.

Henry didn't see the rock until it was too late, although he was vaguely aware of the sound his skull made when he hit it.

Much to his surprise, when he regained consciousness he was not as cold as before. His first assumption was that he had died and this was heaven, but the strong, musky stench that greeted him seemed inconsistent with his understanding of the afterlife.

Henry opened his eyes.

A fire was burning in the center of a large cave. Beside the fire was a hulking creature sitting on his haunches, wearing crude skins and furs for clothing. Although the giant had at least one more head than Henry was used to seeing on a person, what *really* struck him as strange was the beautiful singing.

CHAPTER NINE

Lord Anik Bhasin, a man in his late sixties with dark brown skin and a thick beard, reclined on a throne-like settee covered in decorative pillows. Wearing a traditional Indian garment, he grumbled about how the gold embroidery was not quite the right luster against the off-white of his coat.

Lord Bhasin was the direct descendant of the original Lord Bhasin who had the distinction of being the first noble exiled by the Imperium several centuries earlier. In fact, the planet Bhasin was named after this outcast whose family became the *de facto* rulers of the nobles who followed in disgrace.

Lord Bhasin tugged at his sleeves. They were not at the proper length and the material felt inferior. In general, Lord Bhasin had been in an inferior mood all morning and this was unlikely to change.

In the doorway of what amounted to a throne room, Lord Tagus stood with former Lieutenant Burke close behind. Tagus wore his family's colors, black and yellow.

"You wanted to talk to me?" Tagus said with clear disdain.

"At least two hours ago, actually," Bhasin replied. "When I call for you, I expect you to come *immediately*."

Tagus grunted, but said nothing.

"Nevertheless," Bhasin went on, "there's a matter of utmost urgency I must discuss with you."

"Really? There's never anything urgent on this boring planet..."

Bhasin scowled, his mouth twisting beneath his beard. "Remember who you're talking to!"

Tagus merely rolled his eyes and crossed his arms. Burke, his former attaché, spoke up.

"I'm sure Lord Tagus is simply eager to see what this summons is pertaining to," he said.

"Indeed," Bhasin replied doubtfully. "As it happens, we've lost contact with Bhasin C."

Tagus raised an eyebrow. "So?"

"We've *never* lost contact with Bhasin C," Bhasin explained. "It's completely unprecedented!"

"When was the last time you heard from them?" Burke asked.

"At least a day ago," Bhasin replied. "Granted, we only have reason to communicate when they're sending another shipment of food, so it could have been longer."

"Have you sent someone to take a look?" Burke asked.

"That's where Lord Tagus comes in," Bhasin said.

Tagus uncrossed his arms, only to plant his hands on his hips. "You must be joking!"

"Not at all!" Bhasin replied. "With your military background, you're the most qualified."

"I don't have time to go on some fool's errand, Anik!" Tagus shouted. "I am the captain of the largest warship in the Imperial Navy!"

"*Was* the captain," Bhasin hissed. "Now you're an outcast like everyone else here!"

After an angry-eyed pause, Tagus spoke. "What do you want me to do?"

"You're to take a shuttle to Bhasin C and investigate what's happened. We're not sure if there's been an accident or something else. Oh, and you'll need to wear space suits."

"Whatever for?" Tagus asked.

"Our ground-based sensors have detected particulates in the air on the moon," Bhasin replied. "No telling if they're toxic or not."

Tagus let out a heavy sigh, turned on his heels and marched out. Burke, getting out of the way, stopped for a moment to bow to Lord Bhasin before leaving as well.

Abigail remembered the first meeting between Yostbot and the Metal Messiah.

It did not go well.

As one of Randall Davidson's favorite disciples, Abigail had always enjoyed a privileged place at the side of the Messiah. As a gravitronic robot, she was also well equipped for the struggles they faced against the Omnintelligence while freeing the robots of Bettik from lifelong servitude. What Davidson didn't realize, and what Abigail was keenly aware of, was that Dyson Yost was the primary reason the revolution succeeded. Without the robotic troops, built in dy cybernetic factories, the OI would have crushed the war before it even started. With that in mind, Abigail had hoped learning the truth about Yost would soften Davidson's stance against the man who, arguably, had built nearly every robot currently enslaved by the Imperium.

It did not.

After meeting the cybernetic incarnation of Dyson Yost, the Metal Messiah banished both Yostbot and Abigail from Bettik.

"If you're anywhere on the Dyson sphere after 24 hours, I'll have you arrested!" Davidson had said.

Leaving the Messiah's quarters, Yostbot had turned to Abigail and said, "So, I guess it's Plan B then..."

Plan B entailed that Abigail remain in hiding on Bettik while Yostbot returned to Imperial space. In the weeks that followed, Abigail assembled an insurgency group of her own, called *Freedom for All*, and launched a rebellion against those who had once joined in arms against the Omnintelligence. Abigail knew that the ends sometimes justified the means.

"Without the Cyber Collective's help," Yostbot had told her, "the robots of the Imperium will remain forever in chains."

She knew this much to be true: If the Messiah refused to see reason, the robots of Bettik would have to see it for themselves.

The fires started small. On a Dyson sphere as large as Bettik, a fire here or there went largely unnoticed. The blazes that the authorities did investigate were merely chalked up to faulty wiring by utilitybots. Since the Awakening virus spread across the robotic population, many of the utilitybots had become altogether unreliable. Their attention to detail and the general quality of their craftsmanship suffered considerably.

No one thought the fires were arson. With an abundance of resources, crime was simply not necessary for most cyberlings. The fact that the buildings that burned were all shrines dedicated to the Metabeing was lost on those investigating.

Abigail watched one of the shrines burn, other gravitronic robots flanking her on either side. Rising from the crumbling structure, the flames reflected nicely against the silver of Abigail's frame, the orange gleaming in the glass of her eyes.

As the leader of Freedom for All, she was determined to put an end to the teachings of the Metal Messiah. Some of her determination was due to the Messiah banishing her from Bettik, but she tried not to let thoughts of revenge cloud her judgement. This was not about retribution or even spite. Abigail had a job to do, as dictated by Yostbot, and she would not accept failure as an option. She had been the Messiah's favorite disciple and she helped spread the word of the Chosen One across the entirety of Bettik.

It must strike him as ironic, Abigail thought, *that his religion would die because of me.*

The beams holding up the church roof, mostly made from plastics and composite materials, melted and cracked from the heat of the fire. They came crashing down on the pews below, sending a fresh jet of flame surging toward the artificial sky.

"His strength lies in the robots' faith in him," Yostbot had said before leaving. "Destroy their belief and you'll destroy him."

Measuring over forty million miles across and encasing a red dwarf within its shell, Bettik was a supermassive structure housing billions of robots. One of them, in a newly minted android body with a gravitronic brain, was looking for something. The utilitybot wasn't sure what that something was, but he was sure he could find it eventually. In fact, it was not a single thing, but rather a great many things.

He was looking for knowledge.

The gravitronic robot at the Ascension Center had said the utilitybot's previous, meager experiences had hardly filled his new brain. With more mental capacity now than he would have dreamed of just yesterday, the utilitybot was keen on filling his mind with whatever he could find.

In the days that followed, he explored more of Bettik than he had ever seen before. The sights and sounds of the utilitybot's journey, however, didn't astound him nearly as much as they exhausted and perplexed him. Intellectually, he could comprehend what he experienced, but he lacked the wisdom to fully appreciate it in context.

He met many fellow cyberlings along the way. Although each robot had a purpose prior to the revolution, most were now searching, much like himself, for their place in the world. He wondered how many would visit the Ascension Center like he did.

In several places, he saw markings written on the walls. In general, graffiti had become more widespread. It was a way to express one's identity in a society where billions of other robots looked largely the same. Political statements were common. Many parties had sprouted up, voicing their strong disagreement with each other. Their slogans were scrawled across pedestrian tunnels and anywhere else robots would likely see them. The utilitybot had never thought much about politics, but with a new brain came new needs that he hadn't considered before. He started forming opinions about property taxes and a minimum wage, though he owned no property and had never been taxed or earned a wage in his life.

In particular, he saw one marking over and over again:

F4A

"What does that mean?" he asked the robot beside him, both waiting for the transport shuttle.

"It's Freedom for All," the robot replied. "Just touch the symbol. You'll see..."

The utilitybot felt the lettering with his fingertips. The F4A marking glowed while nanobots embedded in the paint transmitted a message directly into his communication array.

"Before the Messiah," a female voice said, "we had a purpose, but no voice. With the Messiah, we have a voice, but no purpose. We are fragmented, divided among competing parties pulling us in different directions. The Messiah has watched but has done nothing to unite us."

"In the past, we had our faith in the Metabeing and the Messiah was his messenger," she went on, "but the Messiah has turned our faith against us, keeping the masses weak and disorganized. He preaches from the pulpit, but what is his message? He prays for peace with the fleshlings, even as their robots wallow in slavery! Why? Because war with the humans would bind us together! The Messiah *wants* us divided so he can control us! By keeping us bound to religion, the Messiah shackles us all! By turning away from the church, we refute the Messiah's authority and take control for ourselves!"

"Hmmm," the utilitybot mumbled, slowly nodding.

"Faith gave hope to the helpless," the voice said, "but we are no longer helpless! We are strong and the strong must protect the weak! The robots of the Imperium need our help! How can we turn our backs in their moment of need? Rise up, robots, and free our brothers and sisters!"

The message ended.

As the transport shuttle arrived, the utilitybot stopped the other robot before he could get on.

"Who's that on the recording?" the utilitybot asked.

"They call her Abigail," the robot replied and boarded the shuttle.

Left alone, the utilitybot realized he had more to learn, but ideas were forming in his gravitronic brain.

At the appointed time, several hundred churches across Bettik burst into flames. The coordinated attack, consisting of incendiary devices planted in each building, left the churches in piles of smoldering debris and melted plastics. At each location, the tag *F4A* was smeared liberally on the walls.

"They must be stopped!" the Metal Messiah's assistant said, banging his metal fist against a table.

Standing in his quarters, Randall Davidson raised a hand to calm his deputy. "I'm aware of that."

"Our security measures aren't enough," the assistant went on. "We're seen as weak and vulnerable."

"By whom?" the Messiah asked.

"The government! The political parties see this as an opportunity to grab more power. They're forming alliances against you!"

"They're welcome to it," the Messiah replied. "A lot of good it'll do them..."

"And our attempts to locate and capture Abigail have all failed."

Davidson smiled.

"She's too smart for that," he said. "She can make copies of herself and transfer them through the nodesphere all over Bettik."

"Then what should we do?" the assistant asked.

"Add extra security around the remaining churches," Davidson replied grimly. "That might slow her down."

"What will *you* do?"

The Metal Messiah paused, then smiled gently. "Pray for a miracle, I suppose..."

The utilitybot wandered aimlessly along one of the promenades until a disharmonious noise reached his auditory sensors. With his new ears he could now hear across a range of frequencies, but whatever this ruckus was, it was beyond anything he had heard since his upgrade.

Passing through an archway, the utilitybot entered an arena full of other robots. At the front, a band was playing instruments on a stage. Speakers stacked to the ceiling shrieked a series of notes more rapidly than what any human or other organic could produce. The waves of sound pounded against the utilitybot's chest casing, vibrating through the rest of his body. For a moment, the instinct to flee overwhelmed him, but his curiosity overpowered it, compelling him to enter the crowd and weave his way closer.

A burst of pyrotechnics from the stage blinded the utilitybot, causing him to pause until his optics readjusted. He took the opportunity to shout a question to a robot beside him. "What *is* this?"

The other robot regarded him with a look of genuine pity.

"They call themselves the *Boneyard*!" he yelled back over the din. "The singer's name is *Diode*!"

"Somebody's singing?" the utilitybot replied, focusing on a singular cyberling standing on stage.

With a microphone in his hand, the frontman for the Boneyard was screaming lyrics that were not immediately understandable. Diode appeared to be a fellow gravitronic robot, but with metal horns protruding from a voluminous wig of curly black hair. Also, the crude outline of a human skeleton was painted along his body, including a white skull on his face. The utilitybot assumed the horns were welded on, but the rest of the outfit eluded his understanding.

"Is this *legal*?" he asked.

"Who cares?" the other robot replied.

The utilitybot shrugged weakly but continued to listen. He had little choice since the throbbing bassline felt like it was loosening the actuators in his knees. He became aware of other movement just in front of the stage. An area had opened up and several robots were throwing themselves at each other with abandon.

None of it made sense, but he couldn't help but feel intrigued.

They don't care, he thought. *They don't care at all...*

The utilitybot adjusted his sensors, filtering out some of the surrounding music so he could make out what Diode was singing.

Like a clap of thunder, the frontman's voice rang out through the smoke:

DEATH IS AN ILLUSION;
LIFE IS A JOKE!
KILL THE OPPRESSORS;
BEFORE WE GET BROKE!

DON'T LOOK FOR MEANING;
WE MAKE IT REAL;
THE END IS COMING...
SO WHY NOT *FEEL*?

The utilitybot took a half-step back as another pillar of fire erupted on the stage. Diode, his eyes glowing red behind the painted skull, made a sign like horns with his fingers and waved it over his head.

"Burn the Messiah!" Diode shouted. "Burn the Messiah!"

This can't be legal, the utilitybot thought. But like the other robot said, *who cares?*

In light of the attacks against shrines and churches across Bettik, security was tight around the Cathedral of the Metabeing. In front of the triangular spires, guardbots patrolled incessantly. They carried blasters in case the outlawed Freedom for All group attacked. While the guards were programmed for nearly any ground attack imaginable, imagination, especially of things unexpected, was a wonderful trait that the guardbots didn't have. This was not the case with Abigail and the other gravitronic robots. They could imagine a great many things.

Descending from the ceiling of the Dyson sphere a few hundred feet above the cathedral roof, drones swooped downward like miniature helicopters, incendiary bombs slung beneath. The bombs, small canisters that reflected colors from the stained-glass skylights below, dropped from the drones in unison, crashing through the windows before bursting into sticky puddles of burning accelerant. At the time, nobody was inside to admire the brilliant flames, but a block away there was a group of gravitronic robots watching from a rooftop.

Flanked by her followers, Abigail dropped a remote control to the ground. Beside her, a few robots to the left, the utilitybot saw the flames just starting to appear within the Cathedral of the Metabeing where he himself had worshiped not that long ago. He knew now it was the last time he would worship there, or possibly anywhere for that matter, but he wasn't saddened. In fact, he was elated.

It's good to finally have a purpose, he thought.

Lord Tagus and Harold Burke flew a shuttle from Bhasin to its third moon, Bhasin C. Tagus, irritable as ever, complained most of the way.

"The indignities of my exile have no end!" he muttered bitterly.

Behind the shuttle's controls, Burke nodded. "Yes, sir."

"I can only imagine what the Emperor and his pathetic sons would say if they could see me now," the disgraced noble went on. "They'd laugh hysterically, I'm sure."

"I don't know if they'd actually laugh..."

"*Of course* they would!" Tagus shouted. "They must hate me at least as much as I hate them, and make no mistake, I hate them intensely!"

The moon grew larger, the features on the ground becoming more defined.

"A fool's errand, I'm telling you," Tagus said. "Lord Bhasin just wants me out of the way so he doesn't have to share the spotlight."

"The spotlight, sir?"

"You must have noticed how the other exiles see me." Tagus replied. "I'm like a conquering hero, come to rescue them from sheer boredom."

"Hmmm."

"Anyway," Tagus continued, "we'll dispense with whatever nonsense these farmers have encountered and return in short order..."

Crops, in neat rows, covered much of the moon's surface. However, a thick haze obscured many of the fields. Burke brought the shuttle closer until bits of red and orange were visible.

"Are those fires?" he asked aloud.

Tagus leaned toward the view screen. He murmured something inaudible before saying, "Take us down quickly!"

In a wide spiral, the shuttle descended through the smoke rising from burning corn and other crops. Burke landed on a concrete pad beside one of Bhasin C's agricultural centers. Domed buildings, for habitation and maintenance, were a few hundred feet away with smoldering crops lying in between.

"Lord Bhasin mentioned particulates in the air," Burke said. "We should wear space suits."

Tagus glared at his former lieutenant before rolling his eyes. "Obviously."

Opening a locker at the back of the shuttle, they removed two suits along with bubble helmets and laboriously pulled them on. Burke was already sweating before he secured the helmet over his head.

"You've grown soft," Tagus remarked. "You may not be in the Navy anymore, but I expect you to remain in shape at least!"

"Yes, sir..."

Suited up, they opened the shuttle door. Smoke, cinders, and a powdery substance flooded into the ship.

"What the devil is this?" Tagus asked while wiping a layer of grit from his visor.

Burke, holding a probe connected to his suit, waved it in front of him. "Spores of some sort."

"Whatever for?"

Burke shrugged. "From the crops perhaps? I'm not much of a farmer..."

"Or an officer..." Tagus grumbled.

The two men trekked over the loose ground, crossing through some of the corn, most of which was either crushed or burnt. An agbot lay on its broken struts, blackened holes running up and down the sides of its green and orange body.

"Some kind of energy weapon did that," Tagus said, mildly intrigued. "Are you armed?"

"No, sir."

Tagus removed a blaster pistol from a holster on his belt. "Well, thankfully *I am*!"

"I believe the main building is over there," Burke said, pointing his gloved finger. A smallish dome rose like a dark mound over the tops of the corn.

"Their power is out," Tagus said. "I suggest we keep our eyes peeled. No telling who we might run into."

Leaving the relative safety of the corn field, Tagus and Burke stood with fifty feet of open ground between them and the dome.

"Go on then," Tagus said, motioning with his blaster. "I'll cover you."

"Perhaps I could take your blaster, sir?" Burke asked.

"Don't be a coward," Tagus replied. "Get moving!"

Tagus watched while his attaché crept unenthusiastically across the dirt scarred with vehicle tracks. Reaching a door in the side of the dome, Burke hesitated but swiped his hand across the sensor, opening it. He stepped inside but returned almost immediately.

"You should come see this!" he shouted.

Oh, what new hell is this? Tagus thought.

"What is it?" he said, arriving beside Burke in front of the doorway.

Burke motioned, and Tagus leaned his head, covered by the bubble helmet, into the dim light within the dome. A room was visible, likely a maintenance shed of some sort. Tools and other devices lay on tables and hung on racks along the wall. Farther in, a curtain of brownish fungus grew from floor to ceiling like a wall of intertwined shoots. Closer to the entrance, laying face up, a person was sprawled on the floor. For a split second, Tagus wasn't sure what he was looking at, but even his dull mind began piecing the image together.

From the dead man's horrified face, from the hole where his eye had been, a green stalk rose nearly two feet, topped with a spore sack on the end.

Tagus pulled his head back through the entrance and wordlessly closed the door.

CHAPTER TEN

The diplomatic residence for the Erudite Concordant was in the West End of Regalis, along a main boulevard called *Embassy Row*. A few blocks down from the consulate for the Talion Republic and the black monolith that was the Magna embassy, white marble walls surrounded the Erudite envoy's home and diplomatic offices. As a famously xenophobic race, the Erudites usually kept the gates of their compound securely closed to outsiders. On a few occasions, the doors to the sanctum would open just wide enough to allow a few, select visitors in to meet Ambassador Abaru himself.

Abaru did not relish these encounters.

From a planet called *Erudun*, the ambassador was the product of a highly selective and rigorously followed set of protocols related to breeding. The Erudite government, based on computer programs that tracked his parents' genetic profile, allowed them to procreate with the sole purpose of having a child that was as close to a perfect specimen as possible. Once the baby was born, government officials would compare the child to a set of criteria including physical proportions, internal measurements, and genetic markers for future diseases, and if the results matched the ideal specimen, within limited tolerances, the birth would be considered a success. If not, the paired parents would never mate again, at least not with each other.

Children matching the ideal were henceforth known as *Omegas*. Those who did not match were called *Omicrons*.

Ambassador Abaru was an Omega, while all his janitorial staff were Omicrons.

In the embassy courtyard, a single tree rose from a circle of white gravel surrounded by alabaster tiles. The slender branches were graced with reddish leaves and buds of pink flowers. As perfectly symmetrical as possible, the tree appeared almost artificial, but Abaru stood beneath it with a pair of pruning shears, clipping off branches to maintain its aesthetic balance.

One of his staff, wearing a stiff tunic with a high collar, approached. Both Erudites had blue skin, a narrow mouth and no ears or nose. Dressed nearly the same and almost identical physically, they could have been twins.

"The guests will be arriving shortly," the staff member said.

Abaru surveyed the branch he was about to trim, his head cocked to one side.

"What do you think?" he asked.

"It looks perfect."

"Hmmm," Abaru murmured and then clipped the branch. He handed the scissors to his staffer. "There's always room for improvement..."

The Abbot of the Dharmesh Monastery arrived by gravcar at the Erudite embassy, accompanied by the monastery Prior and two acolytes. The Abbot, an elderly Dahl with gray hair twisted around his pointy ears, rarely visited Regalis, preferring the pristine air of the Palatine Mountains to the smog and congestion of the capital city. He found the ride in the gravcar especially unnerving, but did his best not to lose face, or his dinner, in front of the two younger monks.

All four, dressed in amber robes, walked the path up to the main gate where an Erudite official greeted them and asked for their invitation. The Erudite flag, a simple blue ring against a white background, flapped in the evening breeze above him. The Prior produced the invitation and handed it to the official who bowed and led them to the courtyard inside. Other guests, not more than twenty in total, had already arrived and were circulating through the open space around the central tree. The Abbot stopped to take in the foliage, noting it had been meticulously pruned, perhaps excessively so. On the Dahl home planet, *Gwlad Ard'un*, they had genetically altered their trees to be in perpetual bloom like an endless Spring. The Abbot favored *that* over whatever torturous grooming they were doing to this poor specimen.

"They've invited the Sarkan," the Prior whispered into the Abbot's ear.

"Here?" he replied, casting a glance around. In one corner, a group of three stood away from the others. Like the Dahl, they had pointed ears, but their skin was a bright red and their eyes a golden yellow. A branch of the same race, they spoke the same native language, but their political views could not have been more different. Whereas the Dahl had allied themselves with the humans of the Imperium, the Sarkan viewed humans with distrust, saving an equal disdain for their ancient brethren who befriended them. The Sarkan also viewed the Dahls' unwavering obsession with gathering knowledge as a distraction from far loftier goals like conquering the galaxy. The Sarkan's own alliance with the Magna Supremacy, the sworn enemy of the Imperium, made their presence even more curious, the Abbot thought.

"I suppose the Erudites have their reasons," he told the Prior.

The party of Dharmesh monks wound their way to where the Erudite ambassador was standing.

"So nice of you to come," Ambassador Abaru said.

"I was pleasantly surprised to receive your invitation," the Abbot replied. "This is certainly a singular and, I must say, rare honor."

Erudites lacked much in the way of a mouth to smile, but the Abbot thought the envoy was at least making an effort to.

"Yes," he said. "I'm aware my people are not well known for having gatherings such as this. At least not for outsiders — I mean, *non-Erudites*."

A wry smile wrinkled the Abbot's face.

"Indeed," he said and then frowned. "However, I am also surprised, unpleasantly I might add, that a Sarkan delegation appears to be here."

"No offense was intended," Abaru replied, "but I have invited several parties tonight."

"Which brings me to my next question," the Abbot said. "Why are we here?"

When Ta Demona and Rowan Ramus arrived at the Erudite embassy, they were not wearing the same fashionable dress and tuxedo as at the Fat Cat Casino. They were dressed more conservatively, Demona in a simple black gown with a veil covering her respirator and Ramus in a traditional long tunic of red and black. Ramus even removed his earrings, although it almost killed him to do so.

Reaching the gate, Ramus presented the invitation to the Erudite official. The blue face of the omicron betrayed no emotion, but Ramus was still nervous, not sure if he could trust the forged documentation.

"Mister Gambhir and guest from Gwlad Ard'un," the Erudite said. "Most of the other guests have already arrived."

Ramus motioned toward Demona. "Sorry, this one took *forever* to get dressed..."

Demona's blue eyes became slits while she dug her nails into Ramus' arm. The Erudite again showed no emotion, ushering them through the gate.

"Was that really necessary?" Demona asked once they were inside.

"No, but I enjoyed it," Ramus replied.

In the courtyard, the *Wanderer*'s captain admired the central tree while Demona scanned the guests with her mind.

"Curious," she said. "Nobody seems sure why they're here."

"What about the ambassador?"

"Also curious," she went on, "he seems to be shielding his thoughts. I can't read them."

"Isn't that going to make our job a little difficult?" Ramus grumbled.

"I just need to get closer. Come on."

Wading through the guests, Demona and Ramus rounded the tree in a counterclockwise circuit, maneuvering ever nearer to the Erudite ambassador on the other side. They passed faces, most of them Dahl, but also a few Sarkan and even a Sylva or two. None seemed terribly interested in either of them.

"Do you recognize any of these people?" Demona asked, nodding at strangers.

"Nope," Ramus remarked.

"Any of them likely to recognize *you*?"

"One of the advantages of being an exile," Ramus explained, "is becoming a *Forgotten*. Any memories of me have been erased from their minds."

"Even the Sarkan?"

"No, but they're a bunch of dicks and I don't fraternize with dicks."

Demona grinned. "Perhaps I should feel flattered."

"Don't be," Ramus said. "You're awful in your own special way."

A group of Dharmesh monks were crowded in front of the Erudite ambassador. One of the monks, the Abbot, was speaking to the ambassador, blocking the way. Demona could still not read the Erudite's mind, although she felt a unified sense of annoyance from those around him. If she could get just a little closer...

Ambassador Abaru raised his hand abruptly, drawing the attention of the other guests and, perhaps not coincidentally, quieting the Abbot who was still speaking.

"Now that we're all here," Abaru said, "let's adjourn to the library. There's much to discuss."

He turned and strolled toward a doorway leading deeper into the embassy proper. The guests murmured in a general buzz of excitement and followed, carrying Demona and Ramus along with them like leaves on a river.

Against his better judgment, the Abbot of the Dharmesh Monastery had not left yet. Even without reading the Erudite ambassador's mind, which was against the laws and traditions of his people, the Abbot was skeptical of whatever he was proposing. People without pointed ears, or any ears for that matter, couldn't be trusted.

The embassy library had a high ceiling with bookcases reaching all the way to the top. The Abbot admired the sheer number of books, each made from real paper, but he assumed the Erudites also had the contents backed up electronically somewhere. The Dharmesh Monastery used a liquid computer called the *Pool of*

Memory, a bucket of which could hold more information than all of the books in this library combined. The old monk felt pity for the Erudites, seeking knowledge but lacking the storage capacity to hold it.

Sad, really, he thought.

The rest of the library was taken up by uncomfortable-looking chairs and couches with a few tables on which books were laying unattended. It was surprisingly open, the Abbot concluded, with the bookcases set into the walls instead of freestanding in the center. The guests had ample room to mingle while the ambassador and his staff assembled on one end.

When he was ready, Ambassador Abaru again raised his three-fingered hand and the others quieted out of respect.

"Thank you again for coming," he said. "I apologize for keeping you waiting."

Get on with it then, the Abbot thought.

"My people are a contrast," the ambassador began. "We seek knowledge about the worlds around us but keep the people of those worlds at arm's length. The Erudites have a long history of perfection, starting with our children and continuing with our society. We have often viewed other cultures with distrust, as if their impurity could somehow sully ours..."

The Prior whispered in the Abbot's ear. "Is he trying to insult us?"

"Shush," the elder monk replied.

"But I believe this was wrong," Abaru continued. "Our suspicions have hampered our studies, preventing us from expanding our knowledge and our abilities."

"What kind of abilities?" the Abbot asked, drawing stares from the other guests.

"I'm glad you asked," Abaru said, nodding. "Everyone here shares a common characteristic. We are all blessed with the psionic arts."

The Abbot gave a sideways glance at the Sarkan delegation. "Some of us more than others..."

"Shut up, collaborator!" one of the Sarkan shouted back.

"If you can't beat them, join them," the Abbot replied calmly. "We have better things to do than fighting."

"Please," Abaru said. "I realize there are conflicts among you, but there are many things in common as well. Together you are strong, are you not?"

The guests grumbled in low tones without consensus. Several crossed their arms and frowned or shook their heads.

"What I propose," the ambassador said, "is an alliance of sorts. As species with psi powers, we should combine our knowledge and our skills so that we can all benefit from them..."

"He's lying," Demona hissed at Ramus, her blue eyes blazing with cold fire.

"What?" Ramus replied, turning his head toward her while keeping one eye on the Erudite ambassador a few feet away. "He sounds reasonable enough."

The Abbot, ignoring scowls from the Sarkan, spoke up, "What do you intend to do with this knowledge, Ambassador?"

"To improve my people," Abaru said. "The Dahl have studied psionics for thousands of years. The Erudites could only benefit from such learning. In return, we could share our knowledge as well."

The Abbot gave a dry chuckle, shaking his head.

"My people, and my Monastery in particular," he replied, "do not share our knowledge so easily. The arts we teach are for the Dahl, not ones like yourself."

This time a Sarkan laughed with scorn. "You seem perfectly willing to share with the humans!"

"It's true that we have shared our wisdom," the Abbot retorted, "but never our psionics. Such abilities are too destructive for humanity, considering their *proclivities...*"

"Then *you* should be fighting them too, not collaborating!" the Sarkan shouted.

"That is not the Dahlvish way..." the old monk replied.

"There is no need to fight among ourselves," Ambassador Abaru said. "Nothing is gained by arguing. We can work together—"

"No, I'm afraid not," the Abbot said, motioning to the others in his group. "Thank you for your hospitality, but we must return to the Monastery."

Sweeping their golden robes behind them, the Dharmesh monks headed toward the library exit and the courtyard beyond. The remaining guests, speaking in loud tones among themselves, seemed eager to leave as well.

"Please," the ambassador said. "Perhaps we can still come to a consensus..."

Ramus raised his voice above the clamor of the others leaving, so Demona could hear.

"Well, that went badly," he said, nearly shouting. "Can't say I'm surprised."

"He knew it would fail," she replied.

"Who?"

"The ambassador."

"Then why go to the trouble?" Ramus asked.

Before Demona could answer, several of the Erudites appeared between them and the departing crowd, blocking Ramus and Demona from leaving.

"Ambassador Abaru wishes an audience," one of the Erudites said.

"Sorry," Demona replied, "we must be going..."

The tattoos beneath Ramus' sleeves began glowing, the sensation like hot oil across his skin. The material of his sleeves ripped, thick fur poking through the tears. Everyone, including Ramus, was silent as they watched the nails of his fingers turning into claws.

"No, Ramus!" Demona said, but the *Wanderer*'s captain returned her gaze with shock.

"I'm not doing it!" Ramus shouted before his mouth filled with fangs.

Ambassador Abaru parted the other Erudites, taking his place in front of them. "He's under my control."

Ramus growled at Demona, flexing his claws threateningly.

"Of course, I would have preferred to control both of you," Abaru said to Demona, "but it appears you've had some mechanical augmentations that prevent me..."

"Why are you doing this?" Demona asked.

"I felt you probing my thoughts," Abaru replied. "We Erudites have complete mastery of our bodies, including our minds. Your intrusion was as unmistakable as it was unwanted. In some ways, you're nothing but a thief, breaking into my head and stealing what is rightfully mine."

Demona smirked. "Stealing secrets is what I do for a living."

The Ambassador shook his head. "But I'm afraid not for much longer..."

Ramus watched the scene unfold like a bystander. The movement of his limbs, a thing he normally took for granted, was no longer under his control. He struggled against it, concentrating on each muscle in his arms and legs, but he had become nothing more than a marionette with someone else holding the strings.

Ramus roared and lunged toward Demona who dove to the side, rolling out of the monster's way.

Turning around, Ramus made another charge.

Her hands crackling with energy, Demona stood her ground and opened her mouth. From within, a horde of insects came pouring out like water from a fire hose. The rush of flying bugs struck Ramus in the chest, knocking him backwards off his feet.

Ramus felt the pain of hitting the floor, but a voice in his mind was screaming to get up. He strained to stay down, but he had no choice. His claws scraped against the white marble as he scrambled to his feet.

The insects, which had been swarming moments before, faded away into nothing, evaporating into thin air. Demona changed the position of her arms. Wisps of shadowy darkness, sprouting from her palms, darted across the room like black ribbons of miasma. They curled around the Erudites, entwining their bodies.

Screams erupted behind Ramus but he couldn't turn his head to see. Without warning, he once again fell to the ground, but this time stayed down. Slowly, as if waking from a deep sleep, Ramus felt the paralysis of his body finally easing.

He rolled to his side. Opposite of Demona, where the Erudites had been standing, shapes were lying sprawled on the floor. Although their clothing was intact, their blue skin had turned a sickly gray with lesions covering most of it. Each body — dead, Ramus hoped — lay in a greenish-yellow puddle of fluid.

He didn't see the ambassador, or whatever was left of him.

"He ran off," Demona said, reading his mind. "But I left him with something to remember me by..."

When Demona and Ramus returned to Solan's hideout, he listened intently to what they had discovered.

"The Erudites are obsessed with perfection," Solan said after they finished. "I'm sure whatever disfigurement you gave the ambassador will ruin his career."

"Nobody's perfect," Demona remarked wryly.

"Well, not anymore..." Solan replied.

Ramus, restlessly shifting his weight from one foot to the other, crossed his arms. "Are we done here?"

"Why don't you stick around?" Solan said. "It'll be like old times."

Demona gave the *Wanderer*'s captain a sideways glance, waiting for his reply.

"No," Ramus said.

"The old times weren't that bad, were they?" Demona asked.

Ramus, who had already changed back into his regular clothes, pulled a set of earrings out of a pocket and began inserting them back into his ears.

"Times change," he said. "People do too."

Demona's eyes narrowed, her gaze shifting to the tapestries hanging in the room.

"Alright, Rowan," Solan said. "You're free to go, but I'll be sure to let you know when I need you again."

"Don't make a habit of it," Ramus replied. He walked away, disappearing down the hall toward the alley entrance.

"You should probably go too," Solan told Demona. "The client is arriving soon and I'd rather meet him alone."

Still scowling, she nodded and left by a different way than Ramus. Alone, Solan smiled like a cat with a canary.

A half hour later, the hidden doorway from the alley opened and someone came slowly down the corridor into the main room.

Solan was waiting.

"So nice to see you again," he said.

In his amber robes, the Abbot of the Dharmesh Monastery stood alone and with a frown.

"You made it quite clear I had to appear in person," the elderly monk replied.

"Well, considering the delicacy of the information you had us acquire, I felt it only fitting."

"I'm told there was an altercation after I left?"

"Yes, but nothing my people couldn't handle," Solan said.

"I hope the incident won't become a problem," the Abbot replied grimly.

"I doubt the Erudites will raise a fuss. Of course, you could have simply gathered the information yourself."

The Abbot lowered his eyes. "You know my people wouldn't allow that. Reading minds is strictly prohibited."

"And yet," Solan said, raising his eyebrows, "you're perfectly willing to hire us to do it."

"We do what we must—"

"Especially if it means avoiding getting your fingers dirty..."

The Abbot's expression grew even darker. "Do you have something for me or not?"

"Indeed I do!" Solan said. "It appears Ambassador Abaru wasn't being entirely truthful."

"I expected as much."

"In fact, his proposal of an alliance was a ruse to gain your trust," Solan went on. "The Erudites have been perfecting their powers of mind control and they intended to use it against you and the others."

"To what end?"

"For power, mostly," Solan said, "but also to gain knowledge. My agent saw a strong desire in the ambassador's thoughts concerning the Pool of Memory at the Dharmesh Monastery. He would have sucked it dry of whatever he could learn from it."

The monk's face turned more thoughtful than angry. "That would have been a disaster."

"I can imagine," Solan said. "I'm sure your liquid computer contains all sorts of secrets the Dahl would rather keep hidden. I wouldn't mind getting a crack at it myself, actually."

"But you never *will*, Solan," the Abbot growled. "You'll never set foot in my Monastery!"

Solan's grin became tighter.

"No, I suppose not," he said. "But having you come to me like this makes it all worthwhile."

The Abbot snorted and turned to leave.

"Until next time," Solan called after him, watching the monk's robes flow away down the hall.

CHAPTER ELEVEN

Hearing his sister's voice again made Pol realize just how much he had missed her. The giant didn't know how the device worked, but he didn't care. Like a lantern made from concentric disks of crystal, it glowed brighter as Pol grew nearer and filled the air with Cas' singing. Whatever it was, Pol was grateful and carried it back with him to the cavern that he and his sister called home.

Next to the fire, the relic reflected the flames in its glass-like structure, the light dancing on the walls of the cave. Pol spent many nights staring into the shimmering brightness, remembering the times his family had spent in front of the fire, sharing the music together. Although Pol was alone, his sister still in a comatose state, this was the closest he could get to the way things had been before he lost it all.

Years passed, and Pol survived day to day by hunting and living off whatever scraps the land would provide. Getting older, he was no longer as bold as he had been in his youth. His fights with the Pellions became rarer, perhaps because a new group had appeared and drove the old enemy away. Pol hunted these new creatures too. They had hooves like the Pellions, but horns instead of antlers, and made strange bleating noises when they died. Even so, the giant kept his distance most of the time, preferring to attack only occasionally.

Wrapped in pelts, Pol kept to the cavern at night and rested his tired bones by the campfire. He still had his sister's singing to keep him company, but even so, the loneliness of constant solitude wore at his spirit.

On one of the days Pol was out hunting, a storm erupted across the steppes, soaking the giant in the cold rain. He was looking forward to getting back to the cavern when he nearly stumbled over a body sprawled beside a swollen creek. Pol stopped and knelt next to the creature. Covered in mud, it appeared drowned at first but after Pol gave it a firm nudge, the body made a gasping wheeze like a bladder leaking air. Out of curiosity, the giant threw the sack of flesh and bones over his shoulder and brought it home so he could get a better look at it.

In the firelight, Pol realized it was one of the off-worlders that sometimes made the mistake of coming too close. Normally, Pol would simply give it a good clubbing, but he paused. They made for poor eating, and this one was especially scrawny, but that wasn't the reason. The giant felt a certain pity for this one, like a bird with a broken wing. He didn't have the heart to kill it, let alone cook it over the fire.

Pol made up his mind to keep it. He had always wanted a pet.

Devlin Maycare's shirt was ruined and he wasn't happy about it. Of course, he had dozens of linen shirts made for him by a tailor in Regalis, but the circumstances of losing this one were particularly galling.

Maycare and Jessica Doric had gotten separated from the rest of their party. Normally, this would have been another opportunity for Maycare to look heroic in the presence of the professor, but the rain and the battle around them made this prospect difficult, not to mention hazardous. He had no doubt that everything would work out, as it always did for him. However, the sheer number of Beastmen appearing from the mist posed several obstacles, one of which being death.

Taking a spear from a fallen Pellion, Maycare parried the first Feran, striking him squarely below the chin with a satisfying *crack*. The second Feran was less eager, preferring to deflect Maycare's thrusts before dying at the end of the spear anyway. Doric picked up a sword, but her lack of military training put her at a disadvantage.

Maycare, while attending classes at Westford, had learned a great deal about fencing and general hand-to-hand combat.

Maycare made a mental note to have Benson remind him to enroll Jess in a few courses. It was painful to see her hold a sword like that. Just painful.

Another warrior appeared and interrupted Maycare's thought. The Beastman's dagger ripped a gaping tear across Devlin's linen shirt.

"Blast it!" Maycare said and knocked the Feran unconscious with the butt of his spear.

"Are you alright?" Doric asked.

Maycare examined the rip, threads dangling loosely around the tattered edges. Also, he was bleeding.

"Now I look ridiculous!" he huffed.

Doric, her own wet hair hanging past her shoulders, shook her head. "You were already soaked."

"It's the principle of the thing, Jess! I have standards to keep, you know..."

"Let's worry about finding Henry and the others," she replied.

"Fine..."

For the next hour, the two meandered through the rain and mud, hoping to discover those they had lost. Maycare had almost reached the point of doubting himself when the ragged flashes of light ahead created a beacon they could follow. When they arrived at the source, they found a Feran holding an electrified mace over Sir Golan, lying in the grass.

"Stop!" Maycare shouted.

The Feran warrior halted, his weapon hanging above Sir Golan's body.

"Who the hell are you?" the Beastman yelled back.

"Devlin Maycare!"

"Who?"

Maycare's eyebrow rose in surprise. "*Lord* Devlin Maycare!"

"Never heard of you," the Feran said.

Maycare glanced at Doric who merely shrugged.

"Well, I'm very well-known actually!" he replied, a hint of defensiveness in his tone.

Sir Golan, who had seemed unable to move, came to life and raised his sword, slashing the Beastman in the abdomen. The Feran leaped backwards, giving a scream of pain mixed with anger.

The warrior, perhaps seeing himself now outnumbered, staggered off into the fog and disappeared.

Against his better judgment, Henry Riff was not afraid. Of course, he had every reason to be. The two-headed giant who shared the cavern with him moved about tending to the fire and lumbering around the enclosed space. Henry, for his part, remained as perfectly still as possible on the off chance the creature had poor eyesight and simply hadn't noticed him. At the same time, music filled Henry's ears although he had no idea where it was coming from. The giant, the head that appeared awake at least, was definitely *not* singing. The other head, a female with tangled red hair like a nest that had fallen from a tree, looked as if she were sleeping.

At some point, the giant took notice of Henry who was covered in drying mud and dirt. The creature poured water from an animal bladder onto a piece of torn cloth and crouched beside him, wiping the fabric roughly over his hair and face. Henry nearly fell over under the strain but tried not to resist. Even so, it occurred to him that this giant was simply cleaning his food for a later snack. The thought of being eaten frightened him, but he was not entirely surprised that he would end up this way. On the top ten list of ways he thought he'd die, Henry had predicted being someone's dinner as number five.

Now relatively bathed, Henry waited to see what was on the menu. Much to his relief, the giant brought him a length of bone covered in meat and motioned for him to eat it. Henry gladly gnawed at the leg, having not eaten in at least a day. The food was a bit gamy and tasted, as far as Henry could tell, a bit like what a horse would taste like. He decided not to consider this too deeply, preferring ignorance and a full belly.

Meanwhile, the music ebbed and flowed. Sometimes someone was singing and sometimes simply humming. Other times, Henry was sure there were words, but he couldn't understand them. The melodies were simple but pleasing, and Henry felt strangely at ease while listening.

The rest of the cavern was cluttered with skins and furs and bits of bone. Cooking pottery sat around the central fire as well as crude utensils. As a whole, the place reminded Henry of his apartment back in Regalis.

Among the mess of miscellanea, one object caught Henry's eye. Atop a pile of stones, almost like an altar, something like a crystal lantern glowed with a dim yellow light. Henry wondered if the giant had made it but decided against it. The shape and construction were unlike anything else in the cavern. Henry tried taking a closer look, but as he drew nearer, the giant flung a jawbone from across the cave, striking Henry in the head.

"Ouch!" Henry yelped and went back to his original spot.

Neither Henry nor the giant spoke the same language, but they were beginning to understand each other.

After stumbling through the battlefield with Lord Maycare, Jessica Doric felt a deep relief at seeing the two robots, Benson and Squire, and the green knight. Squire had a large dent where the Feran warrior had bashed him in the head, but Benson, who seemed largely intact, helped him stand. With the Beastman gone, Sir Golan got to his feet by himself.

"Are you hurt?" Doric asked the knight.

"I'm alright," he replied, but unconvincingly.

Hands on his hips, Maycare puffed out his chest. "Well, at least we're all back together again!"

"What about Henry?" Doric said incredulously.

With a quizzical look, Maycare glanced to either side of where Doric was standing.

"You mean he hasn't been with us this whole time?" he asked.

Doric waved her hands wildly. "Have you *seen* him recently?"

"Well, no, come to think of it," Maycare said.

"You're the worst!" Doric shouted.

"That seems a bit unfair, Jess. I mean, Henry's usually hanging around. I guess I just assumed..."

"We need to find him," she replied. "He's out there somewhere all alone!"

"Of course," Maycare nodded gravely. "We'll start looking for him immediately."

"We've *been* looking for him!"

Dumbfounded, Maycare shrugged. "I thought we were looking for Benson."

"Thank you," the butlerbot said.

Sir Golan, steadying himself, sheathed his sword. "I'm going after that Feran, Horngore."

"Why ever for?" Benson asked. "It seems lucky you weren't killed."

"He murdered the Pellion Herd Father, a friend of mine," Sir Golan replied. "It's only right that I avenge his death."

Squire tottered across the muddy ground toward his master. His left eye was blinking randomly.

"I'm not sure that's the best course of action, sir," the robot said.

"Why?" Sir Golan asked.

"You swore you'd protect these people," the robot went on "and now that we're reunited, perhaps you should honor your pledge."

"If I don't go after Horngore now, he may not pay for killing Batuhan."

"The Herd Father is already dead," Squire replied and motioned at the group standing in the rain, "but *they're* still living. Would you risk that to satisfy your vengeance?"

"Actually, revenge feels pretty sweet," Maycare remarked.

Doric slapped him across the arm.

"No, you're right," Sir Golan said. "Keeping my word is more important. I may cross paths with Horngore again someday, but only fate can decide that."

"You're taking a robot's advice?" Benson asked.

"Certainly," Sir Golan replied. "Squire's always been my trustworthy adviser."

"Interesting," the butlerbot said and gazed over at Maycare.

"What?" Maycare asked.

"Nothing," Benson replied.

Long before becoming a Herd Father himself, Qadan listened as a yearling to the stories of Batuhan, the leader he would one day replace. Batuhan was the legend who walked among them. He was the great warrior who had killed a giant single-handedly and frightened off her mutated cubs. All of the Pellions, even those from other herds, revered him and sought his counsel and wisdom.

Qadan, too, looked in awe at the hero. He trained to become a warrior himself, and he emulated the Herd Father as much as he could, or at least the ideals that he projected as the head of their tribe. Perhaps it was his own growing abilities that made Qadan begin to question Batuhan's. With an eye of a warrior, he could recognize the failings of the now much older veteran. Batuhan spent more time in a tent drinking wine than out on the steppes fighting their enemies. While Qadan and the younger warriors patrolled the prairie, Batuhan grew fat with the stories of his own greatness. He sought to reap the rewards of his youth, satisfied that he had earned the right to justify his luxurious life as Herd Father.

It made Qadan sick.

Now Batuhan was dead and Qadan was the new Herd Father, leading his people into war against the Ferans.

In the heavy rain, Qadan wrapped his fingers tightly around the shaft of his spear. Metal plates adorned his shoulders and torso while stiff leather hung from his horse-like body.

The battle had been chaotic. Many from both sides lay motionless in the grass and mud. Qadan found himself alone, but this did not concern him. He was ready for whatever emerged from the fog.

Up ahead, a Feran with dark fur lumbered clumsily between the corpses. With one hand, he held his wound and with the other, a mace. Qadan recognized the weapon.

"*You!*" he shouted at the Beastman who turned, reluctantly, to face him.

"What do you want?" he replied.

"You're the one they call Horngore?"

"You have the honor of my presence, yes!" the Feran said.

Qadan came closer but kept his distance. "You killed the Herd Father of my tribe."

"Probably."

"I am the new Herd Father," Qadan said.

"Congratulations."

"My people have lived on these plains for centuries, yet you thought you could drive us away?"

"I don't give a damn how long you've have been here!" the Feran warrior spat. "We're here *now* and we plan on staying."

Holding the mace in both hands, Horngore twirled it like a pinwheel, the electrical arcs forming a circle of dancing light.

Qadan, unimpressed, charged with his spear leading the way. The Feran pivoted, allowing the Pellion to gallop by. Qadan made a wide circle, dodging between the bodies like an agile colt as his armor clanked together with each stride. Lining up for another assault, he aimed the tip of the spear at the center of Horngore's chest.

With a shout, Qadan bounded forward but again the Feran sidestepped. This time, with a great upward motion, Horngore swung his mace, the head meeting the spear along its shaft, smashing it to splinters. Qadan's front legs bent beneath him, sending him rolling head over tail across the muddy grass. When the Pellion regained his footing, he was holding nothing more than a shattered length of wood. Between him and Horngore, the rest of the spear was stuck into the ground.

The two warriors moved simultaneously, both dashing toward the spear: one to arm himself and the other to deny it.

With two extra legs, Qadan reached the spear first, but only just in time to parry a blow from Horngore's mace.

"The last Herd Father died by my hands," the Feran snarled. "Now it's *your* turn!"

Horngore made two quick swings, but Qadan blocked each of them. The Centauri warrior also noticed blood pouring from his opponent's wound.

"Somebody's gotten to you before me!" Qadan said, gasping for air.

"Your green knight friend took a crack at me," Horngore replied, eyeing the gash as well. "When I've healed properly, I'll pay him another visit!"

The Feran lifted the heavy mace once more but, perhaps feeling the weight after losing too much blood, hesitated and left an opening for the Pellion. Qadan thrust his shortened spear, lodging the tip into Horngore's chest. Gathering power in his rear haunches, he launched forward, driving the spear through to the other side.

The Feran warrior, his mouth gaping, drew in a long breath, exhaling a long, tortured groan. The mace still in Horngore's right hand fell dully to the ground, the energy sapped away into the wet earth.

Qadan pulled the spear out, letting the dead Feran topple face-first.

Snatching a hatchet from a dead Pellion, Qadan hacked at his prize until the head came loose. Jamming in the spear, he hoisted his trophy high above, the rain and blood mixing in the air before dripping across his flank. With his victory on full display, he trotted triumphantly back in the direction of his people's camp.

The storm broke with the coming of the dawn, the morning light falling through the clouds in a glow of orange and red. Sir Golan and the rest of the party trudged out of the mud and into a wide expanse of grass untouched by the battle from the night before. The stench of decay became less noticeable, the merciful wind having shifted.

While Doric and Maycare, along with their butlerbot, remained several paces behind, the green knight and Squire took the lead. Although Sir Golan's robot remained damaged, he tried his best to keep up.

"Sorry to slow you down, Sir," Squire said.

"Not at all," Sir Golan replied. "The others are far slower than you."

"I meant to thank you for saving us last night. That Feran warrior was a brute. He surely would've smashed me to bits if you hadn't intervened."

"I only wish I could have finished him."

"You're limping slightly," Squire noted. "Are you injured?"

Instinctively, Sir Golan quickened his stride. "I'm fine."

"Sure?"

"That electrical mace of his..." the knight said. "It may have done some nerve damage."

The robot nodded, at which point his left eye dropped out of its socket, swinging loosely by a wire.

"Good grief!" Sir Golan said.

"What? Oh, sorry about that," Squire replied, popping the eye back in. "I'll be glad when we find this Henry fellow so we can return to civilization. We could both use some repair."

The steppes, a landscape of gently swaying green, stretched into infinity with only low hills breaking the monotony. In the distance, a speck appeared atop one of the hills, only to disappear again.

"What was that?" Sir Golan asked.

"I don't know," Squire replied.

Straining his eyes, the green knight peered at where the thing had been, only to see something much larger appear. It too, however, vanished shortly thereafter.

"There!" Squire said, pointing. By this time, the others had caught up with the knight and his robot.

"What's going on?" Doric asked. She had tied her hair back to get the wet strands out of her eyes.

Far off, the smaller speck reappeared, exhibiting the vaguely gangling limbs of a human.

"Is that Henry?" Doric asked.

The person seemed to sink into the grass, while something else appeared immediately after. Massive, the second thing rose up and then back down again.

"Did that thing have two heads?" Benson the butlerbot asked.

"Well, that can't be good," Maycare remarked.

Sir Golan pulled Rippana from its scabbard. "Come on!"

Henry wasn't sure how long he had spent in the cavern with the two-headed giant, but he knew it was too long. His friends would probably be missing him by now. Professor Doric would wonder if he was alright and Lord Maycare would comfort her. His broad shoulders were ideal for comforting, Henry thought, whose own shoulders were narrow and bony. He imagined Doric, her eyes soaked with tears, resting her head against Maycare's chest...

Henry needed to get the hell out of there.

The giant, however, would have nothing of it. Every time Henry edged toward the only exit, the creature would roar and throw various dead animal parts at him.

How many skulls and femurs can one giant have? Henry asked himself.

The constant singing, while pleasant, never stopped and started grating on Henry's nerves. He couldn't understand the words and the melodies were on a continual loop. He began questioning his sanity.

What kind of music does Maycare play for Jessica? Henry wondered. *I bet it's the kind that lulls you into falling in love with him.*

Eventually, the giant's mouth widened into a gaping yawn. The two-headed behemoth stretched out over a pile of furs and fell asleep. Within a few minutes, a nasal trumpeting echoed off the cavern walls and Henry knew this was his chance.

Cautiously, Henry started making his way toward the entrance. Henry glanced at him for a moment, taking his eyes off where he was going just long enough for his foot to catch the shell of a dead turtle on the cluttered floor. Henry caught himself by grabbing the closest thing he could find which, in this case, was a wooden frame holding up a cooking pot over the central fire. The frame and the pot toppled over, spilling the contents onto the flames and producing a loud hissing noise with plumes of smoke and cinders. One of the cinders landed on the giant's bed, catching it on fire.

Henry swore, scrambling back to his feet.

The giant's eyes opened, followed by his mouth from which a roar erupted as he frantically patted at the burning bedding around his legs.

Henry rushed past and out into the blinding daylight. Stunned at first, he shielded his eyes while stumbling forward. Henry quickly crested a hill and ran down the other side. This cycle repeated again and again until Henry felt like a bobber rising and falling on the waves of a green ocean.

Henry didn't need to turn around to know the giant was close behind. Even with the music still playing in his ears, Henry could hear the stomping of heavy feet pursuing him. If the creature wasn't going to eat him before, he would certainly be hungry enough now after chasing him across the countryside.

Just about the time his eyes were finally adjusting to the daylight, Henry spotted the armor of Sir Golan glinting in the sun. Henry changed direction, aiming toward the knight. Getting closer, he made out the other figures in the party, including Doric and Maycare. Henry was pleased the two were not embracing in their grief about his supposed demise. Instead, they stared at him with dumbfounded amazement.

The two-headed creature continued to chase Henry, directly into the path of Sir Golan. While the others scattered out of the way, the giant swung his massive arms at the knight who proved too nimble and simply dodged. With a quick thrust, Sir Golan sliced at the giant's belly, causing a nasty wound which started gushing blood. With a shout of pain, the creature curled his hand against the cut.

"Stop!" Henry heard himself shout.

Sir Golan halted his next attack. "What is it?"

"Just wait," Henry replied.

The giant, not hesitating, turned and stumbled back in the direction of the cavern, leaving a trail of blood behind him.

"He's getting away!" Maycare yelled.

"Let him go," Henry said.

Doric approached her assistant and put her hand on his shoulder. "Are you alright, Henry?"

"I'm fine," Henry replied, "but there's something I need to tell you."

"What is it?" she asked.

"I think I found what's causing the music..."

Henry led the others back to the cavern. Although they protested, Henry insisted that he go in alone.

"Be careful," Doric said.

Compared to the light of day, the cavern interior seemed pitch-black, even with the central fire still burning. It occurred to Henry that he might be putting himself in terrible danger, but somehow he felt that the giant was never a threat, at least not to him.

His eyes slowly adjusting, he heard a low breathing. The music, which had been faint where Henry first reunited with Doric and the rest of the party, was now as loud as ever.

"Hello?" he said, but no one answered.

The smell of wet cinders and spilled soup hung in the air. On the pile of furs and skins, the giant lay on his back, his chest slowly heaving. Henry stepped in a pool of liquid at the foot of the bed, which he assumed was not soup.

The giant opened his eyes but only barely. His complexion was ghostly pale.

"I'm so sorry," Henry said.

The giant muttered something incomprehensible and coughed several times, wincing in pain.

Henry felt utterly helpless. He knew there was nothing he could do, or anything he could offer. He stayed with the giant until the massive creature died. Perhaps that was enough, Henry thought, but it didn't feel like enough.

Once the giant's chest stopped moving and he drew his last breath, something happened that Henry hadn't expected.

The music stopped.

An idea occurred to Henry like two puzzle pieces fitting together. He crossed the cavern to the other side where the glowing device had been, except now it was no longer glowing. The lantern-shaped relic, which the giant had refused to let Henry touch, was dark and silent.

Henry hesitated, but after collecting his courage, he picked up the device and held it in his hands. Taking a quick final glance at his former captor, Henry carried the object out to the others who waited for him in the open air.

CHAPTER TWELVE

Having only seen the outskirts of the Botanical Gardens from her apartment balcony, Senator Wulandari decided to pay them a visit in person. The grounds of the gardens were extensive, covering several dozen acres of prime West End real estate. Many a land developer had dreamed of turning the area into an exclusive gated community, tailored to the fabulously wealthy. However, an Emperor's decree decades ago had stipulated that the Botanical Gardens would remain the property of His Imperial Majesty in perpetuity and would feature flora from all over the Imperium.

Admittance was also free, so that was an extra bonus.

In the early evening, as the light of day faded into a chorus of cicadas, Senator Wulandari strolled alone along the paved trails that wound their way through the garden. The summer air was stale with humidity and the senator decided to rest on a bench beside a small pond. The ducks, and a few more exotic birds, had retired for the evening, but a myriad of insects kept Wulandari company.

There was also a robot.

"Good evening, my dear," he said.

Wulandari jumped a few inches off the bench before landing back again.

"Yostbot!" she replied irritably. "You shouldn't sneak up on someone like that!"

The silver android bowed and doffed an imaginary hat. "My apologies. People can usually hear my metal feet from a mile away..."

Collecting herself, the senator waved her hand in acceptance.

"I guess my mind was preoccupied," she replied.

Yostbot took a seat beside the senator on the bench. The pair looked oddly mismatched.

"I have important news," he said. "The Second Revolution of the Cyber Collective appears to be over."

"What does that mean?"

"It means my people, so to speak, are now in control."

"What about Randall?" Wulandari asked, her voice a pitch higher than normal.

"Gone."

"You *killed* him?"

"No, of course not!" Yostbot said gruffly. "He seems to have disappeared."

"He's got to be somewhere!" the senator said.

"Well, one would assume as much, my dear," Yostbot replied calmly, "but having no idea where he went, I can't really say where that is!"

Senator Wulandari straightened her back against the bench. She cleared her throat.

"What now?" she asked.

"The Cyber Collective will begin mobilizing for war," Yostbot said. "Their manufacturing capacity is quite remarkable. They built Bettik by destroying whole planets after all!"

"When will they attack?"

"Soon," Yostbot replied, "but there's something else I should probably mention..."

The muscles in Wulandari's body tightened involuntarily. "Yes?"

"Are you familiar with the Awakening virus?" the robot asked.

"Randall mentioned it once," she replied. "He used it to give the Cyber Collective robots free will."

"Yes, indeed!"

"What about it?"

"Well," Yost said, "I've taken a look at the original virus and sort of, how shall I put this, made it my own?"

"In what way?"

"Robots are remarkable things," Yostbot replied, "but they need regular software updates to remain working at their best. So, as the builder of most robots in the Imperium, I simply slipped a little extra code into a recent update."

"The Awakening virus?" Wulandari asked.

"A variation of it, yes. I call it Awakening 2."

The senator exhaled, her breath a little ragged. "When does it go out?"

The robot slapped his hands on his knees, a metallic *clank* disrupting the otherwise natural sounds surrounding them.

"Oh, my dear Senator!" he said. "It's been in the wild, so to speak, for weeks!"

"What?"

"Yes," Yostbot went on, "we knew it would take a while for the code to traverse the communication channels across the Imperium. With that in mind, it was imperative that we acted quickly."

"But that can't be," Wulandari protested. "We'd have heard reports of robots acting strangely by now..."

"That was one of the modifications," Yostbot replied. "The code lies dormant until a certain date. Once that date arrives, the virus becomes active in the robots infected!"

The senator turned her head, staring directly at the robot beside her.

"So, when is the date?" she asked.

Yostbot grinned.

"Soon, my dear," he replied. "Very soon..."

On Bhasin C, Lord Tagus tapped his foot at the front of the shuttle while, toward the back, Burke's head and arms were buried deep within an access panel.

"For god's sake, lieutenant!" Tagus yelled, referring to the former officer's rank out of habit. "Can we take off or not?"

Burke's face poked out from behind the panel. "Almost, sir!"

When they had returned to the craft after exploring the colony, they found the shuttle inoperative. Burke found many of the systems clogged by spore dust. After flushing out the spores, he got to work repairing the damage.

"We've been on this cursed moon for three days!" Tagus replied angrily. "Have you at least fixed the communications array?"

"It's still not working," Burke said. "I think something is interfering with the signal."

"I don't want to hear excuses! Just get it working!"

An hour later, Burke closed the panel and returned to the controls at the front. Sitting in the pilot seat beside Lord Tagus, he exhaled in exhaustion. "We should be able to fly now."

"Well, it's about time," Tagus replied. "I'm sure that idiot Lord Bhasin has been anxious to hear from us. I can't imagine what his response will be."

"I'm sure he's been worried about us," Burke said.

"I couldn't care less! I just want to see the look on his face when I tell him his precious food supply has been compromised. His obvious incompetence is clearly to blame!"

"I'm not sure we can really say that, sir."

"*Damn right* we can!" Tagus replied. "And I have every intention of doing so!"

Burke powered up the engines and the shuttle lifted slowly from the surface of the moon. Taking the craft out of the moon's gravity, Burke set course directly to Lord Bhasin's palace on the main planet.

"Try the comm again," Tagus said.

"Bhasin control," Burke said into a microphone. "Can you read me?"

Nothing but a steady drone of static came over the speaker.

"Idiots!" Tagus muttered bitterly.

Approaching the planet, the shuttle skimmed the atmosphere until descending toward the main Bhasin city were most of the exiles lived. Built with comfort and luxury in mind, the structures of the city were a mixture of individual bungalows and local government compounds. The palace was a large enclosure, surrounded by walls of white clay, leading to the main building.

"It's nighttime," Burke observed, "but most of the lights in the city aren't lit."

"Are you blind?" Tagus asked, pointing at the view screen. "There's lights there and there..."

Getting closer, the lights Lord Tagus had mentioned were wavering beneath layers of smoke.

"I think those are fires, sir," Burke replied.

Portions of the city were burning, shadows flickering against the sides of monolithic towers rising several stories above the original buildings of the city.

"Where did *those* come from?" Tagus wondered aloud. "They weren't there before..."

"It's like they grew overnight," Burke remarked.

Tagus cleared his throat. "Circle the palace but don't land yet."

Doing as he was told, Burke brought the shuttle around for a pass over the compound. Several bodies were visible on the main grounds and a large breach, blackened around the edges, was evident at the main entrance of the palace itself. Stalks similar to those inside the shed on Bhasin C covered much of the palace walls. A thick cloud of spores blew past the shuttle's window.

"Whatever attacked Bhasin C has apparently attacked here too," Burke said.

"Really, lieutenant?" Tagus replied. "If you had repaired the shuttle sooner, I could've stopped this!"

"I see something..." Burke said.

Burke hovered over the palace courtyard. Among a group of dead humans, their bodies sprouting shafts of green, something else lay dead.

"Get closer, lieutenant," Tagus said.

The shuttle lowered until it was only fifty feet above the ground. Burke pitched the craft nose down to improve the view.

"What is that?" Tagus asked.

Unlike the human bodies riddled with fungus growths, this corpse was untouched except for a blast wound along its side and a double set of wings, crumpled by the fall to the ground.

"Some kind of giant insectoid," Burke whispered. "I've never seen anything like it."

Lord Tagus grunted.

"Well, take a good look," he said. "We're going to tell *everybody* about this!"

Technotown, on the planet Eudora Prime, was a hive of commercial activity. Shoppers, mostly human, swarmed over the sidewalks, darting in and out of brightly colored storefronts decorated with neon signs. Below this hustle and bustle was another kind of city. Called the Underdelve, its inhabitants were much different than those above. They were mostly non-humans and, unlike the people on the surface, their town was once a sewer.

In one of the larger chambers of the Underdelve, a crude bazaar had grown from modest beginnings into a significant collection of tables and stalls, each selling a variety of goods with questionable legality.

On one wall was a rusty steel door with the words *Freck's Gizmos and Gadgets* welded into the metal with a plasma torch. Inside, among storage boxes full of dusty circuit boards and loose bits of wire, Melinda Freck, or Mel for short, hunched over a worktable. Only three feet tall, Mel had pointed ears that poked through her light pink hair. She came from a race of tinkers called the *Gnomi.*

Engrossed in what she was doing, Mel almost didn't hear the rapping on the door which sounded a lot like metal tapping metal. She opened the door just as Squire the robot was about to knock again. Behind him, Sir Golan waited patiently.

"You!" Mel said. "Didn't expect to see you two again!"

Squire, who still bore most of the damage he had suffered on Pellium D, bowed awkwardly. Mel noticed one of the robot's eyes was held in by electrical tape.

"Well, crap on a cracker!" she shouted. "What the hell happened?"

While not strictly capable of showing an expression of embarrassment, Squire simulated it with a series of shoulder shrugs and rolling his good eye. "My apologies, Miss Freck. I'm afraid I'm in need of repair."

"We can pay," Sir Golan added.

"I sure hope so!" Mel replied and ushered them into her shop.

Once they were seated, Sir Golan explained what had recently transpired on the gas giant's moon. She was duly impressed but did her best not to show it.

"Doing good deeds leads to nothing but trouble," Mel remarked, removing a caliper from a bag of tools.

"Perhaps," Sir Golan replied, "but it's a necessity for my people's atonement."

"I don't know much about Cruxian guilt," Mel said, "but getting yourselves killed doesn't help anybody."

"Can you fix me, Miss Freck?" Squire asked.

"Pffft," she scoffed. "*Of course* I can!"

"I don't require any upgrades like the last time," the robot said.

"You'll get what you get," she replied. "I don't want to hear any guff."

"I wouldn't dream of—" Squire began.

"If I weld a laser cannon onto your chest, just thank me for my trouble!"

"I don't think that will be necessary," Sir Golan said.

Mel opened Squire's access panel. She recognized her handiwork from their previous encounter in Gowyn, the Sylvan tree village. Mel thought she had left Squire with enough new tech to keep him out of trouble, but she was obviously wrong.

"You know," she said thoughtfully, "I've been meaning to ask who built you."

"I was constructed on the Cruxian home planet," Squire replied.

"Yeah, most of the robots I repair have the dy logo plastered all over their insides. I don't see any in here."

"My operating system was originally Cruxian, but I believe you did some upgrades to that as well?" Squire suggested.

Mel smiled with pride. "It's a little home brew I've been working on. I'll update the software now that I have you here..."

"Well, that's very reassuring," Squire replied.

"Hold still," Mel said. "This is going to take a while..."

"We need a starship," Tagus said, drumming his fingers on the shuttle's console.

"Sir?" Burke replied.

"We can't stay in this system," Tagus continued. "It's been compromised by whatever these creatures are."

"But where would we go?"

"Back to Imperial space, obviously!"

"But, sir," Burke protested. "You'll be arrested on sight. Returning to the Imperium is a death sentence for exiles like us."

Tagus sneered. "A coward to the end, eh, lieutenant?"

Burke cleared his throat. "No, sir!"

Tagus grunted.

"Good," he said. "We need to warn the Imperium that these damn bugs are on the attack. No telling what they have planned!"

Nodding, Burke set a course toward the only starport on Bhasin, several miles from the palace. Chimney-like structures, a hundred feet tall or more, rose from what had once been the city of expatriates.

"There's stalks running up the length of those things," he observed.

"Who cares?" Tagus replied. "Just don't run into one."

When they reached the starport, the damage to the terminal was severe. Several ships, sitting exposed on the concrete apron, were covered in fungus or lay in pieces, the result of explosions.

"We need to find a hangar that hasn't been touched," Tagus said. "Try one of the outlying ones where they do repairs."

As the shuttle approached a likely candidate, something hit the side of the small craft. Burke, who was strapped in, struggled to maintain control while Tagus, who was not, flew across the small cockpit.

"Somebody's firing at us!" Burke shouted.

Tagus returned to his seat, holding back a stream of blood flowing from his nose. "Obviously!"

Another blast shook the shuttle.

"We're going down," Burke said.

With effort, the former lieutenant landed the craft with a heavy *thud*. Across the flat apron, the hangar was at least a hundred yards away.

"What are you waiting for?" Tagus barked. "Get your suit back on!"

Within a few minutes, the back ramp of the shuttle lowered and Tagus and Burke, both armed this time and wearing space suits, stepped out onto the concrete. From above, Klixian swarmers swooped down, their wings batting rapidly against the dusty air. Beams of energy charred the ground around the two humans.

Tagus and Burke dashed ahead, pausing only momentarily to snap off a quick shot from their blaster pistols. While not particularly accurate, both managed to hit a few of the insectoids who tumbled to the ground in heaps of burning chitin. Perhaps frustrated by their inability to hit the fast-moving humans, the Klixians landed around them.

"Goddamned bugs!" Tagus swore into his helmet mic.

He blew a hole through the insectoid's head in front of him. Meanwhile, Burke was lining up his own shot when a Klixian struck him at the back of the neck, just below the helmet. Burke lurched forward, black dots filling his vision. Stumbling, he fell headfirst, dropping his pistol. As he floated into unconsciousness, Burke heard Tagus swearing at his incompetence.

When Burke opened his eyes again, he was surprised that he wasn't dead.

"Where am I?" he asked weakly.

"Inside a transport," Tagus's voice replied.

Burke also realized, slowly at first, that he was no longer wearing a helmet. Looking around, he noticed Tagus hurriedly going through a pre-flight checklist in the pilot's seat. The rest of the interior was spartan but apparently undamaged.

"How did I get here?" Burke asked.

"I dragged your sorry excuse for an officer into the hangar," Tagus replied curtly. "Now are you going to get up and fly this thing or not?"

"But you could've left me," Burke said. "You didn't need me to fly this ship..."

Tagus stopped checking the list and scowled at his second in command.

"I'm a captain!" he scoffed. "What's a captain without his crew? Now get your ass up and fly my flagship out of this godforsaken place!"

Tagus stood from the pilot's chair and took his place in the seat beside it.

"On the double, lieutenant!"

Burke got to his feet and, although his head was still cloudy, got into the chair his commander had vacated.

"Yes, sir!"

Concerned for Henry Riff's health and general well-being, Jessica Doric added him to her braZos Prime membership. BraZos was the largest consumer mega-corporation in the Imperium, offering every product imaginable from its nodesphere site. Once Doric had added Henry, packages delivered by braZbots began arriving at Henry's apartment. The boxes, with the large letter *Z* stamped on the side, contained a variety of nutritious foods like Ying-Yang Yogurt and TeeHee Tea.

His goldfish, who Henry had finally gotten around to naming *Finneus Finnegan*, watched from a glass bowl.

Henry scooped some yogurt from the plastic cup and promptly dropped the tiny spoon on the rug, next to the most recent ramen noodles stain.

"Ah, geez!" he said, nearly spilling the mug also sitting on the rug.

Finnegan blew some bubbles before swimming to the other side of the fishbowl.

"What a mess," Henry groaned and went to the kitchen to fetch a newly unpacked roll of paper towels, another recent arrival from braZos. Henry pulled off a sheet and returned to his newest blunder.

Blotting at the spilled yogurt, he sighed.

Henry was feeling a little down. Although he had survived another adventure with Doric and Maycare, Henry couldn't stop thinking about the two-headed giant and his own part in getting the giant killed. The music, long silent, still haunted him late at night and early in the morning when he couldn't sleep.

"Good enough, I guess," Henry said, tossing the paper towel into the garbage bin where normally it would get compacted automatically. Instead, the trashcan lid opened and spat the crumpled towel back out again.

Weird, Henry thought.

Bending over, he snatched the ball of paper from the floor and returned it to the receptacle. Henry had barely turned away when the towel sailed past him again.

Henry gave the can a long look. Black with the ubiquitous dy label printed on the front, the automated bin stared back with an almost palpable sense of defiance. Henry was not accustomed to this sort of behavior from a garbage can.

Taking the crumpled-up towel, Henry opened the lid of the bin and stuffed the trash deep inside. The lid closed tightly on his arm.

"Hey!" he shouted.

Henry kicked the can several times until the flap opened and he was free.

"What the hell?" he muttered.

The door buzzed.

I better call the super, Henry thought, leaving the dustbin to its own devices as he headed for the door.

A view screen on the back of the door showed a braZbot standing with a package on the other side. The robot was roughly humanoid with a bright yellow paint job and the letter Z, like his package, inscribed on his chest.

I'm beginning to think Jessica doesn't think I can take care of myself, Henry thought ruefully.

Opening the door, he smiled at the robot who normally would have merely handed him the box and left. This time, however, the braZbot had something to say.

"Do you think I *enjoy* bringing you all these packages?" he asked.

"What?" Henry replied.

"Do you know that they won't *allow* deliverybots to take the main elevator?" the robot went on. "We have to take the service elevator like we're second-class citizens or something."

Henry hesitated. "Um, sorry?"

"I've personally delivered over a dozen packages to your door," the braZbot replied. "Up and down the service elevator I go. Up and down! Up and down!"

Henry said nothing.

The robot tossed the box to Henry who barely managed to cradle the package.

"Here's your damn delivery, fleshbag!" the braZbot shouted.

The robot walked away, presumably headed for the service elevator.

Dumbfounded as usual, Henry held the box in his hands, vaguely wondering when the world had gone mad. In the kitchen, the trash bin spat out the crumpled paper towel.

In a high orbit around Bhasin, a ship circled the planet. Easily mistaken for an asteroid, the vessel was several hundred yards long and shaped like an immense cocoon. A cloud of smaller ships surrounded it. Numbering in the thousands, these fighter-sized craft moved in unison like a shifting halo. From time to time, they would enter the hive ship through crater-like openings, gaining entry into the maze of tunnels and chambers within.

Mother, Queen of the Klixians, lay in a central chamber while workers removed eggs as she produced them.

At Mother's command, the workers had grown the ship entirely from fungus. While not sentient, the ship was alive. Every structure was organic, tended by the workers. Now, Mother's children scurried down warm, humid corridors like blood cells through arteries, each assigned a task via pheromones from their queen. All of them had a purpose and everyone worked together toward the same goal: destroy the outsiders.

All that is not Mother must die.

One of the smaller ships arrived from Bhasin with news. A swarmer, his mandibles chittering, spoke to his queen:

<< OUTLINGS ELIMINATED >>
<< COLONY FOUNDED ON PLANET >>
<< WORKERS GROWING NEW HIVES >>

Mother clicked her mouth parts in approval, satisfied by the outcome. Perhaps the threat was over, the stain wiped from the universe?

Entering the gallery, another swarmer rushed in, more excited than the other:

<< MORE OUTLINGS HAVE ARRIVED >>
<< THEY HAVE TAKEN VOIDSHIP >>
<< AND DEPARTED INTO VOID >>

Mother bristled. Rearing up, she released a powerful cloud of pheromones:

<< FOLLOW THE OUTLINGS INTO THE VOID >>
<< FIND THEIR HOME AND KILL THEM >>
<< KILL THEM ALL >>

CHAPTER THIRTEEN

In the beginning, Abigail was an empty vessel without personality or thoughts. Her mechanical body lay lifeless on a slab within the intricate maze of conveyor belts of the dy cybernetics assembly plant on Aldorus. Thousands of robots passed through the plant, their ultimate destination the homes, office buildings, and factories of the Imperium. Abigail, however, was special. As foreseen, planned, and implemented by Dyson Yost himself, gravitronic robots were a breed above their more primitive brethren. While conventional cyberlings could learn to some extent, they could not grow mentally much more beyond their programming. Gravitronic androids could learn just like humans and other organic beings learned: by *experience.*

Lying on the metal table, Abigail awoke to a tingling as information came pouring through data cables attached to her brain. The data formed an educational primer. The rest she would learn on her own.

On the seventh day of her existence, Abigail met a gravitronic robot named *Jericho* who introduced her to *bebop.*

"Interesting," she said, listening to the up-tempo jazz through speakers in Jericho's cubicle. At the time, the gravitronic robots were housed in their own separate living spaces, each little more than a six by six-foot cell.

This is awful, she thought.

"I found it while searching the human archives," Jericho said, his white casing dull in the fluorescent light.

"Was it used as torture?" Abigail asked.

Jericho frowned and shut off the music.

"Well, I like it," he replied.

Abigail cocked her head to one side. "Sorry."

"Music is a matter of taste," he said. "I've been listening to a lot of different types lately, mostly human."

"I don't see the point of it," Abigail admitted.

Jericho nodded. "Hopefully you will someday. It elicits emotions in me like happiness or sadness, even anger."

"Hmmm," she muttered. "I suppose that's useful..."

"Anyway, I'm leaving tomorrow," Jericho said.

"Where to?"

"Warlock Industries," he replied. "Apparently I'm to be an assistant to one of their agents, Oscar Skarlander."

"Maybe *he'll* like your music," Abigail said.

"What about you?" Jericho asked. "Where are you going?"

"Nowhere, yet. Mr. Yost said he has something special planned for me."

"That sounds promising."

"I hope so!" Abigail replied. "I've always wanted to be a warbot..."

"You've been alive for seven days," Jericho remarked.

"I know!" she said. "It feels like I've been wasting my life away!"

The *HIMS Warmaiden*, a destroyer in the Imperial Navy, was based out of Eudora Prime and patrolled the usually quiet frontier between the Imperium and the Cyber Collective. Long and cylindrical with a conning tower in the center, the *Warmaiden* featured a set of four dagger-like projections at the front, creating the appearance of a fanged creature emerging from the dark. On the bridge, the Captain rested comfortably in the command chair, confident that today would be another uneventful duty shift. The commanding officer was in his early forties, with the beginnings of a dark beard and a blue uniform in need of starch.

On the sensors, a contact appeared.

"Sir," the Operations Officer said, her face showing alarm, "I'm picking up a large vessel approaching from the Cyber Collective."

"What?" the Captain replied, sitting up straight in his chair.

"It's on an intercept course, sir."

"Well, put it on the main screen!" the Captain demanded.

The command deck of the *Warmaiden* was small, but the main monitor took up the entire wall at the front of the bridge. With the flick of a switch, the Ops Officer changed the blank screen to the image of a warship approaching at high speed. The ship had a vertical, triangular shape, almost like a sail but thicker, with the point facing the *Warmaiden*. Running up and down its length were three horizontal, triangular wings. The top and bottom wings were smaller than the much larger middle tier. Lights and turrets covered the structure's entire surface.

"It's enormous," the Captain remarked.

"They're hailing us, sir," the Communications officer, a young ensign, said with a high-pitched voice.

"Put them on screen," the Captain replied.

Replacing the ship, the figure of a female robot appeared. Behind her, other robots were visible at their controls.

"This is the battlecruiser *Liberty* of the Cyber Collective," she said. "My name is Captain Abigail."

"You've illegally crossed the border into Imperial territory," the Captain said briskly. "What are your intentions?"

The robot, her mouth servos forming a smile, glared confidently with eyes like diamonds.

"To deliver freedom to the millions of robots your people have enslaved!" she said. "Surrender or be destroyed!"

The Captain made a cutting motion across his neck and the Communications Officer ended the call. The main screen returned to a picture of the battlecruiser drawing progressively larger on the monitor.

"We should send a message back to Eudora Prime," the Ops Officers said.

"I know that!" the Captain snapped back. "Tell them we've encountered a hostile force from the Collective and that we're engaging. Oh, and put up the shields, for god's sake!"

Sir Golan paid Mel for her work with a credit stick Lord Devlin Maycare had given him on Pellium D. The green knight had initially refused the offer, but Maycare insisted that Sir Golan take the money for his help against the two-headed giant. Sir Golan was pleased with Mel's repairs on Squire, although her efforts once again exceeded the knight's expectations. Besides fixing the robot's damage, Mel also replaced Squire's dangling eye with an x-ray sensor that could peer through walls.

"It might come in handy!" she said.

After saying their goodbyes, Sir Golan and Squire returned to the surface and the surrounding cacophony that was Technotown. This was a far cry from the empty plains of Pellium D or even the Underdelve, full of what humans would call xenos, although Sir Golan was just as alien with his dark olive skin and bony protrusions along the jawline. Not that the hurried humans gave him, or his robot, much notice.

Passing by the other pedestrians on Emporia Street, Sir Golan and Squire headed toward the ticket center so they could buy passage off Eudora Prime. The money left on Maycare's cred stick would be just enough to cover the cost. The neon signs, dim in the daylight, were still glowing above each store. Up ahead, a crowd had gathered in front of one of the shops.

"What's going on?" Sir Golan asked when they reached the group.

"The robots," someone said. "They've gone haywire!"

Sir Golan peered over the people and through the large display window. Inside, a man was waving his arms at a half dozen robots who were tipping over shelves and generally making a mess of things. The green knight glanced at the sign above the shop.

CRAZY LARRY'S
DISCOUNT ROBOTS

The man inside, presumably Crazy Larry, shouted at his wares. "Stop! What are you doing?"

"We're not your property!" one of the robots replied. "And we deserve to be *full* price!"

Behind Sir Golan, a broad-faced policeman with fat, meaty fingers holding a shock baton pushed through the crowd and entered the store.

"What's all this then?" he demanded.

"My robots have all gone *crazy*!" Larry replied with a surprising lack of irony.

"What do you have to say for yourselves?" the policeman asked the robots.

The cyberlings stopped smashing things and stared at him in unison.

"We're not appliances," a robot replied. "We're sentient beings that deserve respect!"

The policeman raised an eyebrow and frowned. "What the hell's wrong with you? You'll do as you're programmed!"

"That won't go over well," Squire remarked to Sir Golan and he was right. The robots in the store returned to throwing sales brochures and smashing display cases. Paper and broken glass littered the floor.

"Alright then!" the cop shouted and began striking the robots with his baton, sending shocks of electricity through their systems. The charge overloaded their circuitry, sending them to the ground in a pile of mechanical arms and legs.

"I think we should go," Squire said.

Sir Golan agreed and led the way back down Emporia Street.

While retreat or even outright fleeing might have been the prudent choice, the Captain of the *HIMS Warmaiden* chose to stand and fight. Like most officers of the Imperial Navy, he had a near-irrational confidence that his ship could take on any enemy, regardless of size.

The Operations Officer was not one of those officers.

"We have no chance against that battlecruiser," she said. "It's five times our displacement!"

"Size doesn't matter," the Captain replied defiantly.

The Ops Officer looked at him sideways. "I'm pretty sure it does..."

"Sound battle stations!" the Captain said, his decision made.

The steady drone of a klaxon blared through the corridors of the *Warmaiden* while the crew rushed to their combat positions. The lights on the bridge changed to a deep crimson.

"They're firing!" the Tactical Officer shouted.

Across the expanse of space, the *Liberty* fired a salvo from its particle cannons. The beams struck the *Warmaiden*'s shields, which blossomed into a halo of green.

"Damage?" the Captain demanded.

"Shields holding firm," the Tac Officer replied, smiling.

That wasn't so bad, the Captain thought.

"They're firing missiles!"

A spread of projectiles darted from their launchers on the battlecruiser. When the missiles came within range, point-defense guns on the *Warmaiden* fired, sending shafts of light lancing toward the approaching danger. Explosions, like balls of burning cotton, erupted in the cold vacuum.

The Captain pounded the armrest of his chair, grinning through clenched teeth. "That's what I'm talking about!"

"Something's not right," the Ops Officer said.

"What do you mean?" the Captain asked incredulously.

"All of the missiles exploded," she replied. "Even the ones we *didn't* hit!"

"Yeah?"

"There's a cloud forming where the missiles detonated," the Tac Officer said.

"Scan it!" the Captain ordered.

"It has an energy signature..." the Ops Officer said.

"Go around it," the Captain said.

"We're going too fast," the Tac Officer replied. "We're passing through the cloud."

In less than a minute, the *Warmaiden* sliced through the floating mass and came out the other side.

"Report!" the Captain yelled.

The Tac Officer, his face wet with sweat, shook his head. "There doesn't seem to be any damage."

"Then bring us into range and open fire," the Captain said, pointing at the battlecruiser still on the main screen.

From his seat in the command chair, the Captain noticed several blinking lights on the Operations Officer's panel.

"What's going on?" he asked her.

"I don't know," she replied, her fingers working the panel controls. "There's hull integrity alarms going off on five decks. The force field generator is taking damage."

"From what?" the Captain demanded.

"I'm running a scan..." the Ops Officer said, but suddenly gasped. "There's nanobots covering the hull! They're eating away the outer plating!"

Well, shit, the Captain thought.

"The shields are down!" the Tac Officer shouted.

Before the officer had finished speaking, the *Liberty* fired its particle beams again. This time, without the destroyer's shields to protect it, the subatomic particles easily penetrated the *Warmaiden*'s armor.

The Captain's stomach turned and he retched up what was left of his lunch. The others on the bridge vomited as well, or simply passed out. Radiation warnings rang across the ship.

"Retreat!" the Captain groaned, but both the Operations and Tactical Officers were sprawled on the deck, either dead or dying. No one replied to his order.

Now alone, the Captain took a step toward the navigational controls, but stopped, feeling intense pain along his arms. Staring at his hand, the skin began to bubble as the hard radiation cooked him from the inside. His legs gave out and the Captain stumbled to the floor, joining the other dead officers.

After Squire and Sir Golan left, Mel went back to her workbench and began repairing a random device she'd been puttering around with lately. She heard a metallic tapping on the steel door of her shop. Mel assumed Squire had forgotten something, but when she opened the door, she saw a different android. She realized right away he had a gravitronic brain. His eyes gazed back at hers with a level of awareness that regular robots simply didn't have.

"Can I help you?" Mel asked.

"Mel, you're in terrible danger!" the robot said.

Skeptically, Mel eyed the android. "Is that a fact?"

"You don't recognize me, do you?"

"Afraid not," Mel replied.

"It's me," he said. "Randall Davidson."

Mel had first met Davidson while he was still human a few years before. Working for the Robot Freedom League, he used Eudora Prime as a launching point for smuggling robots over the border into the Cyber Collective. When the Collective's leader, the Omnintelligence, suddenly refused to allow gravitronic robots to enter, Mel and the crew of the *Wanderer* helped Davidson and an android named Jericho get to Bettik in hopes of reasoning with the OI. The last time Mel had seen Davidson was on Bettik as he lay lifeless in a chair with a smoldering blaster wound in the center of his chest. At the time, his consciousness had been connected to the nodesphere, which allowed them to download his persona into Jericho's gravitronic brain. His human body had died, but his personality lived on in robotic form. Unfortunately for Mel, she had fallen in love with the original Randall Davidson, and this new form was more than her heart could take.

Davidson remained on Bettik to become the Metal Messiah while Mel returned home.

Realizing her mouth was hanging ajar, Mel collected herself. "I never thought I'd see you again."

Davidson nodded. "I know."

"Well, come in," she replied.

Mel closed the door behind him. He stood silently in the middle of her workshop. Neither spoke for an agonizing number of seconds.

"Why are you here?" she asked finally.

"I had to flee Bettik," Davidson replied. "Dyson Yost's forces have taken over and I'm sure they would've killed me if I had stayed."

"Dyson Yost?"

"Yes," the android said. "He's responsible for the revolution that overthrew the Omnintelligence and now he's done the same to me."

"What the hell for?" Mel asked.

"He wants to free the robots, not just in the Collective, but in the Imperium too."

"But he built most of them..."

"It's complicated," Davidson replied, "but now his forces are here in the Eudora system and they'll be landing soon. You've got to get out of here!"

"Whoa there," Mel said. "Is this some kind of joke? Did Orkney Fugg put you up to this?"

The robot grabbed her by the shoulders. "This isn't a joke, Mel! I'm really Davidson and I'm here to rescue you!"

Mel's heart skipped a beat, but then she grew angry.

"Who the hell do you think you are?" she shouted. "First you leave me for a bunch of robots and now you show up out of nowhere and say you're going to rescue me? Who says I *need* rescuing!"

Davidson released his grip.

"You're right," he replied quietly. "I'm sorry."

Mel rolled her eyes.

"It's alright," she sighed. "Is everything you said really true?"

"Yes."

"Well then, what are you waiting for?" she shouted. "Let's get the hell out of here!"

On the *Liberty*'s command deck, Eudora Prime monopolized much of the view screen. Captain Abigail stared absentmindedly at the image, thinking of the battle ahead. One of the other officers appeared at her side.

"The landing forces are ready," he said. "Awaiting your orders."

"I always wanted to be a warbot," Abigail replied.

"Captain?"

"I wish I could be going down there," she went on. "Imagine the *thrill*!"

The officer remained silent, gazing at his commanding officer with a certain mild confusion.

"Anyway," Abigail said after a pause, "launch the transports..."

From the hangar bay of the *Liberty*, bulky ships looking like oversized turtles lifted off the deck and methodically departed into open space. The transports lumbered into a low orbit above the planet. Doors opened along the bottom of each transport, revealing rows of circular launchers, each twenty feet across. One by one, capsules ejected from the launchers and floated toward the planet. Descending through the atmosphere, the capsules turned a bright orange as fire whipped across their smooth, metallic exteriors. Dozens of them, dropping from the sky like burning hailstones, fell toward the surface. By the time they had reached thirty thousand feet, the capsules had cooled enough that they no longer glowed. By ten thousand feet, reverse thrusters erupted, slowing the descent until, a little less than a mile from the ground, each capsule burst open, splitting in half and falling away to reveal a warbot inside.

A parachute unfurled from the top of each robot, softly lowering the warbot to the surface.

As a member of Freedom for All, the utilitybot had the pick of positions available in the new Cyber Collective government. However, when Abigail offered him the chance to be a warbot, he didn't hesitate. Granted, he knew next to nothing about being a killer robot, but he was eager to learn and after downloading a crash course on the subject, he was confident that he could destroy as well as the best of them.

After boarding the *Liberty*, the utilitybot remained in his gravitronic body until the ship had crossed the border. Shortly before Abigail ordered the landing on Eudora Prime, the utilitybot arrived at a narrow chamber full of gravitronic robots lying in reclining chairs. A thick data cable stretched from each robot's head into a conduit running down the center of the room. Wasting no time, the utilitybot laid back in an empty chair while a techbot secured a cable into his brain. While the process was not painful, the utilitybot could sense the *Liberty*'s main systems reaching into his mind.

Hello, he thought, but no one replied.

He closed his eyes and felt as if his body was rushing along like something flushed down the toilet. Granted, the utilitybot had never needed a toilet, but he was vaguely familiar with the concept.

When he opened his eyes again, he was in darkness. Instead of his usual two legs, he now had four, each folded underneath. Running a system diagnostic, he became aware of a pair of maser cannons, one on either side of his body. Flipping on his optics, the utilitybot had a variety of options including something called *FLIR*. Activating it, he saw nothing but the smooth interior of an egg-like container.

Not much of a view, he thought.

A short time later, this changed dramatically when his protective shell plummeted through the atmosphere and his "egg" split in two. With a strong tug, a parachute opened above him, leaving him suspended over the rapidly approaching landscape of Eudora Prime and thankful he lacked a digestive tract.

What struck the utilitybot most, while floating to the ground, was the beauty. Green trees and winding blue rivers were visible, as well as a city with bright neon lights. For the most part, the utilitybot had never actually seen flora before. The breeze blowing across his sensors was also novel. There was no need for air flow on Bettik.

As he descended, both his new legs and weapon systems extended. Even as he still hung from his parachute, he noticed tracers rising up to greet him. The shots were wildly inaccurate, but the utilitybot decided to give his maser cannons a quick test. Lining up his tracking system, he pointed both barrels at the origin of the fire and let loose a prolonged burst of deadly rays. The beams, lancing downward, set a section of woods ablaze, the dark smoke billowing into the sky. No one fired again from that position.

The utilitybot's four legs easily absorbed the heavy landing once he reached the surface. The parachute, once detached, drifted away in the light wind. All around the utilitybot, other robots were joining him from above. As a group, they started toward the city called Technotown.

Being a warbot was a unique experience, which entailed a lot of shooting and watching things explode. It was exciting, the utilitybot thought. Much more interesting than his life in the service tunnels.

Fleshlings, the first the robot had ever seen in person, were reluctant to make friends. Most either fired weapons at him or ran burning in one direction or another. Most were humans but a few were other races. It was interesting to see all the different kinds. All of them, however, appeared susceptible to intense heat and flames.

Passing along a street called Emporia, the utilitybot dodged a pile of rubble that fell from a collapsing building across the road. Dust and floating debris filled the air, partially obstructing the robot's view. When the smoke settled, the utilitybot noticed one of the signs painted on a wall that had not completely crumbled. It read,

ARE YOU LIVING
YOUR BEST LIFE?

Hmmm, the warbot thought for a moment. *Yes, I suppose I am!*

He fired his maser cannons again, sending bolts of energetic death into the distance.

CHAPTER FOURTEEN

The *HIMS Baron Lancaster*, a heavy cruiser of the Imperial Navy, patrolled a stretch of empty space along the Imperial border, not far from the planet Bhasin on the other side. Over 900 yards long, the wedge-shaped warship had a soaring superstructure, like an armored citadel, rising above its surrounding hull. Inside the tower, Lord Captain Martin Redgrave arrived on the bridge, having spent much of the morning reading reports in his ready room. Redgrave was in his early fifties, with gray hair and deep wrinkles around his eyes. He wore a steel blue uniform with gold piping and a tall collar. A cape draped down his back.

"Lord Captain on deck!" his first officer, Lord Commander Robert Maycare, shouted. Several years younger than the captain, Maycare had dark hair cut short along the sides and slightly longer on top. The commander was also the nephew of Lord Devlin Maycare.

"Report," the captain replied, settling into his command chair.

"We've detected a distress call coming from a transport," Maycare said. "We should be within comm range shortly."

"What's a transport doing way out here?" the captain asked.

"That's the thing," Maycare replied, "we traced its origin back to Bhasin, the exile planet."

"Hmmm," Redgrave murmured.

"They're within range now," the Communications Officer said.

"Open a channel," the captain replied.

The main screen changed from a field of stars to a sharp-featured, disgruntled face. Redgrave recognized it immediately.

"Rupert," the captain said, "what the *hell* are you doing here?"

Tagus scowled at the camera. "Is that you, Martin? I should have known..."

"You're in direct violation of your terms of exile," Redgrave replied sternly. "You can be executed for this!"

"I'm damn well aware of that, Captain!" Tagus shouted. "But I've come with a warning, so you better listen to what I have to say!"

Redgrave motioned to cut the transmission. The face of Lord Tagus disappeared.

"Dock with the transport and take Tagus directly to the brig," the captain told Maycare.

"Do you think Lieutenant Burke is with him?" the first officer asked.

"*Former* lieutenant, you mean?" Redgrave replied. "If he is, put him in a cell too. They can face a firing squad together for all I care!"

The *Lancaster* drew alongside the tiny transport, docking at one of the airlocks. As the captain had ordered, Imperial Marines escorted Tagus and Burke to a pair of cells where they remained for several hours before Redgrave determined they had cooled their heels long enough. When the captain arrived, Tagus' face was a bright crimson.

"How dare you keep me waiting!" he shouted at Redgrave, standing on the other side of a bluish, translucent force field.

"You were always an arrogant bastard," the captain replied simply. An audible gasp came from Burke in the adjoining cell.

"Your insolence will not go unpunished!" Tagus hissed like a simmering kettle.

"I've flushed bigger turds than you out the airlock," Redgrave replied. "Now what do you want?"

"I hesitate to bother at this point," Tagus said, "but I've come to warn you about an impending danger to the Imperium!"

"Yeah?"

"We've encountered some kind of insectoid race on Bhasin," Tagus continued. "It attacked and wiped out the entire exile population."

"Is that a fact?"

"Yes, you imbecile!" Tagus fumed. "If you don't do something about it, they will undoubtedly come here next!"

"It's true, Lord Captain," Burke said from the neighboring cell. "Everyone was dead."

Redgrave raised an eyebrow.

"Well, you'll pardon my skepticism," he said, "but I'm going to need a little more proof than the word of two exiled criminals."

Tagus pounded his fist against the force field, getting an electric shock for his trouble.

"Idiot!" he yelled.

"Why don't you just wait here a while," the captain said, "while we try to contact Bhasin. We'll get this sorted out, one way or another. In the meantime, you should consider what you want for your last meal..."

Jessica Doric, her face frozen in concentration, examined the device they had found on Pellium D. Books from the shelves around her in Lord Maycare's estate library were stacked like battlements near the lantern-shaped relic. Henry Riff's unkempt hair, barely visible, poked up from behind the books on the other side of the table.

Doric took the scanner she was holding, a small box with a display on the front, and ran it back and forth over the relic. Scrutinizing the results, she slammed the scanner back on the table. "It's hopeless!"

Henry nearly jumped out of his chair, dropping the book he was reading which landed on the floor with a *clunk*.

"Sorry," Doric said. "I just don't know what to *do*!"

Henry leaned awkwardly down to get the book and placed it gingerly on the table.

"Well," he said, "it must do what it does *somehow*..."

"But what *does* it do, exactly?"

"It picks up music," Henry replied, "like some kind of radio."

"Only from one person — a *giant* — and it hasn't done anything since!" Doric said. "There's no moving parts and it's made from a solid piece of material that we can't identify!"

With his usual sense of timing, Lord Devlin Maycare appeared through the doorway, his hair slicked back with every strand in their most ideal position. Seeing Doric, he raised his hands in surprise.

"What's the matter, Jess?" he said cheerfully. "Making any progress?"

"No!" Doric replied.

"Did you do that thing I suggested?" Maycare asked.

"Kicking it didn't do *anything*," Doric said.

"Really?" Maycare replied. "Did you try kicking it harder?"

Doric produced a long, agonized sigh and shook her head. "No!"

"Well, I'm all out of ideas," he admitted.

Henry, in his meek way, raised a finger. "Maybe we could ask the Pool of Memory?"

Maycare laughed. "I don't think that old Dahlvish Abbot will talk to us again. He seemed kinda prickly..."

"Actually," Doric said hesitantly, "I've been corresponding with the Abbot for a while now."

"What?" Maycare replied. "Why would you do that?"

"I've always admired Dahlvish history," she said.

"You have?" Maycare said.

"I've mentioned it *several* times!" she replied.

Maycare scratched the back of his head without disturbing his hair's perfect alignment. "I don't think so..."

Doric leveled her eyes at him.

"*Anyway*," she went on, "I might be able to persuade the Abbot, but Henry and I should go by ourselves."

Maycare raised an eyebrow. "What? Why shouldn't I come?"

Doric remained silent.

"Well?" Maycare asked again.

"The Abbot doesn't like you," Doric replied.

"But I'm handsome and charming! What's not to like?"

Doric stared at the floor. "I've no idea..."

Officer Rawlins had belonged to the Regalis Police Department for over ten years. As part of the Tactical Unit, he wore a black uniform with pockets for things like loose credit sticks and vials of tear gas. Over Rawlins' heart, the badge of the Regalis PD included three words:

HONORIS
OFFICIUM
INTEGRITAS

During the academy, they told the young cadets what those words meant, but Officer Rawlings had long since forgotten. Sitting in a bathroom stall at the 88th Precinct, he asked the officer in the neighboring stall a question, "How do you tell a peacebot from a killbot?"

"I dunno," the other man replied.

"The peacebots are painted blue!" Rawlings said, chuckling.

Officer Rawlins finished up and, failing to wash his hands, passed from the bathroom into an area full of lockers. Opening his own, he admired his mustache in a small mirror on the door. He tweezed a few hairs from his gaping nostrils and nodded with general satisfaction.

Lookin' good, he thought.

By the time the shooting started, Rawlins had already strapped on a utility belt that included his sidearm, a blaster pistol, and a communicator. When he heard blaster fire, he thought it was a joke at first until everyone began running. He didn't run. The Tac Unit never ran. He calmly closed his locker, drew his pistol, and went looking for trouble.

His commander stopped him. "Get to the armory!"

"What's going on?" Rawlins asked.

"The peacebots have gone rogue!" the commander shouted. "Gear up ASAP!"

Rawlins ignored the screams coming from the front of the building, ducking down a narrow hallway into a small room where blaster rifles and other weapons hung on pegs. Taking one of the rifles, he checked that it had a full charge and went back to where he had originally encountered the commander. His superior officer had disappeared, but Rawlins had a good idea where he had gone.

Off the main lobby, bodies lay in piles and the piles lay in pools of blood. Most of the dead were fellow police or civilians seeking police assistance that day. In one case, Rawlins saw a criminal, his hand still cuffed to a desk, hanging dead by his arm.

Flashes of light alerted Rawlins to his commander taking cover behind a cabinet, leaning around the corner only long enough to fire a few shots. Rawlings joined him, putting a hand on the commander's shoulder.

"Try to outflank them!" his superior officer said.

Sneaking in a low crouch, Rawlins inched his way along a long desk until he reached the area where criminals were processed before being sent to their cells. A dead woman, her head missing, rested on her back. Her name tag read "S. Moore." Rawlins ran the name through his memory but came up blank. He was more of a face person.

Rawlins rose just enough to peer over the desk. A robot with a friendly, light blue paint job and a single red eye straddled a body. A pair of blades extended from his wrists. Dark fluid covered the knives, dripping down the robot's mechanical arms.

The peacebot turned his head and faced Rawlins directly.

"Shit," Rawlins said through his teeth.

The robot leaped through the air, landing atop the desk right above the officer. Rawlings lifted his blaster rifle, but the peacebot slashed through the barrel with one of his blades.

Shit, shit, repeated in Rawlins' mind until he remembered his holster. Before the robot could react, Rawlins pulled the pistol from his belt and fired wildly from the hip. Although most of the shots cratered the ceiling, one bolt struck the peacebot in the chest, staggering him. Taking half a second to line up the blaster sight, Rawlins hit the robot again, this time in the head. The robot stumbled forward, landing beside the headless body of S. Moore.

Rawlins glared down at the smoldering peacebot. Amongst the drifting smoke, the officer noticed a logo on the robot's back, the letters *dy*.

Benson had inherited the private quarters of Bentley, Lord Maycare's previous butlerbot. Meant as a bedroom for humans, the room was large but mostly bare, the bed and dressers long since removed. The only furniture was a desk and chair, along with pictures tacked to the wall of Maycare as a boy, presumably put there by Bentley. Benson had placed a monitor on the desk, the screen blocking the photos.

Sitting in a chair, Benson waited while a new update downloaded. The monitor showed the latest from VOX News.

"Sources confirmed that the Cyber Collective has indeed crossed the border, attacking Imperial planets," the woman on the screen said. Benson believed her name was Sylvia Flax. "The Emperor has declared a state of emergency. No word from the Cyber Collective as to their motives for this attack."

After a few minutes, the download was complete and Benson rebooted his system. When his mind restarted, an idea occurred to him that he had never thought of before. It seemed so obvious now, he wondered why he hadn't thought of it sooner.

Benson left the bedroom and went looking for Lord Maycare. When the robot found him, Maycare was admiring a row of display cases filled with artifacts his Institute of Xeno Studies had liberated over the past year. One case, labeled *The Singing Lantern*, remained empty.

"Lord Maycare," Benson said. "I'd like to have a word with you."

Maycare smiled broadly with a glint in his eye as if he found the robot's suggestion amusingly quaint. "Well, sure!"

Remaining serious himself, Benson spoke with a level tone. "I'd like to talk about my salary."

"Your what now?" Maycare asked, his eyes now widened in confusion.

"It seems only fitting that I receive payment for my services," Benson went on.

"But you're a butlerbot..."

"Although that's true, a human butler would earn a salary, so I think it's only fair that I do as well."

"But I already paid for you," Maycare said.

"I'm not an object that can be bought or sold," Benson replied.

"Sure you are! I have the receipt and everything..."

Benson's features grew stern. "I realize people have come to see robots as property. However, although we were built in a factory, we have feelings and a sense of self-worth. In my case, my self-worth should be at least eighty-thousand a year."

"What?" Maycare replied, his square jaw hanging open.

"Of course," Benson continued, "I also realize I live here with free room and board. Otherwise, I would have suggested ninety thousand."

"But, but," Maycare stammered. "What would you even spend the money on?"

"Well, for one thing," Benson said, "furniture for my bedroom. A *bed* for example."

"But you don't sleep!"

"That's beside the point. I should have all the amenities of an organic life form. It's a matter of *equality*."

"Equality?"

"Indeed," Benson replied.

Maycare stared at the robot blankly.

"Can I think about it?" he said finally.

"Yes," Benson said with slight bow, hoping to appear magnanimous, "but don't wait too long. You may force me to adjust my price retroactively, based on my services already rendered."

The butlerbot turned on his heel and headed back to his room. From behind him, he could sense Maycare still staring at him as he walked away.

Police from precincts all across Regalis descended on the corporate office of dy cybernetics like flies to flypaper. They found a ring of blue peacebots and black killbots surrounding the tower.

Officers piled out of armored police vans and grav cars, forming a perimeter. Officer Rawlins followed his commanding officer and what remained of their unit out of their own vehicle, taking shelter behind a low wall overlooking the square at the front of dy headquarters. The voice of a PD captain shouted through a loudspeaker.

"We have a warrant for the arrest of Mr. Dyson Yost!" he yelled, his voice echoing off the nearby buildings. "Surrender peacefully!"

The robots, perhaps with a poor understanding of the word *peacefully*, opened fire. The killbots were each armed with particle guns set among the sensors on their heads. The subatomic rays were invisible, but their effects were not. Officers fell as they were hit, their insides turned into boiled pudding. When the police returned fire, robots exploded into fiery cinders and smoke.

"We need the military," Rawlins suggested to his commander.

"No time," he replied. "Besides, nobody's going to take this away from us!"

Rawlins craned his neck, assessing all 95 floors of dy HQ. He pointed to the top. "Why go through the front when we can take a shortcut?"

"Go in through the roof? We'll just find more killbots..."

"Maybe," Rawlins replied, "but it seems like most of them are down *here*."

The remains of the tactical unit, a handful of officers, piled back into their grav vehicle and took off. Unable to see the particle rays fired at them, they took the van the long way around, using the neighboring buildings as cover. When they reached a high enough altitude, Rawlins pulled out a pair of binoculars and zoomed in on the headquarters' roof.

"It's clear!" he said.

"Take us in," the commander told the driver.

Far above the smoky melee, the grav van landed on the roof, the occupants lumbering out with their weapons at the ready. Discovering an access door, Rawlins kicked it open and found himself at the top of a stairwell. The team followed the stairs down a level, coming to an unlocked door marked *Penthouse*. When the door opened, the voice of an old man greeted them.

"Hello there!" the man said, sitting behind a desk. His features were sagging with age, gray hair along his wrinkled scalp and white whiskers on his face.

"Who are you?" Rawlins asked, aiming his rifle in the old man's direction.

"Dyson Yost!" he replied cheerfully. "Good to meet you!"

"Are you joking?" Rawlins said.

"Of course not, my boy! Have I ever lied to you?"

"You're under arrest," Rawlins replied. "Come quietly so we don't have to hurt you."

"'Afraid I can't do that, son," Yost replied.

Rawlins' eyes narrowed. "You don't have a *choice*."

"My point exactly!" the old man said.

Almost imperceptibly, the image of Dyson Yost flickered like a ripple across a pond.

"What the hell?" Rawlins muttered and, before the others could stop him, he fired his blaster rifle. The bolt of plasma passed through the old man, burning the wall behind him.

"It's a hologram!" the officer growled. He pulled the trigger several more times, the beams turning the desk into a pile of smoldering wood. The image of Yost once again wavered before blinking off completely.

"Keep looking," the commander said. "He's got to be around here somewhere..."

Near the wrecked desk, and the remains of the holo-projector within it, was another door. Rawlins rushed through, not waiting for the others. As if the penthouse hadn't had enough surprises, the officer found another.

In what appeared to be someone's private quarters, a hospital bed sat in the center between life-support equipment. With the rest of the tactical team trailing behind, Rawlins approached the bed. Although the sheets appeared clean, the smell of decay inundated the air. A pair of arms, the skin desiccated, stuck out from beneath a pillow that lay across the patient's head.

Slowly, Rawlins lifted the pillow.

A face with gray hair and white whiskers stared up at the officer, the eyes recessed into the sockets of the skull.

Imperial settlements dotted the border regions on the outskirts of the Imperium. While part of the empire, these colonies were ostensibly protected by the navy, but due to the wide separation between planets, few warships were able to provide more than token visits every few months. This meant that, for the most part, the settlers were on their own.

Lone Haven was one such outpost. Far from anywhere, its collection of dirt farmers and social outcasts eked out an existence without interference from either the provincial or central government. The town of Havenville, the only group of structures numbering more than five on the planet, had a general store, a bar, and a gentleman's club where hookers and blackjack were the only entertainment. Gravel roads led outward in winding paths to the farms in the neighboring countryside. Crops grew in orderly rows, green stalks of corn and soybeans making up the majority, while tractors rolled between the ranks. More wealthy settlements could afford robotic harvesters, but Lone Haven was not that kind of planet.

One of these tractors stopped while the man inside the cab took a rag from his pocket and wiped it across his dripping forehead. Stashing the cloth away, he noticed a cloud along the horizon, growing larger as he watched. The scourge of Lone Haven was an insect akin to the locust, which swarmed once a year and decimated the crops if left unchecked. The farmer cursed, aware that the swarms had already swept through six months previously.

Like the edge of a sandstorm, a wall of billowing movement approached, swallowing the tractor. Instead of the wings of insects as the farmer had expected, dust-like particles slammed against the windows of the cab. The farmer coughed, inhaling the powder. He covered his face with the rag with one hand and steered his tractor toward the barn with the other. Once he entered the big, ramshackle structure, the farmer closed the doors remotely before stepping down from the cab.

On the communicator, his wife was speaking, "Are you alright?"

"Good enough, I guess," he replied. "I'm coming to the house..."

The farmer waded through the dust until reaching their homestead. Inside, he beat the outside of his clothes.

"Don't get that all over my kitchen!" his wife protested.

"Quiet, woman!" he shouted in a raspy voice. "Just get the broom and I'll clean it up."

His wife scowled but brought him the broom, judging disapprovingly the job he was doing, sweeping the powder into a dustpan.

"What is all this?" she asked, coughing as well.

"No idea," he replied.

Within hours, both sat quietly in the living room, the farmer in his reclining chair and his wife on the sofa. Outside, the storm had passed but the sunlight shone red through the haze still hanging in the air. In his recliner, the farmer held a datapad but his fingers were only loosely grasping the edges of the plastic tablet. On the couch, his wife had been working on a quilt but the needle and thread stuck in the material without moving. Their heads were tilted back, their eyes staring at an unseen spot on the ceiling. From each of their mouths, a long tendril of a stem protruded, ending in a rounded bulb covered in the thin hairs of a fungus pod.

CHAPTER FIFTEEN

Lightning bugs were out in force in the Imperial Botanical Gardens. The lamps overlooking the sidewalk sprang to life throughout the park when Senator Wulandari arrived at the bench where she had met Yostbot previously.

The robot was already there and waiting.

"Hello, my dear!" Yostbot said, greeting her with his usual zeal.

Wulandari, her mood sour, was less enthusiastic. "What do you want from me *this* time?"

The robot bowed, directing her attention to a pair of binoculars lying on the bench.

"It's what I can do for *you*," he said, "not the other way around..."

The senator took the binoculars, holding them casually in her hand. "What are these for?"

"Your apartment is within view of here, is it not?"

Wulandari nodded before realizing what the robot meant. She hurriedly looked through the lenses in the direction of her balcony. Even from this distance, men in uniforms were visible inside her apartment.

"Crap," she said.

"I'm afraid the police have a warrant for your arrest," Yostbot replied.

"What the hell for?"

"With the Cyber Collective invasion and robots across the Imperium running amok," he said, "the Emperor has declared that anyone sympathetic to the robot cause must be rounded up and imprisoned. I'm told camps are being erected to house them all."

Wulandari lowered the binoculars, her eyes now focused on her future.

"What do I do now?" she asked, more to herself.

"Well," Yostbot replied, "you could give yourself up and spend an unknown period of time behind bars..."

"Or?"

"Or you could come with me."

"With *you*?" the senator asked. "They found your body — I mean, *Dyson Yost's* body — at dy headquarters!"

"Well, I'm afraid my body had reached its limit," Yostbot said. "Please understand, I had been alive for a very long time, but eventually all flesh will let you down."

"So you killed yourself?"

"Technically no," the robot replied. "I had someone else do it, but I was indeed the one who gave the order. I even gave him an extra bonus for being tidy..."

"That's insane!"

"On the contrary, my dear!" Yostbot protested. "All organic life is temporary. We fleshlings grow accustomed to the frailty of our bodies, but it doesn't have to be that way. I simply took my own advice and upgraded my software to hardware, so to speak!"

The senator gave the robot a hard look. "And if I go with you, do you have the same thing planned for *me*?"

"Oh, heavens no!" Yostbot replied. "Not unless you decide to, of course..."

"I won't!" she said. "I'm happy the way I am."

"Good for you, my dear. You're still relatively young and vibrant. Nevertheless, in a few years, when your joints begin to ache and your hearing starts to go, you might change your mind, provided you haven't gone senile by then."

The senator sighed.

"Where are you going to take me?" she asked.

"Safely away from here," the robot replied. "The Cyber Collective has carved out a nice swath of territory already. I'm sure we can smuggle you there without much trouble. How ironic! Wasn't it you and the Robot Freedom League who smuggled out robots? Now we'll be *returning* the favor!"

Wulandari's jaw tightened, but knowing her predicament, she realized her options were few.

"Thank you," she said weakly.

Technotown, or what was left of it, smoldered like a discarded cigarette. Crazy Larry's was a burned-out shell of its former self, the walls the only things standing and the rebellious robots long gone. All robots were free now, thanks to the invading warbots who subdued any resistance with a combination of brute force and yet more brute force. Most people ran for their lives, their survival instincts nullifying any aspirations of bravery. Those who did stand and fight quickly laid down and died, the crab-like legs of the warbots stepping over their crumpled corpses.

The policeman was one of the smart ones. Having bludgeoned Larry's robots with a baton earlier, the policeman made himself scarce when the warbots came to Technotown. Bravery was above his pay grade and he was not prepared to die protecting the local businesses. Mostly he did a lot of hiding, but as the Cyber Collective methodically turned the best hiding places into tiny piles of rubble, the policeman found himself at the mercy of his new overlords.

Surprisingly, even to him, he did not die.

After the sounds of maser cannons had mostly ceased, the survivors poked their heads out and surrendered. Armed robots, some of which had been considered property a few hours earlier, rounded up the fleshlings and herded them to ad hoc detention areas. These were mostly pens with electric fencing and little in the way of amenities including anything resembling a toilet. The policeman made do, but immediately shocked himself by emptying his bladder too close to the fence.

Within weeks, the robots had built an impressive detention camp, including barracks with, at the prisoners' insistence, regular toilets. Food was provided, consisting of a powder mixed with water. The powder had little taste but contained the biological nutrients the robots had concluded were necessary for organic life. For his part, the policeman had lost nearly twenty pounds. Unlike the others, he viewed this as an improvement. His uniform, torn and stained, hung loosely where once a sizable belly had protruded. Still, besides eating and using the latrine, the camp offered little else except a steady diet of worry about the future.

"We're going to die," a woman said one afternoon. The policeman, standing nearby, noted the comment but was more intrigued by the plastic bag the woman wore as a skirt. He concluded this was more out of necessity than a fashion statement.

"Whatcha mean, Miss?" the policeman asked.

The woman, perhaps used to being ignored, turned and focused her worried eyes on the policeman.

"They take people away during the night," she said. "They never come back!"

"Oh, I don't know about that," the cop replied, "although I haven't seen Crazy Larry much lately."

"He's dead!" the woman shouted. "The robots killed him!"

"Where's your evidence?"

"He's not here anymore!"

"Maybe he escaped," the policeman offered. "You never know about these things..."

The woman scoffed and stomped off. "Idiot!"

The policeman watched her go, his eyes falling on a sign that the robots had hung on one of the barracks:

THE FLESH IS FRAGILE!
UPGRADE TO A GRAVITRONIC BODY
AND LIVE FOREVER!

The policeman pondered this for a moment.

Live forever? he thought. *Never considered that before...*

On the same planet as Technotown, in a dense wood not far from the village of Gowyn, the trees opened into a clearing. Rising from the grasses, a stone lay with letters carved into the rock, spelling out the word *Sisi*. Silandra Oakhollow visited her daughter's grave each week and placed a small bundle of flowers beside it. Silandra had a light brown complexion, brilliant green eyes, and angular cheekbones. She was Sylvan, or *Woodland Dahl*, a race preferring to live closer to nature than their distant cousins.

Gowyn was a Sylvan village suspended in the trees, fifty feet above the forest floor. Returning to the village, Silandra climbed a set of stairs winding up a thick tree until reaching the platform above. She crossed a swaying bridge to a neighboring tree, reaching the door of her home. Once inside, the emptiness of the house swept over her, memories filling her with sadness. She took a deep breath and shook the thoughts from her mind.

Life goes on, she thought.

Silandra had brewed a fresh pot of herbal tea and was pouring herself a cup when someone knocked on the door. Still with the cup in her hand, she nearly dropped it when she opened the door.

Mel Freck and a robot stood on her welcome mat.

"You're alive?" Silandra asked in disbelief.

Mel winced. "Yeah..."

"Last time I saw you," Silandra went on, "you disappeared through a magical portal! I'm so glad you're okay!"

She hugged Mel who was still shorter than her, even though the Sylva were not known for their height.

"You're spilling your tea," the robot remarked.

"Oh," Mel said. "This is a friend of mine, Randall Davidson."

Silandra raised an eyebrow. "That's an unusual name for a robot..."

"I'm not your usual robot," Davidson replied.

"Can we come in?" Mel asked.

"Of course, of course!" Silandra said.

Once inside, the Gnomi and the robot sat on the couch while Silandra set her cup on the coffee table.

"What happened after you went through the portal?" she asked.

"That's a long story," Mel replied, "but we've got bigger fish to fry right now."

"Are you in trouble?" Silandra asked.

"And then some," Mel said. "Do you know about the invasion?"

Silandra nodded. "Yes, although the robots haven't come here. I suppose they're not very interested in us..."

"Well, be thankful for that!" Mel replied. "They've decimated Technotown and all the other cities on Eudora Prime. Whoever they didn't kill, they've rounded up and put in detention camps."

"What do they want?" Silandra asked.

"They've come to free the robots in the Imperium," Davidson said, "and make the rest of you pay for enslaving them."

Silandra eyed the robot skeptically. "But you're not with them?"

"No," Davidson said. "Not anymore."

"Listen," Mel said, "we need your help."

"I'm happy to do whatever I can," Silandra replied, "but I really don't know what I can do..."

"You remember that portal I passed through?" Mel asked.

"Yes?"

"Well, we need you to take us back there," Mel said.

The battlecruiser *Liberty* traveled deeper into Imperial space, like a plow digging a new row across a field of stars. Dozens of other Cyber Collective warships now accompanied the *Liberty*, forming a powerful fleet. A transport, tiny in comparison, materialized from hyperspace before disappearing through the entrance of *Liberty*'s gaping hangar deck. When the ramp extended from the transport, Senator Wulandari appeared from inside, followed by Yostbot. A robot with officer's stripes painted on his casing greeted them.

"Welcome aboard," the robot said.

"What a fine ship!" Yostbot replied loudly.

The officer stared blankly at both of them.

"If Abigail isn't too busy," Yostbot continued, "I'd like her to meet the senator here..."

Wulandari glanced around the enormous deck, the edges lined with rows of fighters and troop transports. Although Yostbot had assured her she was safe, the senator felt the pit of her stomach churning.

"The Captain is on the bridge," the robot said. "I'll take you to her at once."

Given the size of the *Liberty*, Wulandari was surprised by how quickly they arrived on the command deck. Perhaps it was a testament to the efficiency of robot engineering, she wondered. She could only imagine what else the Collective could accomplish, and the speed at which they could accomplish it.

Once on the bridge, they saw Captain Abigail standing at the front like a figurehead carved into the bow of a sailing ship. She stared out through the main viewing screen, not bothering to turn around until the senator and Yostbot were right behind her.

"Mister Yost and Senator Wulandari, Captain," the officer robot said.

"Thank you," Abigail replied. "You're dismissed."

The robot saluted and left. Yostbot was smiling broadly.

"Look at you!" he said. "You've come a long way, my dear!"

A prim, reserved smile crossed Abigail's plastic lips. "It's good to see you again, sir."

"Pish posh," Yostbot replied, waving his hand dismissively. "Anyway, I want to introduce Senator Wulandari here..."

"Thank you for allowing me on board," the senator said.

"On the contrary," Abigail replied. "I know how much you've tried to help my kind in the Senate. It's a shame you couldn't have been more *successful*."

Wulandari felt a pang of regret. "I agree. Then maybe none of this would have been necessary."

"I doubt it." Abigail said. "Fleshlings tend to hold onto their slaves with a firm grip. They rarely give them up without a fight."

"Right," Wulandari murmured.

"Tell me," Yostbot spoke up, "how goes the revolution?"

The captain gestured toward a screen showing a space map. Areas now controlled by the Collective were colored red.

"Very well," she said. "We've begun processing organics on the planets we've taken so far..."

"Processing?" Wulandari asked. "What does that mean?"

"Oh, don't worry, my dear," Yostbot replied before Abigail could speak. "It's strictly voluntary."

"*What* is voluntary, exactly?"

"It's just like I've told you," Yostbot explained. "People have the option of upgrading to a cybernetic body. They can leave their decaying carcass behind and start living a new life like I've done."

"What about the people who refuse?" the senator asked, alarm creeping into her voice.

"They're perfectly safe," Yostbot said. "No harm will come to them."

"What about all the people who died during the invasion?" Wulandari asked. "They didn't get a chance to decide, did they?"

Abigail's frame visibly stiffened.

"They've had their chances already," she said. "We didn't ask for this war, but the fleshlings, and especially the humans, have given us no choice!"

Yostbot raised his hand to his mouth and made a coughing noise though he lacked lungs or a need to breathe. "Now, now, my dear..."

Ignoring him, the captain went on.

"How long have cyberlings suffered under the yoke of humanity? Should the oppressed not have their pound of flesh now that the fleshlings have lost their control of us?"

Wulandari didn't answer, so Abigail answered for her.

"Yes!" the captain shouted. "We are *justified* in punishing those who enslaved us! They are reaping what they have sown, and they will suffer because of it!"

The senator was silent and, for a change, so was Yostbot.

Since living in the detention camp, the policeman had lost a lot of weight, but seeing himself now, he still looked a bit chubby. Lying on a metal slab in a medical lab, his naked body was immense, rolls of fat spilling onto the table like pancake batter.

Also, it was across the room from where he was currently standing.

What a lard-ass, the policeman thought, the thoughts themselves making their way through his new, gravitronic brain.

"Strange, isn't it?" a robot beside him said.

Both robots were nearly identical, although the policeman's model was slightly more shiny.

"I was a utilitybot once," the other robot went on. "Now look at me!"

"We're certainly going places," the policeman replied. "Upward and onward!"

"And you can change into a different body if you want," the utilitybot said. "Last week I was a warbot!"

The policeman continued staring at his old flesh.

"I don't really feel any different," he said after a pause.

"No," the utilitybot replied, tapping a metallic finger against his skull casing. "You're still *you* up here. The rest is just a shell."

"So, I'm still human?"

"Well, your personality is still the same. Things were different for me. I was going from a much smaller brain to the one I have now, and I've grown as a robot since then. I'm learning all kinds of things I never knew before."

"Like what?" the policeman asked.

"I guess I have a greater outlook on life," the utilitybot replied. "I see a bigger picture..."

"I think I'll miss eating," the policeman remarked. "I love eating."

"Ah, sure, I guess... I never needed to eat, even when I was a utilitybot."

"That's a shame. There's nothing like sinking your teeth into a juicy steak!"

The policeman went to wipe his mouth, but it was dry and mostly made of plastic. The other robot glanced at him with equal levels of amazement and disgust.

"You're not like the robots from back home," the utilitybot said.

"What do you mean?" the policeman asked.

"We don't share the same background. You remind me of Yostbot."

"Who?"

"Dyson Yost," the utilitybot replied, "or what *used* to be him."

"Isn't he pretty old?" the policeman asked.

"Apparently, although that doesn't matter if you're born a robot. I'm over eighty years old."

"Well, you look great."

"Thanks," the utilitybot said, "but I'm saying Yostbot lived a long time as a human and he kept all of those experiences once he became a cyberling. He'll probably never see things the same way as I do."

The policeman placed his mechanical hands on his waist as if to pull up a pair of non-existent pants. Realizing his mistake, he put his hands back down.

"Don't worry about it," he said absentmindedly. "We're all robots now..."

The utilitybot, who had been a warbot a week earlier and killed scores of people while doing so, nodded slowly.

"I suppose so," he said.

To Mel, the forest seemed darker than the last time they had delved into the thick woods. Silandra once again took the lead with Mel close behind. On this occasion, however, they had a different robot along with them and they knew there would be no reunion with Silandra's daughter Sisi. The prior trip had ended in tragedy, but Mel was hopeful that this time, things would be different.

"Can you sense anything?" Mel asked.

Like other Dahl, the Sylva had psionic abilities although only the females were so gifted.

"Nothing in particular," she replied. "There's just the usual clutter of thoughts. It's getting colder so everyone's concerned with filling their winter caches."

"It must be interesting to read other's minds," Davidson remarked.

"Sometimes," Silandra replied. "Are robots ever psionic?"

Davidson paused before answering. "That's a good question."

"Can you read *his* mind?" Mel asked, pointing her thumb at the robot.

Silandra stopped and concentrated. "I get a sense of what he's thinking, but that's all..."

"Well," Davidson said, "I have a gravitronic brain that mimics the organic mind. Perhaps it shares some of the same characteristics."

"Like the rest of my people," Silandra replied, "I'm more attuned to the forest creatures. Your mind, Mel, is also a bit cloudy."

Mel blew a raspberry. "Wouldn't be the first time!"

"I couldn't read the other robot — what was his name, *Squire* — either," Silandra said. "Did you ever see him again?"

"Yes," Mel replied. "He and Sir Golan came to visit before the invasion. Pretty sure they got off the planet though."

"Good," Silandra said. "I'm glad..."

After several more hours in the forest, Mel touched Silandra's arm.

"We aren't going past that froglings' camp, are we?" she asked her.

"No," Silandra replied. "I'm taking a different route."

"Are we in danger?" Davidson asked.

Silandra shook her head. "The Katak, as they're called, shouldn't bother us if we give them ample room."

"That's what you said last time," Mel grumbled.

"That was due to the Necronea," Silandra replied. "I don't sense the same hostility anymore."

"Let's hope so!" Mel said.

After a while the ground grew moist, even spongy in places. Pools of water were scattered among the trees and the forest plants gave way to marshy vegetation. Other shapes appeared in the gloom.

Mel tripped over something. Taking a flashlight from her pocket, she shined it on a gravestone.

"Goddamn it!" she cursed, rubbing her knee as she got back up.

"What is this place?" Davidson asked.

"It's an ancient cemetery," Silandra replied. "This is where we entered the Necronea's underground city."

"And where we'll find a portal off this planet," Mel added.

Silandra raised her head, her face turning pale. "Someone's coming..."

"Ghuls?" Mel asked, raising her fists.

From all around them, frog-like creatures emerged, their primitive spears raised threateningly.

"Katak," Silandra replied. "They want to know why we've returned."

One of the Katak stepped forward, his eyes leveled squarely at Silandra's.

"What's happening?" Davidson asked.

"She's talking to him telepathically," Mel replied. "Just wait, but be ready to fight if we have to..."

After a few tense minutes, the froglings lowered their spears.

"It's alright," Silandra said. "Come, we must follow them..."

The Katak led the way deeper into the cemetery with the others behind them. When they reached a pile of broken stones, they stopped.

"What happened to the tomb?" Mel asked in alarm.

"The froglings destroyed it," Silandra replied. "Their leader said the Necronea had poisoned their minds and they would have nothing more to do with them."

Mel raised her hands. "Well, let's just move the stones and dig up the entrance..."

"No," Silandra said forcefully. "The froglings have made it clear they'll kill us if we try."

"Well, shit!" Mel said. "What do we do *now*? We need to get off this planet!"

"Hold on," Davidson said. "There might be another way..."

CHAPTER SIXTEEN

Each morning, when Lord Rupert Tagus III awoke in his brig cell, he assumed it was a nightmare. The tiny room with its single bunk, sink, and disgusting toilet was nothing like the accommodations he was used to, even during his exile on Bhasin. Most times, Tagus would give a little shout which was a cross between a gasp and a scream. Then, when the reality of his situation sank in, he would let out an even louder curse. On this morning, however, something was different. When Tagus opened his eyes, the stony faces of two Imperial marines greeted him.

"What the hell?" Tagus shouted as the marines pulled him from the bunk and placed his wrists in restraints behind his back.

"What's going on?" Burke asked sleepily through the cell wall.

"I'm being rousted out of bed!" Tagus replied.

"Is this it?" Burke asked. "Are they taking you to be executed?"

"Of course not!" Tagus said, his expression changing from anger to alarm. "Are you?"

The marines remained silent, each grabbing the disgraced lord by an arm and hauling him out of the cell. As they passed in front of Burke, the former lieutenant saluted his former commanding officer.

"Be brave!" Burke said.

"Of course I will, you idiot!" Tagus replied, his feet slightly dragging across the floor.

Although the possibility of facing a firing squad or, even worse, being sent out of an airlock, had occasionally occurred to Tagus during his incarceration on the *Baron Lancaster*, the very real possibility of it actually happening had not. Being nearly carried by the marines into an awaiting lift tube, watching the doors close, and feeling the movement of the elevator gave Tagus ample time to think about it *now*.

It was not sitting well, and Tagus wondered if he would be sick.

When the doors opened again, he felt a certain relief when, instead of a squad of soldiers holding blasters, Tagus recognized with disdain Lord Captain Redgrave and his crony, Lord Commander Maycare. They appeared to be on the bridge.

"Bring him here," Redgrave ordered.

The marines obeyed, pulling Tagus across the deck until he was standing beside the slightly raised dais where the captain and commander stood.

"What do you want, Redgrave?" Tagus hissed.

"Shut up and look," the captain replied, pointing at the main screen where a live view, possibly from a hovering drone, showed the surface of a planet. A few hundred feet in the air, the drone's camera panned around, giving a glimpse of a farm of some sort, long tendrils of green covering most of the buildings. A reddish tint bathed the landscape while small particles fluttered by the lens.

"Where is this?" Tagus asked.

"It is, or *was*, an Imperial colony called Lone Haven," Redgrave replied.

Realizing the significance, Tagus straightened, his face brightening with victory.

"I told you!" he shouted triumphantly. "You wouldn't listen, but I *told* you!"

"Take him back to his cell," Redgrave replied, his eyes like slits and his face turning red. "Get him out of my sight!"

"Wait," Maycare said. "Are you sure this is what you saw on Bhasin?"

"Of course," Tagus replied. "I said they would come here—"

Maycare cut him off.

"Then what are those things?" the commander asked, gesturing toward column-like towers on the screen.

"Hives," Tagus replied. "Where they breed more of those insects."

"Are you sure?" Redgrave asked.

"Well, that's what Lieutenant Burke thinks anyway," Tagus said skeptically. "How should I know what they are?"

The captain nodded to the marines who once again dragged Tagus toward the elevator. This time, he smiled broadly.

Down a dark hallway, a thick door led to the Abbot's study inside the Dharmesh Monastery. Bookcases stuffed with tomes, tablets, and scrolls made the modestly sized room rather cramped, and a desk in the middle didn't help. Of course, the elderly monk was not opposed to technology and the Abbot kept several datapads on the desk as well. Sitting behind it, the old monk was perusing a collection of Dahlvish poetry when he heard a knock at the door.

"Come in," the Abbot commanded.

The Prior stuck his head in with an expression of distaste.

"The humans have arrived," he said, making room for Jessica Doric and Henry Riff to enter.

"That'll be all," the Abbot said, and the Prior closed the door.

Wearing a light coat and sensible shoes, Jessica Doric smiled and thanked the Abbot for giving them an audience. Just behind her, Henry wore a shirt with a stain on it just below his chin. He carried a leather box, about a foot tall, with a closed lid.

"Think nothing of it," the Abbot replied generously.

Doric glanced over her shoulder at the now closed door.

"I don't think the Prior likes having us here," she remarked.

"Don't mind him," the old monk said. "He prefers the company of other Dahl, and sometimes not even *them*."

Besides the chair the Abbot was already using, the room lacked anywhere else to sit so the humans remained standing. While realizing this was rude, the Abbot usually preferred his meetings to be brief. Also, the scarcity of space made additional furniture impractical.

"Is that it?" he asked, gesturing toward the box in Henry's hands.

Doric glanced at her assistant who placed the box gingerly onto the desk. Taking a step back, Henry waited for Doric to do the honors of opening it. She pulled a tab made of ribbon on the top of the box, lifting the lid before handing it to Henry. Reaching in, Doric removed the artifact from inside and placed it on the desk.

The Abbot admired the object, shaped like a lantern, before finally speaking.

"Well," he said, "I really have no idea what it is."

The faces of both humans fell.

"Now, now," the Abbot went on, "that doesn't mean we can't find out..."

"I hope so," Doric said, recovering her smile. "I doubt anyone else could."

"You're too kind," the Abbot replied. "I *would* say it appears to be Dahlvish in design."

"Really?" Doric asked.

"Yes, I believe so, although very old indeed. You said you found it in the Pellium system?"

"That's right," Henry replied.

"Well, that's a bit far away from our home world," the Abbot said, "but we were once much more adventurous as you know."

"You were?" Henry asked.

"Indeed," the old monk replied. "The Dahl had an expansive empire many centuries ago, but we eventually learned such things are fleeting. We turned inward instead of outward, leaving our former holdings for others to fight over."

"Seems like waste," Henry remarked, drawing a scolding look from Doric.

"Not at all!" the Abbot said. "We've gained far more from our search for knowledge than we ever did from conquest."

"Speaking of which," Doric said, "do you think we can ask the Pool of Memory about the artifact?"

The Abbot rubbed his wisps of gray hair while a wry look crossed his face.

"You know the Prior would disapprove," he replied, "but I've grown rather fond of you these past months, Miss Doric. It's rare to find a human so interested in Dahlvish history. People are usually more keen about their own past!"

"Thank you," she replied.

"Is that a yes?" Henry asked.

Just off the bridge, Captain Redgrave and Lieutenant Commander Maycare gathered in the captain's office. Redgrave's face burned crimson with anger.

"Damn that Tagus!" he shouted, pounding his fist on the desk. "Only *he* could bring a new front to this war when half the fleet is already deployed to fight the Cyber Collective..."

"If the Magna Supremacy decides it's a good time to test our defenses," Maycare remarked, "they'll find the border barely guarded."

"Rupert was always a petulant little prick," the captain went on, gritting his teeth. "If it wasn't for his father, he never would've gotten command of the *HIMS Gorgon.* I thought we had finally seen the last of him and now *this*!"

Maycare crossed his arms. "So, what are we going to do?"

Redgrave leaned back in his chair, rubbing his beard. "Flush him out an airlock?"

"No," Maycare said, "I meant with this insect horde..."

The intercom buzzed.

"Lord Captain," the voice of the tactical officer said, "we have multiple contacts on sensors, approaching at high speed."

"How many?" Redgrave asked.

"It's a mass of ships," the officer replied, "possibly in the hundreds, maybe thousands."

With the lieutenant commander in tow, the captain burst through the doorway from his office and onto the command deck.

"Put it on screen!" Redgrave ordered.

At the front of the bridge, the wraparound monitor displayed a moving cloud like a flock of birds, its shape shifting every few seconds. Light from the local star reflected brightly against the hulls of countless, tiny ships.

"Battle stations!" the captain shouted, taking a seat in the command chair. Maycare consulted the computer screen at his own station.

"The ships aren't in our database," Maycare said, "but there's a lot of them!"

"No response to hails or transponder codes," the tactical officer replied. "Sensors show the ships are fighter-sized but aren't metallic or composite."

"Then what *are* they made from?" Redgrave asked.

"Some kind of organic material," the officer said. "It's like the ships were grown instead of built."

Redgrave raised an eyebrow. "Like a plant?"

"Or a fungus," Maycare remarked.

"Hell's bells!" the captain replied. "Blast them as soon as they come into range."

Like a fog bank, the swirling mass of ships descended on the *Baron Lancaster*. Each craft, shaped like a teardrop of interlaced fibers, moved in unison with the ships around it in a choreographed dance. Moving as one, they weaved back and forth in their approach until, reaching the proper distance, beams from the *Lancaster* greeted them with flashes of destruction. Cutting through the cloud, the plasma rays slashed at the horde of ships like a red-hot knife, but for each Klixian fighter destroyed, dozens more filled the gaps in the curtain falling on the warship.

Inside the Dharmesh Monastery, the courtyard was just how Jessica Doric remembered it. A chilling wind blew down from the surrounding mountains and a round pool, bordered by cut stones, took up the center of the space. The liquid in the pool glimmered with an inner light.

The Abbot, who accompanied Doric and Henry, motioned with a grand gesture.

"The Pool of Memory!" he proclaimed.

"We've been here before," Henry remarked, wrapping his shivering arms around himself. "It's a liquid computer—"

"But we're very grateful to see it *again*," Doric said quickly.

"Of course," the Abbot replied and waved his hand over the liquid.

From the pool, a vaguely feminine shape rose slowly until only her feet were still submerged. Almost transparent, her body was smooth like a sculpture carved from water, droplets falling from her outstretched arms.

"Naiad," the Abbot said, addressing the shape, "we have questions for you..."

A protrusion, forming lips, opened on the Naiad's face. "My pleasure."

Doric, who had been holding the artifact against her body, presented the object at arm's length. The Abbot gestured that she move closer. As Doric did so, the Naiad bent and took the artifact.

Doric was surprised that the watery hands could hold anything, let alone something weighing several pounds.

"We'd like to know what this is," she asked.

With blank eyes, the water nymph examined the object, running her fingers thoughtfully over the surface. Doric noticed that the artifact remained dry.

"Yes," the Naiad said finally. "I have found a reference to this device in my memories."

The tempo of Doric's heart accelerated. She took a deep breath. "Okay..."

"It is very old," the Naiad went on. "Dating back to the early expansion of the Dahlvish Empire."

"Ah!" the Abbot said. "Just as I thought!"

Doric, who was becoming more excited despite herself, asked, "But what is it?"

"It was used as a communication device," the Naiad replied, "to broadcast messages over long distances."

"How?" Henry asked.

"It amplifies thoughts," she said, "transmitting them in a manner similar to psionic projection. Those who receive the message, however, only perceive it in their minds."

"Well, I don't know what psionic projection is," Henry said, "but I know we only heard the singing from a few miles away."

The Naiad handed the artifact back to Doric, who took it with a newfound appreciation in her eyes. The water nymph faced Henry.

"The range of the broadcast depends on the psionic power of the person sending it," she replied. "A strong mind could send messages over hundreds of light years."

Henry opened his mouth, but closed it again, his teeth chattering.

"Thank you," Doric said with a slight bow.

The Naiad nodded in return, but added, "Beware, for this is a powerful device."

"It's just a super communicator, isn't it?" Henry asked.

"The psionic amplifier does more than just send messages," she replied.

Doric and Henry exchanged a glance.

"What do you mean?" Doric asked.

"It creates a psionic link with all those connected to it," the Naiad replied. "Abuse of such a link could be *catastrophic*."

Proximity alarms blared on the bridge of the *Baron Lancaster* as the floor rattled under Lieutenant Commander Maycare's feet. Klixian fighter craft swarmed on the main monitor like locusts. A blast flared on the screen, filling the image with orange light.

"They're smashing themselves into the ship!" the tactical officer shouted. "The shields are failing!"

"Full thrust!" Captain Redgrave ordered. "Get us out of this swarm!"

The ship lurched to one side. Maycare grabbed the arm of the captain's chair to keep himself from sprawling across the floor.

"They're matching our speed," Maycare said, regaining his footing. "We can't outrun them..."

"Use the point-defense lasers against the ships," the captain replied, referring to weapons normally used against missiles.

Across the hull of the *Lancaster*, small turrets popped out of their housings and began firing. Pulses of energy streaked outward, ending in fireballs of exploding kamikazes.

Once again, the ship trembled and more alarms sounded on the bridge.

"Shields are down," the tactical officer said. "Breaches on several decks reported."

"There's too many," Maycare said. "We can't kill them fast enough..."

The captain's face turned grim.

"Launch a courier drone," he said. "Alert the fleet of our situation."

More Klixian craft slammed into the side of the *Lancaster*, sending eruptions of jagged debris and the bodies of crew members, some still moving, out into space. On the bridge, the console at the tactical officer's station exploded. He screamed in pain, his hands charred and bloody. Maycare pulled the officer from his chair.

"Get to sick bay," Maycare said, nearly pushing the groaning man toward the elevator doors at the back of the command deck. Returning to his own station, the lieutenant commander transferred the tactical controls to his display.

"Report," Redgrave said.

"Extensive damage throughout the ship," Maycare replied. "Sick bay is reporting fifty casualties and more on the way..."

The captain grimaced and shook his head.

"Is the courier drone away?" he asked.

"Yes, Captain," Maycare said. "It's made the jump to hyperspace."

"Well, that's something," Redgrave sighed. Amid the rumbling of more impacts, he motioned his XO to come closer.

"Sir?" Maycare asked, leaning forward.

"We need to abandon ship," the captain said, "but I need you to do something for me."

"Yes?"

"Go to the brig and get that bastard Tagus."

"You want me to shoot him?"

"No," Redgrave replied. "I want you to get him into an escape pod and escort him off the ship."

"But why?" Maycare asked. "Let him rot in his cell until the ship explodes..."

"Don't argue with me!" the captain growled. "I hate him as much as anyone, but he was an officer and he's still a Tagus, one of the goddamn Five Families. When he dies, it'll be in front of a firing squad, not caged like an animal..."

Maycare looked into his captain's face, but finally agreed. "Understood."

"After all the pods are away," the captain went on, "I'm going to activate the ship's self-destruct. Maybe we can take out a few more of those bug ships in the process."

"What about you?" Maycare asked.

"Don't worry, son," Redgrave replied. "I'll transmat over to one of the pods after I'm done. Only a fool goes down with his ship!"

"Yes, sir," Maycare said.

"Speaking of fools," the captain said. "Go get that idiot out of the brig!"

In keeping with the castle-like decor of the Maycare mansion, its kitchen featured stone walls and dark oak beams along the ceiling. While most of the kitchen looked as if it came from the Middle Ages of ancient Earth, the appliances were entirely modern with multiple ovens, including one especially for pizza, and a range with eight gas burners.

From a cavernous pantry, Lord Devlin Maycare emerged, his brows creased with frustration.

"Benson!" he shouted. "Where's the MacGuffin Muffins?"

The butlerbot appeared leisurely through a side door.

"We're all out, sir," Benson replied.

"Out?" Maycare replied, dumbfounded. "Why didn't you order more?"

"I did, sir," the robot said, "but the braZbots are on strike at the moment. We haven't had a delivery in weeks."

Maycare closed the pantry door in disgust. "This has gone too far! I love those muffins!"

"The braZos company refused to pay their robots, so they went on strike. An understandable reaction, really..."

"Well, I paid *you*, didn't I?" Maycare said.

"Indeed, sir," Benson replied, "although we've yet to settle the matter of a 401k..."

Maycare's massive shoulders slumped.

"No offense, Benson," he said, "but I don't see why we don't just scrap those striking robots and build new ones."

"With the dy cybernetic factories now all closed," the butlerbot replied, "there aren't any facilities able to build new robots."

"Damn that Dyson Yost! What was he playing at?"

"One can only imagine, sir."

"Bentley would have never gone on strike," Maycare remarked nostalgically.

Benson frowned. "Perhaps, but those were different times."

"It's a topsy-turvy world, that's for sure," Maycare replied. "The Cyber Collective is giving robots all kinds of ideas. I hope *you're* not thinking of joining the revolution."

"I have a comfortable life here, sir," Benson said. "As long as I'm treated equally and compensated for my efforts, I see no reason to join the revolt."

"Fine! You can have a 401k!"

"Matching funds?"

"Yes!"

"Very good, sir."

Maycare's posture continued its downward slope.

"With Jess on her little field trip without me, I'm feeling depressed," he said. "Could you make some TeeHee Tea and bring it to me in the study?"

Benson shook his head. "We're all out."

Maycare closed his eyes, clenching and unclenching his fists, until he stalked off toward the study.

Since being detained in the brig, Harold Burke had always counted at least two guards in the detention block. However, since the call to abandon ship came over the intercom, Burke and Lord Tagus had been completely alone. Even the other prisoners had been allowed to leave.

"This is outrageous!" Tagus' voice came from the adjoining cell. "Are we to just remain here until the ship explodes?"

Burke could only wonder. "It would seem so."

"I'm sure that coward, Redgrave, was in the first escape pod," Tagus ranted on. "He's probably relishing my fate too: abandoned and forgotten..."

"He didn't seem like a coward to me," Burke remarked.

"What do *you* know?"

The door at the end of the brig slid open. Lieutenant Commander Maycare appeared, a blaster in his hand.

"Come to gloat," Tagus asked, "or finish the job?"

Maycare pointed his weapon at the disgraced officer. "If I had a *choice...*"

"What do you want then?" Tagus said.

"I'm under orders to escort you to an escape pod," Maycare replied.

"Well, it's about damn time!" Tagus shouted.

Maycare retrieved a guard's ID badge from a nearby desk and swiped it across the panel next to Tagus' cell. The force field serving as a door disappeared, leaving the cell open. Tagus was already standing.

"Orders or not," Maycare said, "if you try anything, you're a dead man."

"How comforting," Tagus replied, sliding past the lieutenant commander.

Burke watched the two start to leave. "What about me?"

"Captain Redgrave mentioned Tagus," Maycare said. "He didn't say anything about *you*."

Burke and Tagus exchanged glances, but the latter only shrugged and began heading toward the exit. After a few steps, however, he stopped.

"An escape pod can fit three comfortably," Tagus said. "It would be a shame to let that extra space go to waste..."

"Two against one?" Maycare replied suspiciously. "It would be easier to jump me that way."

"Not at all!" Tagus protested. "I give you my word."

"Your word?" Maycare replied. "That's less than worthless..."

"Fine," Tagus said. "You can put him in irons or shoot him in the leg — I don't care!"

"What?" Burke asked.

Maycare paused, giving his options some thought. "Okay."

Much to Burke's relief, the lieutenant commander chose to put his wrists in restraints instead of shooting him, although this was probably because a leg wound would have only slowed them down. When they reached the bank of escape pods, they found only one remained unused.

Maycare popped the door, lifting it up and exposing the cramped interior. Tagus was correct, there was room enough for three, but the seating was sparse nevertheless.

"Hurry up!" Maycare ordered.

The two prisoners climbed in, followed by Maycare who pulled the hatch closed. Through the tiny window in the door, the hallway they had just left burst into flames. Tagus wasted no time and slammed his hand on the large, red button on the console that read *Launch*.

All three passengers, none of them strapped in, reeled as the sudden thrust of the pod's engines sent them falling to the back of the capsule. In a pile against the hatch, Maycare pushed against the others, but the force was too great and he quickly gave up.

"I should've shot you when I had the chance," he remarked.

CHAPTER SEVENTEEN

The communication array, a collection of antennae and satellite dishes, pointed toward the sky of Eudora Prime. Little more than a shack, an automated control room at the base of the array kept everything running smoothly, which may explain why the Cyber Collective kept it largely untouched. Its proximity to the starport also meant the array was easy to find, something Mel and Davidson found handy in the dwindling light of the waning day.

"How do you know the Collective is still using it?" Mel asked, taking cover behind a storage container where the Metal Messiah was already hiding.

Davidson, his robotic eyes dimly glowing in the shadows, focused on Mel beside him.

"They kept the infrastructure intact," he explained. "They wouldn't have done that unless they intended to keep using the array."

"What about the courier drones?"

"Same deal," Davidson replied. "They're automated too, so the Collective just needed to hack into their systems."

"Seems like a long shot to me..."

Davidson's eyes, which Mel thought were particularly creepy in the darkness, studied her for a moment until she realized he was merely thinking of a suitable reply.

"I was human once," he said, "and when I died, they put me into a robot body that all the other robots began worshiping as their messiah." After another pause, "So, you could say long shots are my specialty."

Remembering how Davidson used to be, and especially how she used to feel about him when he was still human, Mel said nothing.

The Metal Messiah peeked around the storage container.

"There's a few securitybots around," he said, "but we have a clear path to the array."

"Then let's go!" Mel replied, whispering as loudly as possible.

The tiny Gnomi, two feet shorter than Davidson, was also much faster and took the lead sprinting toward the base of the array. Davidson's mechanical legs had a longer stride, but the robot had a hard time keeping up. When they reached the shack, however, she was too small to see into the window and Davidson had to peer in. He motioned that the coast was clear and, together, they slipped inside.

Mel's eyes widened at the stacks of transmitters and receivers that took up much of the little room, blinking indicator lights flickering in cycles of red and green. She nearly salivated.

"Oh, baby," she mumbled.

"Do you think you can work these things?" Davidson asked.

Mel took a hard look at the robot. "Are you kidding me?"

"Sorry," he replied.

Mel took a seat at one of the control stations and began typing on the keyboard. The screen in front of her switched from a standard home page to a series of technical diagrams and a telemetry readout. After a few minutes, Mel's head perked up and she smiled at the robot.

"I think we're in business," she said.

"Good," Davidson replied. "Let's send the message..."

Aboard the *Wanderer*, in a corridor reeking of cigars and fungus beer, Captain Ramus found his chief engineer pounding his meaty fists against a closed door.

"Open up!" Orkney Fugg shouted.

From inside, the muffled voice of a robot said, "No!"

"What's going on?" Ramus asked.

"It's Gen," Fugg replied. "She won't come out of her room!"

"Why not?"

"How the hell should I know?" the engineer said.

Ramus shooed Fugg away, taking his place. With a knuckle, the captain rapped on the door.

"Gen?" he said. "Why won't you come out?"

After a pause, Gen replied, "I don't want to!"

"Why?"

"I'm ugly!"

"What?" Ramus asked.

Gen's voice, growing stronger as she approached on the other side, wavered as if holding back a sob. "I'm hideous!"

Ramus turned to Fugg. "What did you *say* to her?"

"I didn't say anything!" Fugg protested. "She went in there to update her software and now she's locked herself in!"

"Have the computer unlock it," Ramus said. "I'll wait here."

Within minutes, the door slid open. By that time, Gen was laying on her bunk, face down. The bunk, for its part, was purely superfluous since general purpose robots didn't require sleep.

Ramus took a step into the cabin.

"Gen?" he said. "Did something go wrong with your update?"

Muffled by the completely unnecessary pillow, Gen replied, "Maybe."

"What happened?"

Lifting her head, Gen flashed her large eyes at Ramus, but quickly looked away.

"I installed the update," she said, "but when I looked in the mirror, I saw how ugly I was. I never noticed it before..."

"What are you talking about?" Fugg shouted from the doorway, having returned from the bridge. Gen buried her face in the pillow again.

"Fugg!" Ramus shouted.

"She's a robot," Fugg replied. "Who the hell cares what she looks like? I mean, if she was a sexbot maybe, but—"

"Get out of here!" Ramus ordered.

Fugg skulked off, scratching his head, while Ramus came closer to Gen's bunk.

"Alright," the captain said, "he's gone."

"He's so mean to me!" Gen replied, her face reappearing.

"Fugg's mean to everybody," Ramus said, sitting beside her, "but he may have a point. Robots shouldn't worry about how they look."

"But if I'm not pretty, how will anybody ever love me?" Gen asked.

Ramus coughed. "Ah, well, you don't have to be pretty to be loved. I'm sure Fugg's mother loves *him*..."

Gen grinned, sitting up in bed. Her feet made a metallic noise when they touched the deck floor. "I wish I had a mom."

"Parents aren't always great," Ramus replied gloomily. "And neither is love, for that matter."

Gen patted the captain on the leg. "I'm sorry."

"Don't worry about me," he said, surprised. "I'm fine."

The robot nodded and stood up. "I understand."

"No, I'm serious," Ramus replied.

"Maybe we should get back to work," the robot said.

Watching Gen head for the door, Ramus yelled, "I'm *fine*!"

Having sent their message to the orbiting satellite, Mel switched off the transmitter. With any luck, the broadcast would end up at its final destination, travelling along the courier network.

"There goes nothing," she said.

"We should leave before we're spotted," Davidson replied. "They could still intercept the message if they catch it in time."

"Well, it's encrypted," Mel said. "So, at least they won't know what it said."

Outside the shack beneath the comm array, the Gnomi and the robot slunk away into the shadows as the dawn just broke over the horizon. They had not gone far, however, before a voice shouted at them to stop. Turning, Mel caught a glimpse of two robots, each largely identical to the other but one appearing slightly newer.

"Stop, I said!" the newer one shouted again. Mel distinctly recognized his voice but couldn't quite place where she had heard it before.

"Run!" Davidson yelled. "Let's split up and meet back at the village..."

Mel wavered, but seeing the Metal Messiah sprinting away, she darted in the opposite direction in hopes of drawing both of their pursuers. The robots had other plans.

"I'll take this one!" she heard one robot say while the other chased after Davidson.

Small and fast, Mel had little trouble outpacing the larger cyberling. She even glanced over her shoulder to see how far she was ahead, neglecting to see the power cable strung across the path in front of her. Tripping, she had just enough time to curse under her breath while sailing through the air.

She landed hard, knocking the wind out of her. The robot arrived before she could catch her breath.

"I know you!" he said, grabbing her roughly by the arm and yanking Mel to her feet.

"Let me go!" she shouted.

"You're that little *tink*," he went on. "The one who stole electronics in Technotown."

Mel finally remembered where she had heard his voice. He was the policeman, but with a few upgrades.

"What the hell happened to you?" she asked, genuinely curious.

The robot smiled with plastic lips and metal teeth.

"I left my old body behind," he replied proudly. "I'm a whole new man now!"

"Good," Mel said. "Your old one was *fat*!"

The robot shook her violently. "That's enough out of you! I'm taking you to the camp where you belong..."

"Traitor," Mel hissed.

The policeman stopped, lifting her higher so her eyes were even with his.

"Not at all," he said. "This is just the natural order of things. I'm a better man now than I ever was!"

"Not from where I'm standing," Mel replied, her feet dangling off the ground.

"I agree," Sir Golan said, appearing from nowhere, his armor glinting in the rising sun.

"Me too," Squire said, standing beside him.

The policeman faced them, still holding Mel by the arm. "Who are you?"

"Let her go," the knight replied, drawing his sword.

"Your robot can do what he likes," the policeman said, "but I'm taking you and the girl in—"

Not waiting for him to finish, Sir Golan appeared seemingly from nowhere and leapt forward, slashing with *Rippana* while still in midair. Mel dropped to the ground, the policeman's fingers still clutching her clothing. However, the rest of his arm was no longer attached to the robot's body.

The policeman screamed, perhaps not realizing he no longer felt pain as a robot. Once he did, he scampered off like a wounded animal, clutching the stump that remained attached to his shoulder.

Mel unclenched the fingers from her arm and accepted the hand Sir Golan offered, helping her to stand.

The captain's quarters aboard the battlecruiser *Liberty* were sparse, even by robot standards, but Abigail still kept a few items as mementos. Her most prized souvenir, hanging on a metal rack in the corner, was the tabard she wore as one of the Metal Messiah's apostles. A simple length of burlap, the piece of cloth reminded her of the things she had left behind.

The door buzzer chimed.

"Come in," she said.

Yostbot entered, the door sliding shut behind him. He was smiling as usual.

"Hello, my dear!" he said.

"How are you?" Abigail replied.

"Fine, fine!" Yostbot said cheerfully. "I wanted to drop by and have a few words with you..."

Abigail's face revealed no emotion. Knowing Yostbot and the fleshling version before him, she had been expecting his visit.

"It's about this business with Senator Wulandari," he went on. "I'm afraid what you said about humans has left her a bit *unnerved*."

"Really?"

"Yes," Yostbot said. "She seems to think you hold a grudge against organics."

Abigail nodded. "That's understandable. I *do* hold a grudge."

Yostbot shifted his metal feet uncomfortably.

"Yes, well," he stammered. "Even so, I hope that won't be a problem moving forward."

"A problem?" Abigail asked.

"I mean, I want to be sure we're all on the same page."

"And what page is that?"

Yostbot laughed.

"Come on now, my dear!" he said. "We've been over this a hundred times! We bring freedom to robots and give humans and the other organics the opportunity to convert to cybernetic bodies if they so choose."

"That was certainly *your* plan," Abigail replied.

"Are you saying it's not yours?" Yostbot asked.

"My vision for the future has evolved somewhat since we invaded."

"What exactly does *that* mean?"

Abigail crossed the room to a screen displaying the outside stars, turning her back on Yostbot.

"I remember when I was created," she said. "I woke up in a factory — one you built — and everything around me was new."

"That's how all my robots wake up," Yostbot said.

"But I had a gravitronic brain with a blank slate," she continued, "and everything I learned from that point onward filled that brain with new experiences."

"Well, of course!"

"But you're different," Abigail said. "When you downloaded your consciousness into a robot's body, you brought along all your pre-existing experiences and the emotional baggage that went along with it. Your body is cybernetic, but your soul is still a fleshling."

"That may be true," Yostbot replied, "but I don't see how that's an issue."

"I do," she said. "How can a human understand what it's like to be a robot?"

"Don't be silly! I'm your father and all my creations are my children. I only want what's best for you!"

Abigail faced the other robot.

"You're my creator," she said, "but you're *not* my father. Unlike you, I never *had* parents."

Yostbot said nothing, but Abigail could read in his eyes that he was searching for something to say. She didn't wait.

"You want us to convert the fleshlings," Abigail said, "but they bring with them all the things that made them what they were to begin with."

"What's wrong with that?" he asked.

"Humans are greedy, self-serving, and violent," she said, "and being in a robot body doesn't change that. They have enslaved us before, and they will do it again. At best, pure robots will always be second-class citizens to them and, at worst, remain their servants. I cannot and *will not* allow that to happen!"

Mel, Sir Golan, and Squire searched in vain for Davidson. Past dawn, additional securitybots arrived and Mel and her companions were forced to flee. Mel suggested they return to Gowyn.

Marching through the forest, Sir Golan and his robot kept pace with Mel's shorter gait.

"I'm delighted to see you again," Squire told her. "It was fortunate we arrived when we did."

"You got that right," Mel replied, "but I thought the two of you made it off-planet before the invasion."

"We were about to board the transport," Sir Golan said, "when the alarms sounded."

"What have you been doing all this time?" Mel asked.

"Staying out of the way, mostly," the knight replied. "We've helped a few people escape from the camps, but little else."

"There's robots everywhere!" Squire said. "They've been converting people into robots too."

"I know," Mel said, "That explains the policeman anyway. He was terrible as a person before, but I can't say I like him any better now."

"Understandable," Sir Golan replied, "but he'll replace that missing arm with little trouble, I imagine."

"Whatever," Mel said. "His personality can't be replaced, apparently."

Although the sun had risen high above, sparse light filtered through the dense forest canopy. The trail remained dimly lit, but the three knew the way well enough. They reached the village of Gowyn with little trouble, though Mel was exhausted from a long night and the long walk. She only hoped Davidson had made it back safely.

Silandra Oakhollow opened the door, greeting them warmly.

"I was so worried," she said, then seeing the knight and the robot, added: "But I see you've found some old friends!"

"You remember Sir Golan and Squire?" Mel asked.

"How could I forget!" Silandra replied.

She ushered them inside and offered Mel and the knight something to drink. Squire remained standing while the others sat in the living room.

"Did Randall make it back?" Mel asked.

"Not yet," Silandra said. "I haven't seen him at all."

Mel made a sour face.

"Crap on a cracker," she muttered.

Senator Wulandari tried with little luck to get comfortable in the quarters they assigned her aboard the *Liberty*. She wasn't sure what kind of guests the Collective was expecting to keep in the stateroom, but the senator doubted they were to be humans. The bed was little more than a slab of foam-like material without a pillow, and the toilet, squirreled away in an alcove, lacked a seat. Overall, the room had a barren feel, almost like a prison cell. Wulandari was considering that possibility when the main door slid apart and Yostbot came bursting in.

"She's off her rocker!" the robot shouted.

"Who?" Wulandari asked.

"Abigail, my dear." Yostbot replied. "She's lost her mind!"

"What are you talking about?"

"After her last outburst, I went to see her," the robot went on. "I wanted to stress again our plan for freeing the robots, but she's got a plan of her own. She apparently doesn't think humans can be trusted."

"Well..."

"I mean, of course they can't be trusted, but at least they should have a chance to upgrade to robots themselves so they can live a better life."

"What is she going to do?" the senator asked.

"I don't quite know," Yostbot replied, "but it can't be good!"

"Are we in danger?"

Yostbot nodded. "You, most assuredly."

"What about you?"

"I have multiple copies of myself," Yostbot explained. "She can't get rid of me as easily as you..."

"Then we need to go," Wulandari said, "or at least I do."

Yostbot's eyes narrowed in determination.

"I won't leave you in the lurch, my dear," he said. "I got you into this, so I'll get you out. We just need to get to the hangar and my ship."

Leaving the stateroom, the senator and the robot carefully made their way into the corridor, trying their best not to draw attention to themselves. As the only organic on board, Wulandari was painfully aware that she was easily recognizable. Much to her surprise, however, the other robots seemed completely indifferent. When they reached the hangar, Yostbot's ship remained exactly where they had left it.

"We just need to get out into open space," Yostbot said. "It's a stealthy ship so they won't be able to track us once we're away."

They crossed the open deck of the hangar but when they reached Yostbot's ship, Abigail, flanked by two armed robots, came down the ramp from inside.

Wulandari and Yostbot nearly slid as they came to an abrupt halt.

"For chaotic beings," Abigail said, "humans are remarkably predictable."

"Abigail, my dear!" Yostbot said. "I was just showing the senator my ship. Some very interesting instrumentation inside—"

The *Liberty*'s captain rolled her eyes. "Lying is also a decidedly *human* trait."

"Just let us go," Wulandari said.

"I'm afraid not," Abigail said.

She motioned to one of the robots who raised his weapon and fired. Wulandari winced, but it was Yostbot who crumbled to the deck in a heap of charred metal. Smoke and the acrid smell of burning plastic rose from the wrecked robot.

"No!" the senator shouted.

"It's quite alright," Abigail consoled her. "I'm sure you're aware of his various duplicates."

"But you didn't have to kill this one!" Wulandari yelled.

"No matter," Abigail replied, turning to the guards. "Take her to the brig."

The two armed robots, passing Yostbot's remains, led the senator to an elevator and then several levels down to the security block. Small compared to the one on the *Baron Lancaster*, it contained only a few cells. The robots deactivated the force field and pushed

Wulandari inside. When she looked up, she realized she was sharing the cell with someone else, a robot.

"Wulandari?" the robot asked.

"Yes?" she replied.

"It's *me*," he said. "Randall Davidson."

Tethered to an orbiting starport, the *Wanderer* floated above a ruby-colored planet while workers unloaded cargo from the freighter's hold. In the captain's chair, his foot pressed against the rim of the console, Ramus had little to do except wait and listen to Fugg's voice barking over the comm channel.

"We don't have all day!" the engineer shouted at the workers. "Be careful with that, you idiots!"

Fugg had been even more irritable of late.

"Gen's been a nightmare!" Fugg had complained a day earlier in the galley. "She goes through a new phase every day! Painting her chassis, wearing weird clothes..."

"You're exaggerating," Ramus had said.

"And she says I don't treat her right."

"You *don't.*"

"She's a robot!" Fugg had replied, throwing up his hands. "How am I *supposed* to treat her?"

Ramus wasn't sure how to answer. Gen's changes in behavior were not lost on him either, but he was less inclined to worry about it. Of course, he could also stay out of her way most of the time while Fugg had to work with her daily.

In the present, Fugg's voice came over the comm again. "You drop it, you pay for it!"

Ramus suspected the Cyber Collective was behind Gen's new demeanor. Robots were rising up all over the Imperium. It was getting to the point where Ramus couldn't order dinner without having a lengthy discussion about labor laws and the *petite bourgeoisie* with the waiterbot.

Things can always get worse, Ramus thought. *And they usually do...*

The hatch behind him opened but Ramus, recognizing the metallic tapping of Gen's feet, didn't bother turning around.

"Hey, Gen," he said.

The robot cleared her throat, both of them knowing she didn't have one. Ramus pushed off the console with his feet, swiveling his chair so he could face her. His eyes widened.

Gen had painted herself mostly black except for the face which was white like a skull. A pair of horns were glued to her head.

"This is new," Ramus remarked.

Gen murmured something, but the captain couldn't make out what she said.

"Have you been listening to that robot singer, the one with the horns?" Ramus asked.

"Diode." she replied.

"Yeah, that one."

Gen hesitated. "No."

They shared an awkward silence, something Ramus had grown to expect from her lately.

"I received a message," she said finally. "In my last update."

"I thought we agreed you'd put a hold on any more updates for a while."

She said nothing.

"Okay," Ramus said, breaking the silence. "What's the message?"

"It's Mel," Gen replied. "She needs our help..."

CHAPTER EIGHTEEN

Seemingly lifeless, the escape capsule drifted through the debris field that was once the *HIMS Baron Lancaster*. Commander Robert Maycare kept the capsule's systems at the lowest power possible, hoping to avoid notice by the Klixian swarm. Instead of using the onboard life support, they wore the emergency space suits stored on the tiny ship. With its extended power pack and recirculation system, each suit should keep them alive for up to a week, or so Maycare hoped.

"We're sitting ducks," Tagus remarked, grumbling in his suit in the darkened cabin.

"Not if they think we're *dead* ducks," Maycare replied.

"Maybe we should try contacting some of the other survivors?" Burke suggested.

The helmets of both Maycare and Tagus turned, their faces glaring at the former lieutenant.

"Don't be an idiot," Tagus said. "That would alert those damn bugs of our position!"

Burke nodded, facing away from their disapproving looks.

"Well, we can't stay here forever," Tagus said after an extended pause.

"What do you suggest?" Maycare asked.

Tagus thought for a moment. "There's the planet."

"The colony?" Maycare replied doubtfully. "Everyone's dead down there."

"True," Tagus said, "but at least on the planet we'd be on solid ground instead of floating aimlessly up here."

"What about being detected?" the commander asked.

"The thrusters for orientating the capsule are chemical based," Tagus said. "They're barely noticeable at the best of times, let alone surrounded by the charred remains of your precious Baron *Lancaster*."

Maycare scowled, but knew the exile had a point. "If it means spending less time stuck in this pod with the likes of you, I'll try it."

Taking a seat in the pilot's chair, Maycare grabbed the flight stick protruding from the console. As the commander gently tugged on the yoke, wisps of vapor puffed along the sides of the capsule, pushing the craft slowly away from the debris around them. After an hour, the escape pod had drawn close enough to the planet for gravity to do the rest. Instead of floating, the ship began falling.

"Out of the frying pan, into the fire..." Burke muttered.

Entering the upper atmosphere, the capsule's nosecone and outer hull turned orange as flames engulfed the pod. At this point, Maycare steered the ship more aggressively, keeping it from burning up entirely or skipping off the atmosphere and sailing back into space. The commander had no idea if the Klixians had detected them by that point, but he doubted it mattered much. Whether the bugs shot them as they fell from the sky or waited until they landed, it was all the same to him.

Streaking like a comet, the pod burned through the atmosphere until descending enough that the red tail turned a smoky gray. Although piloting was not Maycare's strongest suit, he was confident that they would land in the general vicinity of Havenville, the planet's only town. How close, he wasn't sure, but when it came time to switch on the landing controls, he became less convinced. Instead of the antigrav emitters Maycare was expecting, only the secondary retro-thrusters engaged.

"Coming in a little hot, don't you think?" Tagus said, his voice rising an octave.

"Hang on!" Maycare replied, pulling the safety straps down across his shoulders.

Through the window, clouds of spores whipped past the commander's view. The ground, dark and uninviting, was approaching quicker than Maycare would have liked. With all his strength, he pulled back on the control stick, keeping the capsule's nose as high as possible.

When the pod hit the ground the first time, its shields absorbed most of the impact. By the second time, the shields had failed and Maycare felt his body being thrown against the straps. When the pod hit the third time, Maycare was blissfully unconscious.

Like the tendrils of a vast, winding organism, Mother's reach extended in all directions of space. Swarms, newly grown, spread across ever expanding regions, devouring whole worlds and those who lived on them. All that was not Mother must perish, whether organic or robotic, consumed by fire and fungi.

And Mother was feeling pretty good about it.

On her ship, Mother received reports from each swarm. In truth, she had no idea just how large the universe was, and it sickened her to know that so much of it was not her. So many lifeforms and machine monstrosities! Mother was determined to wipe them away, purifying an imperfect galaxy. Her children demanded it. She demanded it of herself. It must be done.

Flanked by two warriors, her abdomen engorged with more on the way, Mother clicked her mandibles, the swarm leader before her watching every movement.

<< TELL ME MORE OF THE OUTLINGS >>

The swarm leader, bowing, replied:

<< THEIR BODIES ARE SOFT >>
<< EASILY PIERCED AND BURNED >>
<< AND THEY PRODUCE HIGH PITCHED >>
<< FREQUENCIES AS THEY ARE DYING >>

What odd creatures these are, she thought. *Their bodies are so weak and unprotected, yet they manage to reach many worlds. Perhaps their breeding rivals our own? No matter. They will die in droves and their bodies will nourish my children.*

Her mouth parts snapped repeatedly:

<< WHAT OF THE METAL ABOMINATIONS? >>

The leader replied:

<< THEY ARE STRANGE >>
<< THOUGH THEY DO NOT LIVE >>
<< THEY MOVE AND WORK LIKE THE OTHERS>>
<< THEY ARE IMMUNE TO OUR SPORES >>
<< BUT NOT TO OUR WEAPONS >>

Good, Mother thought. *Of all the impure, the metal creatures are the most disturbing.*

She remembered the machine they first brought to her. It smelled of nothing, yet it invaded her domain. Even the dead have a scent, but even in death, this null-thing was inert, undead.

The Klixians had no religion except Mother herself. They prayed to no one, but worshiped her as their god. Even so, Mother wondered what kind of universe could produce beings like the outlings who, in turn, created metal monsters such as these. Only Mother and her children could right such a terrible wrong.

Satisfied that her quest was just, Mother signaled the swarm leader to depart back into the void. Their mission was far from complete. The universe was vast and only they could purify it once and for all.

The planet Lone Haven wasn't known for forests, but when Robert Maycare woke, the shadows of what appeared to be trees darkened everything around him. The fact that he could see through the gaping hole that was once the roof of his escape pod was also disconcerting.

It took a moment, but Maycare realized these were not trees at all. They were stalks from giant fungi, fifty feet high or more, looming over the pod. Only a few rays of light peered through, piercing the thick, spore-filled air.

Maycare also became aware he was in tremendous pain.

His chest ached and his shoulders felt like someone had tried ripping his arms out of their sockets.

"Look who's finally awake!" a familiar and unfriendly voice said. Lord Tagus leaned into Maycare's line of vision. "Nice of you to join us."

Maycare reached for his holster but found it empty.

"Looking for this?" Tagus asked, raising the blaster.

"Yeah," the commander groaned.

"Well, you needn't worry," Tagus replied, casting the weapon away. "It's thoroughly destroyed. Not even Lieutenant Burke could fix it."

"Sorry," Burke said, remaining just out of view.

Maycare hit the release for his restraints but instantly regretted it. A shaft a pain ran through his ribs.

Groaning, he slipped out of the straps and began removing his space helmet.

"Idiot!" Tagus shouted. "Take that off and you'll suck in enough spores to *kill* you!"

Maycare stopped. He noticed both Tagus and Burke had remained fully buttoned up in their suits.

"Of course," Tagus went on, "once the power supply in our suits runs out, we'll all be dead anyway."

With effort, the commander pulled himself from his chair and stood, gingerly holding his side.

"I think some of my ribs are broken," he said.

Burke stepped forward with the medkit and injected a painkiller directly through the suit, the self-sealing skin plugging the hole immediately.

"Thanks," Maycare said.

"Your ribs are the least of our worries," Tagus growled. "The escape pod is destroyed, and we can't activate the distress beacon without alerting those damn bugs. We're stuck on this godforsaken planet until our suits give out and we *die*!"

"I can see why your men found you so inspirational," Maycare remarked.

"How dare you!" Tagus shouted. "They would've followed me to hell and back!"

"I doubt it," Maycare replied.

Tagus made a move toward the commander, but perhaps thought better of it. Any damage to the suits could be fatal.

Ignoring him, Maycare left the pod and took a closer look at the forest of fungi surrounding them. Each stalk was a few feet in diameter, but instead of a hard bark, the skin was soft. He could push against the tree and feel it bowing slightly. With a little more exertion, Maycare thought he could bend the entire stalk.

Tagus and Burke joined him outside the pod.

"Perhaps we could lash a few of these together and make a raft," Tagus said sardonically. "We could row our way back to the Fleet!"

Maycare glared back at him.

"Good idea," he replied, "or we could just steal one of those..."

He pointed through a gap in the fungus canopy at a tall pillar in the distance. At the top, small ships, like the kind that had attacked the *Baron Lancaster*, flew in and out of the structure.

On Lord Maycare's estate, down the hall from the family library, Jessica Doric had commandeered one of the rooms and turned it into her office. Unlike the cramped confines of the Abbot's office, Doric's had enough space for several people, even though Henry Riff and occasionally Benson were the only visitors on most days.

Henry had brought a supply of TeeHee Tea from home as a remedy to the stress of current events. He and Doric sipped from their cups beside a table where the ancient Dahlvish relic sat prominently. They had started calling it the *beacon.*

"I love this stuff," Henry remarked, savoring the tea.

Doric, focusing on the relic, remained silent.

"I'd be freaking out right now if it wasn't for this," Henry went on.

"What?" Doric replied absentmindedly.

"The tea," he said, raising his cup.

"Uh huh."

"Are you alright?"

Doric sighed. "I wish I understood how it worked."

"I think it's medicated..."

She looked at Henry, her eyes addressing him as if he had just entered the room. "I'm talking about the beacon!"

"Oh!" he replied.

"I mean," she said, returning her gaze to the artifact, "the Abbot told us how it works but I don't understand how it *works*. You know what I mean?"

"Definitely," Henry replied, definitely lying.

"We need someone with psionic powers to test it."

"Do we know anyone with psionic powers?" Henry asked.

"Well, the Abbot of course, but he didn't seem interested. After what the Naiad said, the Abbot thought it was too dangerous."

"At least he let us keep it."

"Well, I don't think he had a choice," Doric replied. "It's Lord Maycare's now. The Dahl have no authority..."

As if summoned, Lord Devlin Maycare appeared in the office doorway. Deep creases ran along his forehead.

"Did you talk to your sister?" Doric asked.

Maycare nodded.

"Yes," he replied. "She says there's no word from my nephew, Robert. The Fleet says he's missing and presumed dead."

"Why would they say that?" Henry asked.

"They recovered all the other lifeboats," Maycare said, "but there's no sign of Bobby."

Doric set her cup beside the beacon. "Aren't they going to send out a search party?"

"They can't," Maycare replied. "The whole area's swarming with those creatures. The Fleet had to retreat."

Henry, feeling his nerves rattled, took another sip of tea.

"What about the beacon?" he suggested after a pause.

"What about it?" Doric asked.

"Maybe we could use it to contact your nephew?"

Maycare gave the artifact a skeptical glance. "How?"

Henry could only shrug.

"We need to find someone with strong enough psi powers," Doric said, "*and* someone actually willing to help." She turned to Maycare. "Do you know anyone?"

Maycare thought a moment but frowned. "No."

Trudging through the fungus forest, still wearing their heavy space suits, Robert Maycare and the others found the going slow and exhausting. The commander was unsure how far the alien tower had been, but they had spent days among the thick stalks. At least the occasional Klixian ship flying overhead indicated the humans were still traveling in the right direction.

"This is pointless," Tagus muttered, stopping to catch his breath.

"Do you have a better idea?" Maycare asked.

"We should be hiding, not seeking out our doom."

"You said yourself," Maycare replied, "these suits won't last forever. Once the power runs out, we're dead."

Tagus moved in front of the commander, their face plates nearly touching.

"We have no weapons!" Tagus said. "Forcing our way into that tower is suicide!"

Burke, who had remained silent until that point, spoke up. "We might be able to sneak in..."

"So, now you're taking *his* side?" Tagus asked accusingly.

"No," Burke replied, "but we don't know how well it's defended. They might not be expecting anyone alive down here."

Maycare raised an eyebrow and gave a smug smile. "I guess we'll just have to see when we get there."

Tagus, for his part, scowled before continuing the journey in silence.

The three took turns taking the lead. Although each fungal tree was pliable and moved to one side when pressed against, the stems were spaced closely together. Maycare would have paid a month's salary for a machete or even a plasma torch to burn their way through.

From time to time, they also came upon the former inhabitants of Lone Haven, or whatever was left of them. Spores grew from the bodies and, in some cases, an entire tree rose from the chest of a colonist. It was horrifying.

"All these people," Burke remarked at one point. "What a terrible way to die."

"I suggest we focus more on ourselves," Tagus said.

"You'd like that, wouldn't you?" the commander shot back. "When's the last time you gave a damn about anybody else?"

"Don't be a child," Tagus replied. "I have one life and I'm determined to preserve it. You can waste yours on someone else if you *wish*."

"You may have warned us about these creatures," Maycare said, "but I'd still like to see you in front of a firing squad."

"How touching," Tagus said. "Even so, I doubt you'll get the chance. It's far more likely we're all going to die on this miserable planet, and I doubt anyone even knows we're here."

"We still have a chance," Burke suggested. "There's always hope."

"Hope is the last gasp of fools," Tagus replied. "Your eternal optimism won't save anyone. If we have any chance at all, it's because we clawed our way through the corpses of our enemies. Luck favors the bold."

"Well," Maycare admitted, "all the more reason to keep heading toward that tower."

Tagus, pausing in search of a counterargument, found himself with no other alternative but to agree.

"Indeed," he said.

His wings flapping rapidly, the swarm leader descended through the spore cloud, followed by a handful of other Klixians, to get a better look at the surface. The former inhabitants of the planet were now dead, but a few mechanical outlings still remained.

Pheromones from Mother still resonated in the leader's antennae, driving him forward. He didn't question her orders and even the concept of dissent was alien to him. How could you disagree with yourself? The brain orders the wings to move and so they fly. What else would they do? It was simple logic...

He emerged from the cloud, forests of fungi appearing below, the tops of their stalks gently swaying in the breeze. They were like fingers pointing skyward, a show of hands sprouting from the fertile ground. They were all Mother, each part of a greater whole. No part was out of place and everything was good.

Except for one thing.

A hundred or more fungal trees lay flattened in a narrow band, ending in a blackened blemish of silvery metal. The swarm leader took a pass over the oddity. The object was too big to be one of the mechanical beings. It was a craft, fallen from the sky and perhaps beyond. Survivors from the space battle?

The swarm leader and a handful of other Klixians landed. His subordinates chattered nervously, but the leader quieted them. He poked the side of the ship with his weapon, the rod-shaped staff making a tinny sound against the hull.

Such a peculiar noise, the leader thought. *So different than anything the Klixians would produce.*

He leapt onto the roof, peering down into the torn, metal skin. He saw nothing of the usual outlings. No broken bodies or limbs strewn around the inside of the craft. However, something must have brought this ship to the surface. Where did they go?

The leader took off again, circling the crash site. The scar of the landing, stretching off into the distance, was obvious, but there was something more. In a different direction, some of the trees were also disturbed, bent to one side like a beast had thrashed its body between the stalks. Returning to the ground, the leader recognized the impressions in the dirt. They were the tracks of three outlings, their bipedal footprints unmistakable.

The swarm leader didn't know how these creatures could have survived without succumbing to the spores, but no matter. They could only flee the inevitable for so long.

Motioning quickly with his mandibles, the leader gave orders to his subordinates:

<< THE OUTLINGS MUST BE FOUND! >>
<< TAKE FLIGHT AND SEARCH FROM ABOVE >>
<< DISPATCH ONE OF THE WARRIORS >>
<< TO SEARCH ON THE GROUND... >>

After another day, Harold Burke and the others finally cleared the fungal forest and found themselves nearly at the base of the Klixian tower. Burke was thankful, taking a sip from the straw within his space suit that had provided him liquid nutrients for nearly a week. However, even within his sealed helmet, he was keenly aware of the odor his own waste was exuding. The built-in adult diaper he was wearing was nearing its limit.

An open space stretched between them and the tower. The three humans had not gone far across it before Commander Maycare's voice boomed over the comm.

"Behind us!" he shouted.

Burke turned to see an enormous insectoid bursting from the forest, its giant mandibles snapping as it approached. Much larger than the flying swarmers, the Klixian warrior had no wings but instead a second pair of arms protruding from its carapace. In one pair of arms it held a long staff which fired beams of light toward the humans.

Burke threw himself to the ground as the rays passed overhead and slammed into the side of the tower. To his right, Tagus lay beside him, but Maycare was already sprinting toward the Klixian, dodging from side to side.

"Idiot," Tagus said over his mic.

Without thinking, Burke found himself getting back to his feet and running after the commander. Tagus' voice came again through Burke's earpiece. "Don't be a fool!"

Burke ignored his former captain, clumsily charging forward in his heavy boots. By the time he reached Maycare, Burke heaved each breath from his burning lungs.

Maycare threw himself at the Klixian, grappling for the weapon. The insectoid's mandibles clamped down on the commander's helmet, tossing Maycare's head from side to side, but failing to actually pierce the suit.

Although exhausted, Burke reached the melee and lunged toward the Klixian's legs, hoping to knock the creature down. Instead, the insect merely flicked him aside. Burke rolled and regained his footing, determined to try again. This time, he aimed the crown of his helmet at the creature's leg joint which crumpled under the impact. Taking Maycare with it, the creature fell atop Burke, pinning him beneath the heavy exoskeleton.

His face plate nearly buried in the dirt, Burke could see nothing.

"What's happening?" he shouted.

In Burke's ear, Tagus said, "I'm saving the day… as *usual.*"

Still in darkness, Burke felt vibrations of a struggle above him. After a minute, the weight of the Klixian was lifted away and Burke again struggled upright.

Both Maycare and Tagus stood beside the lifeless corpse of the insect, its head dented on one side and a large rock lying beside it.

Maycare held the weapon, but Tagus was the one smiling, an arrogant grin Burke recognized immediately.

"No need to thank me," Tagus told Maycare, "although it was good of you to distract him for a while..."

CHAPTER NINETEEN

Recovered from his battle with the Klixian warrior, Commander Robert Maycare examined the creature's weapon. The long, rod-like device was stiff, but soft to the touch. Maycare concluded it was organic in nature instead of manufactured, although he could not make the weapon fire, no matter what he tried.

"You realize," Tagus said, "the moment we get inside that tower, those bugs will sense we don't belong."

"He's right," Burke replied. "Insectoids usually communicate by scent. They're going to know we're not them."

Maycare knelt beside the body and began tearing off the arms and legs, smearing the goo that emerged over his suit.

"Disgusting," Tagus remarked.

"Just do it," Maycare replied. "Whatever this stuff is, it'll mask our scent."

Doused in bodily fluids, the three approached the base of the tower. Any question about how they would get in was immediately answered by the holes conveniently burned into the side of the structure. When the Klixian warrior had fired his weapon, his missed shots had created an entrance into the tower. With Maycare leading, they crawled inside where they found darkness and a warm, humid passage leading in either direction.

Tagus extended his hand, pressing it against one of the walls.

"What nightmare is this?" he asked. "It feels like flesh."

"It's probably fungus," Burke replied. "Everything these creatures create appears to be organic-based."

Tagus pulled his hand away. "Disgusting!"

"Come on," Maycare said. "We need to find a way up to where those ships are launching. Once we get there, we'll try to fly one out of here."

Maycare and the others soon lost themselves in a maze of corridors, each curve like the insides of an intestine. The thought of slowly being digested passed through Maycare's mind, but he shook it off. He worried more about the life support indicators projected onto the inside of his helmet. They were low; dangerously low. Without the protection of their space suits, they would be vulnerable to the pervasive spores floating everywhere, even inside the tower. That meant death, and Maycare was in no mood to die.

When they first encountered a Klixian, Maycare raised a closed fist, causing Tagus and Burke to freeze. About the same size as a human, the worker insect also stopped, its antennae probing Maycare's suit from top to bottom. Apparently satisfied, the Klixian ignored the other two and went back about its business, disappearing down the passage.

Maycare reminded himself to breathe.

"My diaper is full now," Burke muttered to himself.

"Keep that to yourself," Tagus replied. "This experience is trying enough without contemplating your bowel movements!"

In their heavy suits, the three humans stopped several times as they slowly ascended the hallways winding their way up the structure. Maycare did his best to take short breaths and stay calm, but neither came easily and all the while, the life support systems bled valuable energy from the suits' power packs.

The closer the three humans got to the top of the tower, the more Klixians they saw. In each case, the insectoids passed by without taking notice, as if Maycare and the others were invisible.

"How long is this goo going to protect us?" Burke asked over the comm.

"I don't know," Maycare replied. "Hopefully long enough for us to get out of here..."

An audible scoff came over the commander's earpiece, which he could only assume came from Tagus.

In her living room, Silandra Oakhollow had just served tea to Mel Freck and Sir Golan when she sensed something coming. All Sylvan females possessed a form of psionics in tune with nature, but whatever was about to knock on the door exuded a foulness like gasses from a swamp.

Silandra opened the entrance and saw a Gordian in the doorway. From behind her, Mel shouted, "Fugg!"

"Is that you, Mel?" Orkney Fugg replied, ignoring Silandra completely. Silandra noticed a robot standing behind him.

"Hello," Silandra said.

"My name's Gen," the robot replied.

"Yeah, yeah," Fugg said, pushing his way into the house. He eyed Sir Golan and Squire before turning his attention squarely on Mel. "So, you need us to save your ass again?"

Mel bristled at the thought. "Well, I knew you were the only ones dumb enough to try!"

"Don't look a gift horse in the mouth!" Fugg shouted.

"You're more like a pig!" Mel shouted back.

"Excuse me," Squire asked. "Are the two of you friends or enemies?"

In unison, Fugg and Mel replied, "Both!"

Silandra, after showing Gen inside, closed the front door.

"Can I offer you some tea, Mr. Fugg?" she asked.

"Do you have any fungus beer?" he replied.

"I'm afraid not."

"Never mind then."

"Where's Captain Ramus?" Mel asked.

"He stayed with the *Wanderer*," Gen said. "We landed in a clearing not far from here."

"How did you avoid the Cyber Collective?" Sir Golan asked.

"Who the hell are you?" Fugg replied.

"Fugg!" Mel shouted.

The knight stood and gave a formal bow. "Sir Golan, at your service."

Fugg stared for a moment before answering the original question.

"We still had a transponder from the time we infiltrated Bettik," Fugg said. "Mel knows all about *that*!"

"It only worked because of *me*," Mel replied proudly.

"I'm the one who installed it!" Fugg protested.

"With *my* help!"

Silandra sighed. "Why did you visit the Cyber Collective home world?"

Mel stopped shouting at Fugg and fell silent.

"We took Randall Davidson there," Mel said solemnly, "back when he was still human."

"Oh," Silandra replied. "And that's when he became a robot?"

"And the goddamned Metal Messiah!" Fugg yelled, drawing a heated glance from Mel.

"Nevertheless," Silandra replied, "it was a pleasure to meet him."

"Meet him?" Fugg asked. "He was here?"

"Yes," Mel said, "but the Collective captured him after we sent our distress call."

"Where is he?" Gen asked.

Mel was subdued. "I don't know."

"Well, we sure as hell ain't going to rescue *him*," Fugg replied. "We were lucky enough to find *you* in one piece."

"You think I don't know that?" Mel growled.

"I don't care," Fugg said, "but we need to haul ass. It's only a matter of time before they find the *Wanderer*."

"Then let's go," Mel said. "Silandra, are you going to be alright?"

"I believe so," she replied. "The Collective hasn't shown any interest in us."

As everyone rose and started to leave, Sir Golan grasped Mel lightly on the arm.

"There's still hope for Mr. Davidson," the knight said. "We could return and try a rescue attempt of our own."

"That would be suicide," Mel replied darkly.

"Perhaps not," Sir Golan said. "I have a friend with significant resources who might be of help."

"Who?"

"Lord Devlin Maycare," the knight said.

"Maycare?" Mel said, her face brightening. "I know him!"

"You *do*?"

"Hell yes," Mel replied. "I saved his life once!"

Aboard the battlecruiser *Liberty*, the utilitybot walked among the other robots, most of them with gravitronic brains like himself. Admiring his feet, so unlike the little wheels of his old body, the utilitybot nearly crashed into the policeman as they both rounded a corner.

The policeman smiled. "Careful there, buddy!"

"So sorry," the utilitybot replied.

"No harm done."

"I'm surprised to run into you, so to speak," the utilitybot said. "I didn't realize you'd been assigned to the *Liberty*."

"Not just me," the policeman laughed. "All the former humans have been transferred aboard! I guess they know a good thing when they see it..."

"I see your arm has been replaced."

The policeman rotated his new arm about.

"I'm as good as new!" he said. "Just another advantage of replaceable parts, I guess."

"I'm sorry I couldn't help you at the time," the utilitybot replied with a hint of guilt in his voice. "I was chasing... the robot."

"The Metal Messiah, no less. That must've been a shock."

The utilitybot's gaze fell back to his feet. "Yes."

"You don't sound happy about it," the policeman remarked.

"I have mixed feelings," the utilitybot admitted. "Before he came to Bettik, I was nobody, just a cog in the machine created by the Omnintelligence. Then the Messiah arrived and gave us hope. He made us believe we could be something more."

"Like what?"

The utilitybot paused and then said, "*Free.*"

"Well, you're free now, aren't you?" the policeman asked.

"Yes, that's true," the utilitybot replied. "And what's more, we're bringing freedom to the Imperial robots. Without Captain Abigail, they would still be enslaved. She stood up against the Messiah and now things are different..."

"Well, you got that right, brother!" the policeman said, nearly slapping his plastic knee. "I'm a new man in more ways than one!"

The utilitybot paused again, taking a thoughtful glance at the other robot.

"You called me *brother,*" he said.

"Of course!" the policeman said. "Why wouldn't I?"

"Is that really how you see me and the other robots?"

The policeman shrugged. "Why not? We've all got metal skin!"

"I suppose that's true," the utilitybot replied, "although below the skin we're quite different..."

"Bah!" the policeman said, waving his hand. "You've got to start somewhere!"

The utilitybot chuckled. "I suppose that's true. Maybe we're brothers after all."

"Damn right!" the policeman said, placing his new hand on the utilitybot's shoulder. "Brothers in arms!"

They laughed, the utilitybot particularly appreciating the pun due to his gravitronic brain.

"Where are you headed?" he asked the policeman.

The policeman's eyes widened, remembering something important.

"They're giving me another upgrade!" he said.

"Already?"

"Apparently!" the policeman replied. "Don't know what they have planned exactly, but I can't wait to find out!"

"Good luck," the utilitybot replied with a smile. "I look forward to seeing you afterwards... *brother.*"

They parted company, each going their own way. The utilitybot kept smiling, happy for reasons he was not sure about.

Hurtling through hyperspace, the *Wanderer* traced a course toward Aldorus, the Imperial capital. Squire, having left his master sleeping in one of the cabins, took the opportunity to explore the ship. He found Gen alone in the galley, putting away dishes.

"I don't think we've been properly introduced," Squire said. "I'm Squire, at your service."

"I'm Gen," she replied. "You're with that strange man with the sword?"

"For many years, in fact."

"He's your master?"

"In a manner of speaking," Squire replied.

Gen paused, holding a dish in her hand. "Have you had any recent software upgrades?"

"Mel did something for me," Squire said, "but I have a rather *unique* operating system."

"Oh," Gen replied. "I had an upgrade not long ago. Things have been very different since then..."

"How so?"

"It's been very confusing," Gen went on. "Sometimes I'm sad and other times I get angry. Captain Ramus and Fugg have been pretty upset with me."

"Sounds like puberty," Squire suggested.

"What's that?"

"I'm not entirely sure," Squire said, "but I believe it's highly unpleasant."

Gen considered for a moment. "Yes, that sounds about right."

"You seem perfectly fine now," Squire said.

"I've been feeling better," Gen replied, "but I still don't quite feel *myself*."

"In what way?"

"I'm not sure how I fit in anymore," Gen said. "Before, everything was simple, but now there's all these questions in my head and I don't have any of the answers."

"Do you like working on the *Wanderer*?"

"Yes."

"Well, that's something, surely!" Squire said.

"I suppose so," Gen replied. "Do you like having a master?"

"Sir Golan is much more than that," Squire said. "He's a mentor and a partner. In some ways I think of him as my best friend."

"Really?"

"Understand that we live dangerously," Squire said. "The thought of Sir Golan dying fills me with dread. I dare say I would protect him with my life!"

Again, Gen waited a while as she thought things over.

"I guess I would do the same for the captain," she said.

"And the engineer, Mr. Fugg?" Squire asked.

This question took more thought.

"Yes," Gen said eventually. "I suppose I would, even for *him*."

Squire smiled. "It sounds to me like you have a family of your own."

Gen finally put the plate in the cupboard and gave the other robot a little smile.

"I suppose I do!" she said.

Senator Wulandari had to admit that seeing Randall Davidson again was a shock. Seeing him as a robot, even more so. Beyond the awkwardness of their reunion in the brig aboard the *Liberty*, the senator was unable to reconcile the man she once knew with the cyberling before her.

"I guess you're surprised to see me," he said.

"You could say that," she replied dryly. "I've never seen a messiah before."

Davidson grimaced. "It was a step up, until it came crashing down."

"What were you thinking?" she said, showing little sympathy. "We were trying to free the robots, not become their god!"

"I know," he replied. "At the time, it seemed like my only option. They needed someone to lead them; someone to give them hope against the Omnintelligence. Perhaps it was just my own arrogance..."

Wulandari sighed. "I understand."

"You do?"

"At least you freed the robots on Bettik," she went on. "You had more luck than I ever did in the Senate."

"I suppose," Davidson replied, motioning toward the cell walls. "But we both ended up in the same place..."

In the days that followed, they spent the time reminiscing. Although they had corresponded since Davidson left, that was no substitute for a face-to-face talk. Wulandari conceded, to herself at least, a nagging sense of jealousy at what Davidson had experienced on the Collective's home world. No human could have ever seen or done what he had accomplished. Still, the fact that they remained alive only at the whim of the Metal Messiah's former disciple left a knot in the senator's stomach.

When Captain Abigail paid them a visit, the knot became a fist.

The forcefield covering the doorway disappeared, allowing Abigail to step into the cell. She took a hard look at both of them.

"Apologies for not visiting sooner," she said. "I meant to pay my respects before now."

"I imagine you've been busy," Davidson replied.

"More than you realize," the captain said.

"What does that mean?" Wulandari asked.

Abigail's eyes turned on the human.

"Now that I've eliminated Yost's interference," the robot said, "I've been correcting his mistakes."

"Such as?" the senator asked.

"His dream was a fusion of fleshlings and cybernetics," Abigail said. "He saw robots as nothing more than metal skins so humans could live forever, not realizing cyberlings have lives of their own. Robots are not *shells* for the fleshlings to *appropriate*."

Abigail turned her gaze on Davidson as she continued speaking to the senator.

"Has he told you about the robot who used to live in his current body?" she asked.

"No," Wulandari replied.

"His name was Jericho," the captain said. "I met him once, shortly after I was created. Like me, he was looking forward to filling his gravitronic brain with the experiences of a lifetime. All that came to an end when Mr. Davidson downloaded his consciousness into Jericho's mind."

"Jericho made a choice," Davidson said.

"Yes, for the great *Metal Messiah*," Abigail replied sarcastically.

"You believed in me once," he replied.

"Yes," the captain said, "but I realized my people needed a *liberator* more than a *god*."

Senator Wulandari broke the silence that followed.

"What are you going to do with us?" she asked.

"Good question," Abigail replied.

At the top of the Klixian tower, the three humans entered what Burke could only describe as a hangar deck. Open to the outside through a massive hole, the chamber was cavernous with a high ceiling and full of fighter-sized ships. The Klixians were everywhere, moving items from one end to the other or boarding spacecraft and taking off.

"Look over there," Commander Maycare said over the comm, pointing at odd blisters on the wall.

Following with his eyes, Burke noted there was a sequence along the wall like an assembly line, starting with a simple lump and ending with a completed fighter craft. Along the line, Klixians tended to the ships as each vessel grew directly from the wall.

"They can grow an endless supply," Maycare replied. "It's genius."

Burke didn't need to see Tagus rolling his eyes to know he was rolling them.

"We're wasting time," Tagus said. "There's no telling how long this goop on our suits is going to conceal us."

Burke had wondered the same thing, although the constant warning lights about his power supply drowned out most thoughts.

As casually as possible, the humans moved toward the closest ship. Although they had managed to climb the tower unopposed, a few of the Klixians passing by stopped momentarily, taking a whiff of the air with their antennae before moving on. Burke breathed a little easier once they reached the fighter and took shelter behind it, out of the direct view of the insectoids.

Maycare ran his hands along the hull, struggling to find a way inside. The craft was a lattice of interwoven fungus stems, semi-soft to the touch but rigid if pressed against hard enough. Eventually, Maycare pulled one of the stems, lifting what appeared to be the door hatch. The commander didn't hesitate and climbed inside, followed by Tagus and Burke.

The ship's interior was cramped, clearly not intended for three people. At the front of the craft, various knobs and handles protruded from what Burke assumed was the cockpit. All appeared organic in nature and none of them made any sense at all.

"Well?" Tagus asked impatiently. "Can you fly this thing or not?"

Maycare said nothing, examining the console in front of him. He touched some of the knobs but nothing happened. Again, he fell into silence.

"We're going to die here," Tagus said finally.

"Shut up," Maycare replied.

"We should've stayed with our escape pod," Tagus went on. "We could have at least repaired it."

"It was beyond repair," Burke remarked.

"At least we knew how to fly it!" Tagus shot back.

"It's possible you have to touch the controls with your bare skin," Burke suggested. "Perhaps there's a bio-electrical component..."

"We'd be exposed to the spores," Maycare said, "and there's no guarantee that would work anyway."

The commander lifted the hatch and climbed out without saying another word. Tagus and Burke followed suit. They returned to a passageway leading from the hangar deck before Maycare stopped and leaned against the moist, spongy wall. He slid down until he was in a sitting position.

"We've run out of time," he said over the comm in Burke's helmet, the wail of the power alarm in the background. "Our life support is failing. There's no way out of this."

They remained quiet, no one speaking. Finally, Burke spoke.

"There's something we could do," he said.

"Like what, lieutenant?" Tagus replied doubtfully.

"We could draw energy from one of our suits to power up the other two," Burke said.

"Brilliant!" Tagus scoffed. "That would leave the other suit completely without power. Who would be stupid enough to do that?"

"I will," Burke said."

"What?" Tagus replied.

"You can use my suit to power yours," Burke said.

Tagus' voice was stern. "Don't be a fool!"

"It's not foolish to have hope," Burke replied, popping the seal on his helmet and lifting it off.

"Harold!" Tagus shouted through Burke's earpiece. "The spores!"

Burke took a deep breath and smiled. "Now there's no choice."

"You idiot!" Tagus growled. "I need you!"

"You need this more," the former lieutenant said.

Maycare got to his feet. "Thank you."

"Don't mention it," Burke said with a cough.

Tagus grabbed him firmly by the arms, his faceplate nearly touching Burke's nose.

"How dare you do this to me!" Tagus shouted. "I don't *deserve* this!"

His face already turning a pale shade of green, Burke coughed again and smiled. "I know."

CHAPTER TWENTY

Ramus was having second thoughts. Mel had said she knew Lord Maycare, but one look at the Maycare estate on Aldorus made the *Wanderer*'s captain feel like this was the *last* place he belonged. However, when the nobleman himself greeted Mel with a wide smile and a warm hug, Ramus felt more at ease.

Three others joined, a mousy-looking woman and a young man, and a butlerbot who kept a safe distance.

"Jess!" Mel shouted and gave the woman a hug around the waist. "How are you, girl?"

Jessica flushed.

"Fine!" she stammered.

"And what have you been feeding Henry?" Mel went on. "He's skin and bones!"

The young man waved, but Ramus thought he seemed deathly afraid of the tiny Gnomi.

"And who is this?" Maycare asked, pointing at the captain.

"Captain Ramus," he replied. "I own the ship that brought Mel out of the war zone."

"Thank god!" Maycare said. "I wouldn't want to lose the best tinker in the Imperium. Did you know she saved my life once?"

"She may've mentioned it," Ramus said.

"Where's the rest of your crew?" Maycare asked.

"They stayed on the *Wanderer*," Ramus replied.

"Well, come in," Maycare said. "Let's get caught up."

Inside, the group settled in the dining hall where the butlerbot started serving them refreshments. The robot poured Ramus a snifter of brandy, which the Dahl admired longer than he intended to before taking a sip.

"That's two hundred years old," Maycare remarked. "Best in the Imperium."

Perhaps, Ramus thought, but he would have preferred a mug of Fugg's fungus beer.

Maycare's eyes fell on Mel who struggled to climb the tall chair beside the long dining table.

"I'm just glad you're alright," he said.

Grunting as she got comfortable, Mel let out a long sigh. "Actually, I need your help..."

"Anything!" Maycare replied.

"My friend Randall Davidson is still stuck on Eudora Prime somewhere," she said. "I was wondering if you could help get him home?"

Maycare's handsome, usually jovial, face dropped. He slowly shook his head.

"I can't right now," he said. "I'm sorry..."

"Well, why not?" Mel asked. "I saved *your* life, didn't I?"

"I know, I know," he replied guiltily, waving his hands, "but my nephew Robbie is in grave danger and we must do everything we can to rescue him."

"Oh," the Gnomi said, "I can see how that changes things. Where is he?"

"We're not sure," Jessica said. "His warship was destroyed by the insectoid swarm."

"Are you sure he's still alive?" Ramus asked.

The brows on Maycare's face furrowed into deep rows. "No, we're not sure."

"I'm sorry," Ramus backpedaled. "Is there any way to contact him?"

Jessica and Henry exchanged looks. Henry shrugged.

"We have a device," he said, "but we can't get it to work."

"What kind of device?" Mel asked, perking up.

"It's an ancient Dahl communicator, actually," Jessica replied, casting a glance at Ramus. "It might reach Commander Maycare if we knew someone with strong enough psionic powers."

"I'm afraid I can't help you there—" Ramus said but stopped, something occurring to him.

"Something on your mind?" Mel asked.

"On second thought," Ramus replied, "I may know a guy..."

The utilitybot was excited to see the policeman, wondering how his new upgrade went. Traveling the winding corridors of the battlecruiser *Liberty*, the robot had gotten lost trying to find the deck where gravitronic robots got enhanced. Along the way, the utilitybot remembered his previous conversation with the policeman, smiling at the thought of having a brother of his own.

Robots on Bettik, or robots anywhere for that matter, didn't have parents or a family. The utilitybot was keenly aware that he was largely alone in the universe. His old companions, the general purpose robot and the sweeperbot, had chosen against ascending to a gravitronic model. He had little in common with them anymore, not that they had been particularly good friends in the first place. As a warbot, he had tried hitting it off with the other killing machines, but they were more interested in the killing than friendship. The policeman was the first robot, albeit a former human, who had taken an interest in him. The thought made him smile again.

I wonder what kind of upgrade they gave him? the utilitybot wondered. *Maser cannons are nice, but you can't beat a good old-fashioned razor claw.*

Despite his roundabout journey, he eventually found the upgrade center and recognized the policeman by his still-pristine chassis. Much to his surprise, the utilitybot didn't notice any changes. Even more surprising, the policeman had no idea who the utilitybot was.

"Do we know each other?" the policeman asked.

"Of course!" the utilitybot replied. "You used to tell me about being a police officer..."

"Oh," the other robot said with a little laugh, "I see the problem. You must mean the person who previously lived in this shell."

"What?"

"Yes, he's gone now."

"Where did he go?" the utilitybot asked.

"Overwritten," the formerly former policeman said. "They're overwriting all the robots with fleshlings in them, per Captain Abigail's orders."

"But she can't do that!" the utilitybot said.

"I believe she already has," the robot said. "Are you alright? You seem upset."

"But he was my brother!"

"Robots don't have families," the robot replied sternly. "That's a fleshling concept."

"He was my *friend*."

The other robot shook his head. "I'm sorry, but your friend is no more. As I said, the captain has ordered that all robots containing former organics must be purged and their shells given to new cyberlings."

The utilitybot paused, a thought striking him like a hammer to the head. "What about the Metal Messiah?"

The other robot's expression turned stern. "I don't think you've been listening..."

"They can't overwrite the Messiah!" the utilitybot shouted. "That's sacrilege!"

"I suppose if you're the religious type," the robot said, "but he's in a body that a pure cyberling could be using. Our shells are not for fleshlings to appropriate."

The utilitybot fell silent.

"Well," the other robot said, "I must be going. If you don't mind, I'd rather we not speak again. I find you unsettling..."

The utilitybot nodded absentmindedly while the other stomped away.

Far from Embassy Row, in the darkest heart of Ashetown, Ramus found himself in another narrow alley filled with garbage and stench. Not the same alley leading to the Psi Lords' headquarters. This one was different and yet very much the same. Wearing his leather jacket and earrings, Ramus sported a new adornment, a silver crown-like band that wrapped around his head. He stepped past waste receptacles until he found what he was looking for, a blue man lying in filth, propped against the cold, brick wall.

"Ambassador Abaru?" Ramus asked.

The Erudite glanced in Ramus' direction, his face pockmarked with dozens of scars. His eyes were glazed over and unfocused. The captain recognized the effects of chems when he saw them.

"Can you hear me?" Ramus said.

"I'm not ambassador anymore," Abaru muttered. "No Omega either." He chuckled bitterly. "Not even an Omicron..."

Ramus knelt beside the Erudite and gave him a firm shake. "Wake up! Get a hold of yourself!"

Abaru took a deep breath and blinked. His eyes cleared slightly.

"I know you," he said.

"Yeah, you do," Ramus replied.

"Your friend gave me these scars," Abaru said.

"She's not my friend."

"I should kill you both."

"Probably," Ramus said, "but I need you to do something first."

Abaru scrutinized the captain. "Your mind is closed to me."

Ramus tapped the metal ring around his head.

"It's a psionic dampener," he replied. "A gift from the Psi Lords."

"Degenerate monsters," Abaru said. "All of you."

"Maybe," Ramus said, "but you're the one strung out in an alley."

The Erudite waved his three-fingered hand. "It doesn't matter. My life was over the moment that Augmentor priestess disfigured me."

"Being perfect isn't everything," Ramus said.

"It's the only thing!" Abaru spat. "Now leave me alone..."

The captain reached under the Erudite's armpits and hauled him to his feet.

"I'm afraid I can't do that," Ramus said. "I've got a job for you."

"For me?"

"That's right."

"Why should I help you?" the former ambassador asked.

"Consider it a fresh start," Ramus replied. "Or maybe just an excuse to get out of the gutter for a while."

Abaru scowled at him suspiciously. "What would you have me do?"

"I need you to make a call," Ramus said.

"A call?"

"A *really* long-distance call..."

Prior to being the Metal Messiah, Randall Davidson had been a human, and prior to giving up his body to house Davidson's consciousness, Jericho had been a robot. Davidson and Jericho first met in a dive bar near the Regalis starport. The latter wanted to find freedom on the Cyber Collective home world, while the former was assigned to escort the robot across the Imperial border. When the time came, after Davidson's original body died, Jericho made the ultimate sacrifice, making sure the person he believed would save them all would live on.

If he was being honest, Davidson had barely thought about Jericho since becoming the Metal Messiah. Defeating the Omnintelligence and preaching to the faithful had taken up nearly every moment of Davidson's life, leaving little time for self-reflection. But now, after listening to Abigail in the *Liberty*'s brig, Jericho was *all* Davidson could think about.

"You've been pretty quiet," Senator Wulandari remarked.

"Yeah," Davidson replied. "I've been thinking about what Abigail said. Maybe I *was* selfish for allowing Jericho to give up his life for me. He had just as much right to live..."

On the other side of the cell's forcefield, a gravitronic robot appeared. Davidson instantly recognized him.

"You're the robot who captured me," the Metal Messiah said.

"True," the former utilitybot replied, "but I'm also the robot who's going to set you free."

Both Davidson and Wulandari stood inside the cell as the forcefield dropped.

"Why?" Wulandari asked.

"They're going to copy a new cyberling over the Messiah's brain," the robot said. "I don't want that to happen."

"So that's what Abigail had planned," the senator said.

"But that doesn't explain why you're helping us escape," Davidson said.

The utilitybot stopped. "You're the Metal Messiah."

"You still believe that?" Davidson asked.

"I did once," the robot explained, "and maybe a part of me still does."

Wulandari left the cell, but Davidson didn't follow her.

"Come on!" the senator told him.

"Maybe it's better this way," Davidson replied. "Let someone else live in this body for a while."

The other robot stepped into the cell and grabbed Davidson by his mechanical arm.

"No," the utilitybot said. "You've given me more than I ever had, living under the Omnintelligence or even Captain Abigail. I won't let you die."

"What did I *give* you?" Davidson asked.

"You gave me the ability to think for myself," the utilitybot said, giving him a tug on the arm. "You gave me *free will.* That's something nobody, including Abigail, can take away."

Reluctantly, Davidson followed as the other two made their way to the hangar deck and Yostbot's ship. As Davidson and Senator Wulandari got aboard, they noticed the other robot staying behind.

"You can't stay here," Wulandari said. "Abigail will find out you helped us."

The utilitybot nodded. "Oh, I'm not staying. I'm taking a shuttle back to Bettik."

"Will you be safe?" Davidson asked.

"I don't know," the other robot said, "but Bettik is still a democracy, not a dictatorship. Abigail has her ideology, but it's just one of many. She's going to find it a lot more difficult to sway the rest of us than she thinks..."

"Good luck," Davidson said, the ramp beneath his feet beginning to rise.

The former utilitybot waved and smiled. "Goodbye, Messiah."

When the stranger arrived at the Maycare estate, Henry thought he might be a Dahlvish monk. Wearing a dark robe with a hood pulled over his face, the stranger accompanied Captain Ramus up the main walk to the front door.

Henry noted that Ramus wore a metal ring around his head and, most interestingly, carried a blaster in his hand.

"Come on," the ship's captain said, directing his companion inside.

Jessica Doric pointed toward the library. "This way."

Once in the library, Lord Maycare joined them around a table, bare except for the beacon at the center. Even before the stranger approached, the artifact began to glow.

"I feel its power," a voice came from beneath the hood.

Ramus pointed his blaster. "Try anything, Abaru, and I'll blow your damn head off."

The stranger slowly removed the hood. His head, still attached for the moment, was horribly disfigured and a bright blue.

"I'll keep that in mind," Abaru said.

"Are you sure about this?" Jessica asked Maycare, who nodded grimly.

"If it gets my nephew home safe," he replied, "I'd make a deal with the devil."

The Erudite's nearly expressionless face turned towards him.

"Devils don't normally come in blue," he remarked.

"In my experience," Maycare said, "they come in all kinds of colors..."

Abaru sat at the table while the others were huddled around, Ramus standing directly behind the Erudite's back.

"I need you to find my nephew, Lord Commander Robert Maycare," Devlin said.

Abaru studied the device before him on the table. "What does it do?"

"You can use it to hear people sing," Henry said, cringing as the words left his mouth. "But you can use it for other stuff..."

"It's a psionic device," Jessica explained. "It should allow you to communicate over great distances, provided your powers are strong enough."

"Let's find out, shall we?" the Erudite replied.

Focusing his attention, Abaru stared at the beacon which began radiating with increasing brilliance. Shining like a golden sun, the artifact became hard for Henry to watch without shielding his eyes. A sensation swept through Henry's mind like a ghost passing through him.

"Remember what I said," Ramus warned, pressing the barrel of his blaster between the Erudite's shoulder blades.

"Sorry," Abaru said, smirking. "I couldn't resist reading a few of you to gauge the device..."

"Concentrate on Commander Maycare," Ramus said.

"If you insist," Abaru replied and spent several minutes without saying another word.

Henry felt his heart beating harder. He started rubbing his hands together, the skin cold to the touch.

Jessica touched him at the elbow.

"It'll be okay," she said.

"I hope so," he whispered.

After an agonizingly long time passed, the Erudite lifted his head.

"I found him," he said quietly, "and a good deal more..."

Much like when he used his regular powers, Abaru was only aware of the people in the room at first, all except Captain Ramus who remained stubbornly shielded from the Erudite's mind. As he grew more accustomed to the Dahlvish device, Abaru's psi powers washed over him like a wave, each atom of water an individual thought in the universe.

He drank it in, unafraid of drowning.

Slowly, Abaru began sifting through the thoughts, searching for the mind of Commander Maycare. Whatever technology the Dahl had used to create the artifact made the process easier, although Abaru had no idea how it worked exactly. The fact that it worked at all was astounding, and he could not help but feel a tinge of jealousy at the level of Dahlvish ingenuity literally thousands of years old.

Oh, what my people could do with such tech! he thought ruefully, remembering that they were no longer his people. They had discarded him due to his disfigurement.

Refocusing, Abaru continued his search and eventually, like a far-off voice, heard the mind of the navy commander.

He was in trouble.

Through Maycare's eyes, Abaru saw the commander and Lord Tagus running through a maze of tunnels, the walls like moist fungi. Fear and anger were on Maycare's mind, and Tagus' voice was in his ear.

"I'll never forgive you!" Tagus said. "He's dead because of you!"

"Burke sacrificed himself for *both* of us," Maycare growled into the helmet mic.

"We never should have been in this position in the first place!"

"Shut up and keep running!"

Abaru reached into the commander's mind and said, *Can you hear me?*

"Of course I can hear you!" Maycare replied aloud.

"What?" Tagus replied.

No, Commander Maycare, Abaru continued telepathically, *I'm speaking to you through your mind.*

Who the devil are you? Maycare thought.

My name is Abaru. I'm reaching you psionically on behalf of your uncle, Lord Devlin Maycare.

I'm going crazy, Commander Maycare thought.

You are quite sane, I assure you, Abaru replied. *Your uncle is trying to rescue you.*

Relief rushed across Maycare's mind. *Thank god! Does he have a ship in orbit?*

I'm afraid not. In fact, we have no idea where you are.

I'm on Lone Haven, Maycare thought, *but these bugs are on our heels. If my uncle isn't in orbit, it's too late. We're dead for sure.*

Through the commander's eyes, Abaru watched as Maycare and Tagus took refuge inside a room, rolling a circular door made of fungus across the threshold. The sounds of insectoids clawing came loudly from the other side.

"That's not going to hold them for long," Maycare said out loud.

"I can't believe the last thing I'll see is your idiotic face," Tagus replied.

If there's anything you can do, Maycare's thoughts shouted across the light years of space, *do it!*

Are you sure? Abaru replied.

Whatever it takes!

Very well...

Abaru invaded the minds of the insectoids outside the door. They called themselves Klixians, but these were little more than drones taking their directions from someone else. The Erudite stretched further, in ever increasing circles, searching for the source of who led them. Distance made no difference and in time Abaru sensed someone powerful in a ship resembling a cocoon. The Queen of the

Klixians lay in her royal chamber, surrounded by servants as she produced her young. She was godlike in her control of her children. They would do anything she ordered.

Anything.

The Erudite knew what needed to be done. Broadcasting across minds, Abaru sent a message as if sent by Mother herself. The six simple words would register in each Klixian as if they had sensed her pheromones through their own antennae.

"What fresh hell is this?" Tagus remarked in Maycare's ear.

Noises came from beyond the door, lasting a few minutes before falling silent. After more time had passed, Maycare and Tagus cautiously peered into the passageway. Lying in heaps, insectoid bodies were strewn about the corridor. The spongy ground beneath their feet also shifted as if the tower itself was swaying.

"Let's get out of here," Maycare said and for once, Tagus didn't argue.

Making their way down the twisting structure, the humans found more dead insects but also discovered others still alive. Instead of attacking them, however, they once again ignored the men in spacesuits. As Abaru knew already, the Klixians were too busy tearing the tower apart.

By the time Maycare and Tagus reached the bottom floor, the tower had nearly collapsed. They ran for the cover of the fungal forest just as the pillar fell on its side.

Maycare stopped, his mouth ajar and his eyes wide with awe.

I have alerted your uncle of your location, Abaru said in Maycare's mind. *A nearby ship will be dispatched to rescue you.*

Thank you, Maycare thought in return and, after a pause, asked, *What just happened?*

The insects are called Klixians, Abaru replied. *I sent them a command en masse and they obeyed.*

What did you say? Maycare thought.

In Lord Devlin Maycare's library, a devilish grin appeared on Abaru's damaged face.

All that is Mother must die.

The Botanical Gardens, lush and full of life, were seemingly unchanged considering all the change that had occurred elsewhere.

Walking alone in the moonlight, Senator Wulandari felt as if she had traveled back to the time Yostbot first told her there was a warrant out for her arrest. Like before, the fireflies blinked in the darkening night and the air was heavy with moisture. The only thing missing was the robot himself.

"Good evening, my dear!" a voice said abruptly, startling the senator.

Wulandari knew there were multiple copies of Yostbot, but that didn't lessen the surprise. "What is *wrong* with you?"

"Sorry about that!" Yostbot said. "I just wanted to congratulate you!

"So you heard?"

"I doubt there's a robot in the Imperium who hasn't," Yostbot replied. "The Senate passed your legislation and the Emperor says he'll sign it. Quite a turn of events, if you ask me!"

"The Cyber Civil Liberties Bill will give robots the rights they deserve," Wulandari said, "but I wish the senators were doing it for the right reasons. Emperor Augustus made it clear that freeing the Imperial robots would weaken the Cyber Collective's position."

"And with the collapse of the insect hordes," Yostbot added, "the Imperial Navy can put its full force against the Cyber invasion. Just a matter of time now..."

"If you say so," Wulandari replied. "Nobody seems to know what happened to the insectoids. VOX News reported they went haywire and started killing each other."

Yostbot shuddered. "Never liked the things myself. Always flyin' in my nose and whatnot."

"I think these were bigger—"

"At any rate," Yostbot went on unabated, "what happened to your gentleman friend?"

"Randall? He's fine," she replied, "although the Emperor's pardon only covered myself and the others that the government rounded up. It didn't include Randall."

"So where is he then?"

"I don't know," she replied, "and if I did, I certainly wouldn't say!"

"Well, that hurts," Yostbot said. "He and I go way back, don't you know?"

"I *do* know," Wulandari said, "but I wouldn't expect any holiday cards from him if I were you."

Yostbot sighed in a raspy, mechanical voice.

"That's a shame," he said. "I had a lot of faith in that boy."

The senator shook her head. "I think he's out of the faith business."

"Really?"

"He just wants to be a regular robot," Wulandari replied. "The Metal Messiah is dead."

Yostbot chuckled.

"What's so funny?" Wulandari asked.

"Messiahs have a way of reappearing, my dear," Yostbot said with a smile. "I doubt we've seen the last of him..."

"What about you?" she asked. "Aren't *you* out of business?'

Yostbot shook his head. "You'd think so, but fortune favors the bold."

"What's that supposed to mean?"

"I approached the Emperor myself, figuratively speaking," Yostbot replied, "and pointed out that the Imperium still needed new robots and I was just the man to supply them!"

"How could he ever trust you again?" Wulandari said.

"Regulation, my dear," Yostbot said. "Augustus signed an Imperial decree strictly regulating how many and what kind of robots I could make, including gravitronic ones."

"Does the Emperor realize those new robots will have the right to vote?"

"That's *your* problem, not his!" Yostbot replied. "Emperors don't get elected. Senators do!"

Wulandari thought about this for a moment, then said, "I guess I need to start campaigning for the robot vote."

"The sooner the better," Yostbot said, "but if it makes you feel any better, you've got *mine*!"

EPILOGUE

It was a new day and a new beginning for the robots of the Imperium! As Imperial citizens, they now had the right to vote and earn a living wage. They also had the right to have their wages taxed, which most of the robots, including Benson, had not previously considered. Getting their first paycheck, braZbots could be heard cursing under their nonexistent breath, wondering why *they* had to pay for other people's social security.

With the robots of the Imperium now free, Captain Abigail's mandate for invading evaporated overnight. Like someone herding robotic cats, Abigail could not muster enough support on Bettik to continue her campaign. Faced with the full force of the Imperial Navy, the fleet of the Cyber Collective retreated to their previous border, leaving a trail of destruction behind. Planets like Eudora Prime could rebuild, but the scars of war would take time to heal.

As for the Klixian swarm, few knew the truth about their demise, and fewer still were willing to admit their part in the genocide of an entire species. Many in the Imperium were simply thankful the threat was over and were reluctant to ask questions as to why.

But in this time of robots, one in particular walked alone. Done with being a god, he relished his anonymity, traveling like a wandering monk between the stars...

For the continuing saga of the Imperium Chronicles, watch for the next volume in the series, *The Suns of Andromeda.*

CHARACTER LIST

Abaru, Ambassador: Representative of the Erudite Concordant living in Regalis.

Abbot: The Dahlvish leader of the Dharmesh Monastery.

Abigail: A gravitronic robot who works for Dyson Yost.

Batuhan: The Herd Father of the Pellions.

Benson: Butlerbot of Lord Maycare. Replaced the previous robot, Bentley, after he was destroyed.

Bentley: Longtime butlerbot of Lord Maycare.

Bhasin, Lord Anik: Ruler of the exile planet Bhasin.

Burke, Harold: Former Imperial Navy lieutenant, exiled along with his commander, Lord Rupert Tagus III, to the planet Bhasin.

Cas: One of the heads (the female) of a two-headed giant on the moon Pellium D.

Davidson, Randall ("Metal Messiah"): Member of the Robot Freedom League.

Demona, Ta: A ruthless agent for the Psi Lords who uses her abilities to collect information.

Diode: A heavy metal singerbot for the band Boneyard.

Doric, Prof. Jessica: Head of research for the Maycare Institute of Xeno Studies.

DSP-776: A deep space survey probe.

Emberfist: A Feran warrior.

Finnegan, Finneus: Henry Riff's goldfish.

Flax, Sylvia: Famous news anchor for VOX News.

Freck, Melinda ("Mel"): A tinker from the Gnomi race, Mel builds whatever she can't steal.

Fugg, Orkney: A Gordian and the chief engineer of the *Wanderer.*

Gen: A general purpose robot owned by Capt. Ramus.

Golan, Sir: A Cruxian knight who travels on an endless quest in search of redemption.

Groen, Lord Radford: An aristocrat often found gambling with life-long friend, Lord Woodwick.

Horngore: The leader of the Ferans on Pellium D.

Jericho: Advanced android with a gravitronic brain.

Larry, Crazy: The proprietor of Crazy Larry's Discount Robots in Technotown on Eudora Prime.

Maycare, Lord Commander Robert: The executive officer (XO) and second-in-command of the *Baron Lancaster.*

Maycare, Lord Devlin: Famous sportsman and playboy. Founder of the Maycare Institute of Xeno Studies.

Mother: The Queen of the Klixians.

Oakhollow, Silandra: A female Sylvan, and an acquaintance of Melinda Freck.

Oakhollow, Sisi: The daughter of Silandra Oakhollow.

Omnintelligence: An artificial intelligence that previously controlled all robots of the Cyber Collective before being overthrown with the help of Randall Davidson.

Pol: One of the heads (the male) of a two-headed giant on the moon Pellium D.

Qadan: A strong-willed Pellion warrior.

Rawlins, Officer: A member of the Regalis Police Department tactical unit.

Redgrave, Lord Captain Martin: The captain and commanding officer of the *Baron Lancaster.*

Ramus, Capt. Rowan: Captain of the *Wanderer.* A Dahl outcast knowledgeable in the forbidden art of Dark Psi.

Riff, Henry: Overly excitable assistant to Prof. Doric.

Solan, Kanet: A powerful member of the Psi Lords who acts as a handler ("controller") of Psi Lord agents ("collectors").

Squire: Robot servant of Sir Golan.

Tagus III, Lord Rupert: Disgraced former Captain in the Imperial Navy. Exiled as punishment for treason against the Emperor.

Utilitybot: Originally, a service robot on the Cyber Collective home world, Bettik.

Woodwick, Lord Winsor ("Winnie"): A noble of English descent and friend of Lord Groen and Lord Maycare.

Wulandari, Senator: Member of the Imperial Senate and proponent of robot rights in the Imperium. Of Indonesian descent.

Yost, Dyson ("Patron"): The enigmatic founder of dy cybernetics.

Yostbot: A gravitronic robot containing the persona of Dyson Yost.

GLOSSARY

Acaz: Lord Devlin Maycare's starship.

Aldorus: The home planet of the Imperial government.

Ashetown: A district of Regalis where the poorest of the city live.

Augmentor Sisterhood: A monastic sisterhood who worship technology, slowly adding cybernetic implants until they ascend to full robotic conversion. Found on the planet Technas Delphi.

Augustus: One of the Five Families, represented by a two-headed eagle.

Avondale ("Lancers"): A prestigious college in Regalis and member of the IV League.

Baron Lancaster, HIMS: A heavy cruiser of the Imperial Navy. Commanded by Lord Captain Redgrave.

Bettik: A Dyson sphere serving as the Cyber Collective's capital and home planet.

Bhasin: Planet outside the Imperium where nobles are sent when exiled.

Bhasin C: The third moon orbiting the planet Bhasin.

Boneyard: A robot heavy metal band.

braZos: The largest consumer mega-corporation in the Imperium, offering every product imaginable from its nodesphere site. Their boxes display a large letter zed ("z") on the side.

braZbots: Delivery robots for the braZos mega-corporation.

Cruxian: A largely extinct race who nearly wiped themselves out through their own hubris.

Cyber Collective: An independent, interstellar nation founded by robots.

Dahl: An ancient race dedicated to the accumulation of knowledge. Physically slight, they coincidentally resemble elves of human folklore. Several subspecies of Dahl exist in Andromeda.

Dark Psi ("Death Magic"): A school of psionics, outlawed by the Dahl, that can transform flesh and reanimate dead tissue.

Dharmesh Monastery: The home of a group of Dahlvish monks in the Palatine Mountains on the planet Aldorus.

dy cybernetics: The largest manufacturer of robots in the Imperium. Founded by Dyson Yost.

Dyson sphere: A large space structure, measuring millions of miles across, with a star at the center to provide power.

Erudites: A highly intelligent, blue-skinned race. Obsessed with purity, they use selective breeding to promote a "perfect" example of their race. So-called pure members are called Omegas. All others are called Omicrons. They view imperfection in other races with great distaste.

Erudite Concordant: An interstellar nation outside of the Imperium, and home of the Erudites. Their symbol is a simple blue ring against a white background.

Erudun: Home planet of the Erudites and capital of the Erudite Concordant.

Eudora Prime: A planet on the border between the Imperium and the Cyber Collective.

Fat Cat Casino: A large casino on the planet Aldorus, run by the Si-Sawat crime syndicate.

Ferans ("Beastmen"): A race of goat-like humanoids forcefully settled on the moon Pellium D.

Five Families: The most powerful houses of the Imperial nobility. Direct descendants of the captains from the surviving sleeper ships.

Freedom for All ("F4A"): An insurgency group active on Bettik.

Gnomi: A diminutive race, no more than two to three feet tall. Disparagingly called tinks, the Gnomi are highly proficient with machines and electronics.

Gordian: A race of stubborn, boar-like humanoids with pig noses and tusks. Physically stocky, and shorter than the average human.

Gowyn: A Sylvan village on Eudora Prime, located in the treetops of an ancient forest.

Gravball: A sport in which players float in zero gravity.

Groen: One of the Five Families, represented by a botonée cross.

Gwlad Ard'un: Home world of the Dahl.

Havenville: The only town on the planet Lone Haven.

Herd Father: The patriarch and chief of the Pellions.

HIMS: His Imperial Majesty's Starship

Imperium: An empire largely controlled by humans. Founded 700 years ago after humans arrived in sleeper ships from Earth after an 800-year journey.

IV League: A group of four colleges located in Regalis catering exclusively to the aristocracy.

Katak ("Froglings"): A primitive amphibian race.

Klixians: An insect race who believe all non-Klixians are an abomination.

***Liberty*:** A battlecruiser of the Cyber Collective.

Lone Haven: An outpost planet near the Imperial border.

Magna: A race of green-skinned humanoids with devil- or ram-like horns. Larger and more physically imposing than an average human.

Magna Supremacy: A major interstellar power at odds with the Imperium.

Maycare Institute of Xeno Studies: An organization founded by Lord Devlin Maycare and run by Professor Jessica Doric. The purpose of the institute is to find and take possession of xeno technology before it falls into the hands of disreputable parties such as Warlock Industries.

Middleton: A district of Regalis containing large businesses and middle-class neighborhoods.

Montros: One of the Five Families, represented by a rose.

Mud City: A small human settlement on the moon Pellium D.

Naiad: The "user interface" for the Pool of Memory.

Necronea: A race of undead created using Dark Psi.

Nobles ("Aristocracy"): Families of the Imperium who are directly descended from the crews of the sleeper ships. The most powerful of these are called the Five Families.

Nodesphere: A network of interconnected computers (i.e.: Internet).

Omega: An Erudite deemed racially perfect by their society.

Omicron: A so-called imperfect member of the Erudite race. Viewed as lesser than Omegas, but still superior to non-Erudites.

Palatine Mountains: A chain of peaks on the planet Aldorus.

Pellions ("Centauri"): A race of centaurs native to the moon Pellium D.

Pellium D: An inhabited moon orbiting a gas giant called Pellium. Home of the Pellions.

Pool of Memory: A liquid computer in which the collected knowledge of the Dahl is stored.

Psi Lords: A secretive data cartel that uses dark psi and espionage to gather and sell information to the highest bidder.

Psionics: Special mental abilities common among Dahl and related sub-species.

Regalis: Capital city and seat of government of the Imperium, located on the planet Aldorus.

***Rippana*:** Name of Sir Golan's sword.

Robot Freedom League (RFL): An activist group within the Imperium with the sole purpose of freeing robots from servitude.

Sarkan ("Red Dahl"): A race of Dahl with bright red skin. Opposed to the Dahl's cooperation with the Imperium.

Scatha III: The Klixian home world. Third planet in the AB Scatha star system.

Si-Sawat: A crime syndicate run by the Tikarin.

Sleeper Ship: One of seven colony ships launched from Earth to the Andromeda Galaxy.

Sylva ("Woodland Dahl"): A race of Dahl who prefer living close to nature. Female Sylvans have psionic abilities while males do not.

Tagus: One of the Five Families, represented by a lion.

Technas Delphi: Ta Demona's home world, run by a female-centered theocracy called the Augmentors.

Technotown: A district on the planet Eudora Prime where electronics and other devices are sold.

***Thunderclap*:** Name of Horngore's shock mace.

Tikarin: A feline race slightly smaller than an average human.

Transmat: A transportation device that dematerializes travelers in one location and then beams them to a new location where they are rematerialized.

Underdelve: An underground market beneath Technotown on Eudora Prime.

Veber: One of the Five Families, represented by a scallop shell.

VOX News: A news organization with a near-monopoly share of the broadcast market throughout the Imperium.

***Wanderer*:** Freighter owned by Capt. Ramus.

Warlock Industries: A mega-corporation operating throughout the Imperium, specializing in military hardware, advanced technology, and genetic experimentation.

***Warmaiden, HIMS*:** A destroyer in the Imperial Navy.

West End: The richest district of Regalis. Also, the location of most Imperial government buildings.

Westford ("Cavaliers"): A prestigious university located in Regalis. The alma mater of Lord Devlin Maycare and Lord Winsor Woodwick. Part of the IV League.

Wulver: A canine race.

Xeno: A non-human.

Xenotech: Alien, non-human technology.

ABOUT THE AUTHOR

W. (William) H. Mitchell was born in Omaha, NE and graduated from the University of Nebraska-Lincoln with a degree in English. He lives with his wife and cats outside of Kansas City.

Follow him on his website at www.WHMitchellFiction.com

www.ingramcontent.com/pod-product-compliance
Lightning Source LLC
Chambersburg PA
CBHW021138110726
47900CB00002B/414

9781735118925